THE NIGHT BLADE QUEEN

THE NIGHT BLADE QUEEN

JADE LOUISE

SHADOWKISSED PUBLISHING
STORIES OF MYTH, MOONLIGHT, AND SHADOWED DESIRE

Copyright © 2026 by Jade Louise.

All rights reserved. No part of this book may be reproduced in any form or by any means, electronic or mechanical, including photocopying, recording, or by any information storage and retrieval system, without written permission from the publisher/author.

This novel is entirely a work of fiction. The names, characters and incidents portrayed in it are the work of the author's imagination. Any resemblance to actual persons, living or dead, events or localities is entirely coincidental.

Jade Louise asserts the moral right to be identified as the author of this work.

Jade Louise has no responsibility for the persistence or accuracy of URLs for external or third-party Internet Websites referred to in this publication and does not guarantee that any content on such Websites is, or will remain, accurate or appropriate.

ISBN: 978-1-7644757-0-9

First edition, published in Australia in 2026 by
Shadow Kissed Publishing
PO Box 5011, Canning Vale South, WA, Australia, 6155
www.shadowkissedpublishing.com.au

Copy Editing by English Proper Editing Services

DEDICATION

This is for you. To all of you who were ever faced with a daunting task and thought you could not go on. Even if you're not through the tunnel yet - you are amazing. You are what fuels this world and I am proud of you. Know, the darkness isn't always the end - sometimes you need the dark to see clarity.

Oh, and to my mum. Her strength and character are where Zoryana gets it from. Love you Mum.

CONTENTS

Content Warning i
Map of the Dusklands and Solnyr iii
Historian's Note iv
Prologue vi
The Prophecy of Reforging ix
Chapter One: Ascent 1
Chapter Two: My Queen 10
Chapter Three: Sunrise in Solnyr 17
Chapter Four: The First Seeds of Doubt 26
Chapter Five: The Envoy 33
Chapter Six: Sun in the Dark 42
Chapter Seven: Shadows and Sundrops 51
Aurelian's Ledger: Day One in the Dusklands 60
Chapter Eight: Flame 62
Chapter Nine: The Rite of the Shadowborne 70
Chapter Ten: The Garden of Obsidian Roses 80
Chapter Eleven: Sovereign Proposition 88

Aurelian's Ledger: The Queen's Proposition 95
Chapter Twelve: The Golden Spires 98
Chapter Thirteen: The Traitor Prince 105
Chapter Fourteen: The Oath 115
Chapter Fifteen: Battle Weary 123
Aurelian's Ledger: The Return to Nightfell Castle 130
Chapter Sixteen: Training 132
Chapter Seventeen: Aftermath at the Front 138
Chapter Eighteen: Fractures 145
Aurelian's Ledger: The Night of the Storm 153
Chapter Nineteen: Receding Blight 155
Chapter Twenty: The Three 163
Chapter Twenty-One: Coming Together 168
Chapter Twenty-Two: The Silence Never Lasts 175
Aurelian's Ledger: The Battle at The Thorned Vale 182
Chapter Twenty-Three: The Summons 184
Chapter Twenty-Four: The Dawn Reclaiming 194
Chapter Twenty-Five: The Day the Sun Fell 203
Aurelian's Ledger: Reclaiming the Night 211
Archivist's Addendum 213
Glossary 215
The Vesmoran Calendar 218
Acknowledgements 221
About the Author 223

CONTENT WARNING

THIS STORY WALKS THROUGH SHADOWED terrain. Within its pages you will find depictions of war and violence; death both spoken of and shown on the page; and a culturally rooted, fully consensual branding rite of passage. Themes of misogyny and sexism thread through the world as the characters push against the forces shaping them.

On the sensual side, this book carries a 3–4 Spice level: graphic sexual content; FM and MFM relationships; oral pleasure (for all genders); and elements of shadow play woven into intimacy and power.

EXPLICIT CHAPTERS

The below chapters contain explicit, on-page spice. If that is something you don't want to read, take note of the page numbers below so you can skip.

1. Ascent - Pages 4-6
2. My Queen - Pages 15-16
3. Sunrise in Solnyr - Page 17-18 (mention), and pages 23-25

4. The Envoy - Pages 38-41
5. Sun in the Dark - Page 42-43
6. Flame - Pages 62-65
7. The Oath - Pages 120-122
8. Receding Blight - Pages 161-162
9. The Three - Whole chapter - Pages 163-167
10. Coming Together - Whole chapter - Pages 168-174
11. The Summons - Pages 189-193

A NOTE ON SPELLING AND GRAMMAR

This story was written in Australian/UK English—there are words like 'centre' and 'colour', and a whole host of others. I am Australian and we learn the Queen's English—that is how I write.

HELIOVAR

SOLNYR

VEKARION

DUSKLANDS

HISTORIAN'S NOTE

THIS STORY IS COMPILED PRIMARILY from journal entries and letters discovered in Nightfell Castle and the Solnyrian royal seat, with some creative liberties taken to fill in the story while translating and transcribing.

The writing of Aurelian, Prince of the Sun, as he was known while the majority of the entries were being written, can be highly lyrical and while translating to blend into the overall story, some of that was lost. We attempted to preserve as much of it as we were able, but not all of it survived the final edit. Some full entries of his works are published within these pages to show contrast and aide in understanding.

Much of the descriptions and general activity of High Queen Zoryana and Aris, her Shadowsworn, were taken from the writing of Prince Aurelian and other historical documents. We did discover some letters in her hand, and some annotations in Aris' voice that we were able to use to build their characters further.

The works by King Aurastes IV were sycophantic and sometimes indecipherable. Great effort was given to translate as much as possible to give a full understanding of the story.

A NOTE ON MEASUREMENTS

Some of the original documentation was unable to be translated fully. Liberty was taken when translating in those cases. A lot of the words unable to be deciphered were relating to measurements, of distance, time, and ages. The most accurate sounding modern alternative was chosen if we could not discern from the pages. A calendar is included in the back of this volume to assist in discerning the timeline based on Prince Aurelian's writings.

In twilight we trust,

Archivist Lyra Daeven

Keeper of the House of Memory

Year 472 of the New Vesmoran Age

PROLOGUE

THEY WILL SAY SHE WAS A MONSTER.

They will carve it into temple stone, into children's lessons, into the mouths of priests who never tasted ash. They will name her the Wound of the World, the Witch Queen, the Storm That Devoured an Age. But that is not the truth.

The truth is this: She was a woman who loved too much and was destroyed for it.

1,000 years ago - The Breaking

(as it truly happened, not as it was recorded)

The moons should not have been red. Their silver magic and majesty were stained red by the blood of her people. Of the people he had also sworn to serve and protect.

Seravine stood on the shattered balcony of the citadel, her hands trembling around the last letter he sent—the one where he said he would come back to explain why he had done what he had done. He did not return with his arms open, not with apologies, not with the future they had planned. He had returned with soldiers. With fire and sun sigils. With the crown she had helped him earn.

"Stand down, Seravine," Caelen said. Her fellow ruler, the man she thought she had loved—his voice was shaking like *his* was the heart that was breaking, not that he was the one doing the breaking. "You know I do not want to do this."

She laughed, because grief had already burned past reason, her restraint starting to unravel. "You do not *have* to," she said. "You *choose* to. No one forced you to use my power for your own gains. No one forced you to steal from me. Steal a vital part of me."

Behind him, his generals waited, clad in shimmering gold, suns emblazoned on their breastplates, the sign of *his* court, not *theirs*. Behind her, everything she loved was already dead. The court they had built together. The gardens she had raised from the stone and nurtured to bloom. The cradle that would now forever lay cold.

He had told the world she was unstable. Dangerous. Unfit to rule. A threat to peace. Sewed lies to create a tapestry where he was the hero, and she was a demon for him to slay.

But the worst lie was this: That he ever loved her at all.

He had told himself he was saving the world. That the magic she carried was too wild—that the storms were *her* fault, not the wound he had cut into her heart. That the lengths he had gone to secure her magic for himself had not fractured her control, making her unstable and every inch the danger he had claimed she was. If he believed it hard enough, maybe history would too.

His men waited for the order. Just one word: *Execute*. But his voice failed and his breath hitched. Because even now—ash and blood in her hair, rage in those eerie, quicksilver eyes, shadows and magic pulsing around her—she was still the only person who had ever looked at him and saw a man instead of a throne. And he had betrayed her. Betrayed her to become that throne. Betrayed her instead of loving her the way he knew she had loved him. Because he was jealous of the power she possessed.

"Seravine." His jaw tightened and his hand shifted to the blade at his side. "Please...do not make me do this."

And that was when he knew—he was not the hero of this story. He was just the one who would survive it. He would be the one left to tell the historians the story—no matter the truth of it.

The letter slipped from her fingers, fluttering to the floor, like it was the last remnant of her love for him. The last thread of control she held over the tide building inside her, despite his best efforts to drain the well dry.

Her magic did not roar—it wept. Grieved for the heinous act that had been committed against it. The ground cracked. The air pulsed. Lakes recoiled like frightened beasts. She screamed his name—not to curse him, but because she had once loved him so deeply it could tear the world in half.

And it did.

A dense, impenetrable forest rose in a single night, roots drinking centuries of blood. Magic rewrote itself like a wounded animal, lashing out in blind fury. Fae and all manner of other creatures warped, creating what the world would learn to call monsters.

He fled. He ran from the woman he had condemned, while her power remade the world around him. They would paint her as the beast.

But the truth was simpler: She broke the world, but he had broken her. And the world learned to blame only her.

When the land finally stilled, when the new map of the world cooled in molten lines of ruin, when her magic burned itself out, Seravine whispered, her voice ash-soft, "Let him live long enough to drown in what he has done."

And then she vanished, leaving behind her heartbreak and the devastation her magic had wrought upon the land, no longer able to exist in the world that caused her so much pain and stripped her of her power. Some say she died. Some say she sleeps beneath the broken earth. Some say she is still screaming in the storms. All the stories are wrong.

The only truth is this: The Breaking was not the end. It was the first lie.

The Prophecy of Reforging

"When the lie has lived longer than the truth,
When light burns colder than shadow,
When the crown that shines is rusted through with silence,
And the crown that mourns is heavy with unspoken names,
Then shall the Heir of the Blame and the Heir of the Burden
Stand together upon the wound of the world.
Not to rule—but to remember.
Not to conquer—but to unmake.
For kingdoms built on falsehood are not toppled by war,
But by a single, unbearable truth."

CHAPTER ONE
ASCENT

A THOUSAND YEARS AFTER THE Breaking, the world still pretends it has healed.

Borders have new names. History has new heroes. And the name Seravine is only spoken in two ways: as a curse or as a prayer. But none of them knows the truth.

Not Solnyr, who claim their lineage is pure. Not the Dusklands, who wear rebellion like a crown. Not the scholars, who insist the past is sealed.

Because the past is not dead. It is merely waiting. And tonight, in the ruins of the old capital, beneath a sky split by the twin moons, the first thread of that buried truth begins to rise in the form of a woman who refuses to bow.

ZORYANA

The air tasted of old magic. I drew in a breath, letting it settle in my lungs like stormfire. My boots crunched over the broken tiles of what was once the Throne Hall of Vesmor—now only a shattered skeleton of stone and vine, half-swallowed by time. Growing up, we had all been told this place was haunted. Those who told us were wrong. It was not. It was watching and waiting.

My hand settled on the hilt of my weapon—obsidian-forged, night-sung, alive in ways steel could not be. The wind caught my cloak, whipping it and my dark hair around me. Somewhere in the shadowed wreckage, something shifted. It did not feel like another living being—not animal or fae. It was a feeling…an awareness.

Good, I thought to myself. *Let it come.*

I had not crossed my entire land, defied my council and Aris, or trespassed on the oldest ruin in the world to tremble before ghosts. I was born into a world built on the bones of a queen they called mad. I had promised myself I would not repeat that history. I was determined to rewrite it.

A whisper rippled through the air, like the memory of a voice rather than the voice itself. "Daughter of defiance…"

I froze. Not from fear but from recognition. It was not possible. And yet, every bone in my body knew it had to be. This was not the voice of the living. It was older than any kingdom that now stood. Older than the lies written after the Breaking. Older than the silence that followed.

It was her. The first and last unbowed queen. *Seravine.*

A pulse of cold magic rolled across the ruins—not hostile, but testing. Like a hand brushing the edge of a blade. I stood firm, determined not to bow or shake. That was how a queen was supposed to react, right?

"You would claim a throne built on ruins," the voice murmured, echoing through broken pillars and torn banners. "Do you know what was stolen…to make *you*?"

I shook my head, but I was thankful to hear my voice was steady. "No. But I intend to learn." And I really did. I wanted to know how to fix my dying land.

The wind stilled around me. Then, sounding almost like approval, the voice spoke again "…Good."

The ruins of the old Throne Hall trembled. The past, it seemed, was no longer content to sleep. All at once, the wind picked up again, swirling around me, and the haunting sounds of the Spine Choir joined in, surrounding me in a cacophony of sound and air. It felt almost like a hug from my long-dead ancestor. Like she approved of my path forward.

"I will make you proud," I murmured as I left the ruins, heading for the clearing where I had left Vecheryn, my loyal and beautiful Shadowmare that I had raised from a foal. She had been with me for so long, I was pretty sure we could actually communicate beyond what was normal.

"So, did you have fun breaking the laws you are about to swear to uphold?" The deep, male voice made me jump and yelp in a very un-Queen-like way.

Clutching my chest, I turned to the voice, finding Aris, my Shadowsworn warrior, best friend, and lover, leaning against a tree. His arms were crossed across his broad, armoured chest, and he had a stern look on his scarred but gorgeous face, obviously annoyed at the fact I had given him the slip earlier. The scowl softened slightly, and I could tell he found himself highly amusing. Vecheryn, who had been munching happily on the surrounding foliage, looked up and leaned in to nuzzle the side of Aris' face. The scowl slipped altogether, and he reached up to stroke the mare's nose. He was a sucker for that move... from me, or the horse.

"I am not breaking any laws," I replied, now that my heart had stopped pounding in my chest. "As the Queen, no part of my land is off limits to me."

Aris turned his attention back to me with a look that could only be described as mischievous. "You are not Queen *yet*," he quipped. He dropped his hand from Vecheryn's muzzle, making the mare huff her disapproval before she went back to munching on the grass.

"What is an hour in the grand scheme of things?" I replied, unable to stop myself from rolling my eyes.

"When it is the difference between being a princess and the ruler of our land? I would venture that an hour means a lot," Aris said, his tone teasing.

"Does becoming Queen mean you stop being so disrespectful?" I grumbled, making him laugh at me. He straightened up and moved towards me. A better way to explain what he was doing was stalking—I had seen him move like that many times before when we hunted together, and sometimes in the bedroom…or wherever we were.

"I seem to remember that you like it when I am disrespectful." Oh, did I ever. Not when we were in front of other people of course, it was difficult to explain why my Shadowsworn was allowed to speak to me like that, but behind closed doors… yes, I very much liked it when he was disrespectful. Honestly, it made me feel like I did not have the weight of the world on my shoulders.

"Aris Veldoran…how dare you presume to know what your Queen is thinking or what she likes." I tried my 'Queen' tone out for a laugh. I had been learning how to command the respect of my subjects from my advisers, and I would like to think I was beginning to perfect it. Not with Aris of course, the male just grinned.

"I would never presume, my Queen," he replied, reaching out to push back a lock of hair behind my ear. "I do not presume…I know."

I felt those words deep in my belly; the kiss that followed…I felt that all the way to my toes. Aris kissed like he wanted to feel my soul, not just my lips against his. It had been that way since our very first kiss shortly after I had turned eighteen and we had put our arrangement in place. As the future High Queen, the people I kept close to me were highly scrutinised; any relationship I had was judged for how it could affect the land— even just friendships. No Queen of the Dusklands since the Breaking had married. They had all taken strategically chosen lovers, usually multiple, resulting in generally murky parentage of the heir, and no one but the Queen being able to claim the youngling she birthed. If no one knew who the father was, no one else could exert any control over the crown.

There was no one in Nightfell that was high enough ranked

to marry me, and I was not able to go to the other kingdoms to find a spouse—the Thornwood prevented me from leaving Nightfell or other royalty from coming through from the other side. Not that anyone would welcome me anyway—The Devourer of the Sun. Aris, and our arrangement to be each other's physical comfort, just made sense. I had chosen Aris—my best friend. It had felt like a perfect idea at the time, though my mother had cautioned me due to our friendship. He had become my Shadowsworn not long afterwards, making our relationship border on taboo, but I did not know how to give him up. He was a link to my humanity that I was so scared to lose, just like all my ancestors had, including my own mother.

I let myself forget that I was due to attend my own coronation in less than an hour and reached up to sink my hands into his hair. Shadowsworn tended to cut their hair close to their scalp to reduce the chance of making noise when they were coming in for the kill, or giving an enemy a way to hold them back, but Aris kept his a little longer purely because I liked running my fingers through his hair—it just was not the same when he cropped it like the others…I liked to keep him in line every now and again and my fingers in the soft strands was a sure-fire way to make him cave. The moan that was muffled in our kiss proved my theory.

His hands slid down my back to my rear, squeezing a little as my feet left the ground and I found myself with my back against the trunk of a tree. We kissed and ground together like starlings until we were panting for each other and I could definitely feel how much he wanted me.

"I should…I should let you down. We… You still have to get ready," Aris groaned against my neck when he pulled away.

I needed him… As it was the day of my coronation, I had been required to spend the night attending a sacred ritual, then slept in a different room, meaning that our usual ability to sneak in some time together after the world went to sleep, or before it woke had been taken from us. I ground my hips against his again, gratified when he pushed me further into the tree.

"No, you really should not. Unless you are putting me down to get your pants off." Mischief lit his features.

"Is that an order, my Lady?" His hand slid between us, fingers brushing my centre through my dress as he started to unlace his pants.

"Yes." My simple, commanding word was all the prompting he needed. His pants were open in a blink, and my dress was bundled around my waist. His first thrust slammed my back against the tree as he entered me. My arms and legs tightened around him, revelling in the feeling of being full of him. Sliding my fingers into his hair, I pulled him in, catching his lips with mine. The kiss was all-consuming, flaring my passion as much as the feeling of his cock moving inside me. Aris' hand slid between us, over my chest to loosen the front of my dress. A sharp moan left me when his fingers closed over my nipple. The sharp, pleasurable pain sent a shot of desire to my core. My passion exploded, muscles tensing around him. He joined me in ecstasy not long after and as we rode out our climaxes, he continued to palm my breast, prolonging my pleasure.

Now sated, it was definitely time I needed to get back to the castle. I had less than an hour until the ceremony started and half of that would be spent riding back home, let alone actually getting ready. "Do you think they will care if I am late for my own coronation? It is not as if they can start without me." I attempted some levity. He let out a huff of a laugh.

"I do not think that is the best way to start your reign, my Lady…as much I want to stay inside you right now, I would be remiss in my duty if I did not get you back in time." Aris—always the voice of reason. We shared another quick kiss, and he pulled out of me. Setting my feet on the ground, Aris made sure there was nothing in my hair. We adjusted our clothing and made sure Vecheryn was ready as he hoisted me up onto her back, before he leapt up behind me.

"How did you get here? Where is Sumerak?" I asked him as Vecheryn took off towards the castle. His Dusk Stallion was nowhere to be seen.

"I sent him back when I saw Vecheryn. I thought that if we went back together, I could make sure you did not escape," he replied, making me laugh.

"Good thinking," I agreed. The coronation had been looming since my mother passed to the realm of the ancestors two years ago. At twenty-seven years old, I was finally old enough to rule in my own right and wear the Rooted Crown, fully taking on the burden of my family's past.

In what felt like no time at all, I was standing in front of the Thornwood, the scar Seravine's magic ripped into the land, separating us from the rest of the world. Her grief and anguish could still be felt throughout the Dusklands, but it was felt strongest at the barrier. Her magic had caused the forest to sprout overnight, and all manner of mangled creatures to be created. History says the creatures were once fae, like us, but Seravine's grief turned them into something other. That same power flowed through me, straining to be let loose. From birth, all children in Nightfell are taught that grief is power; it is not weakness. We are encouraged to experience the full spectrum of emotion and on this night, I would take on the grief of a broken and dying land. I just hoped it would not split me apart.

Before me, at the edge of the wood, but not within her borders, the scholars of the Memory Circle stand—keepers of memory for all aspects of life in the Dusklands. As a matriarchal society, only women were appointed to the Circle, and only women could assist and serve them—to keep the memories pure. During this ceremony, only I and one person of my choosing could stand within the trees. The Thornwood would accept no other at this time. Behind me stands Aris, his presence always a beacon of strength and support, steadfast and comforting. He reached out to press his hand to the small of my back briefly to calm me, like he could feel the roiling storm inside me. The women in my family had a habit of exploding, and that was the last thing I needed. I took a deep breath and nodded. As the moon showed herself from behind a cloud, the Memory Circle began to sing the histories I was inheriting. As their voices rose to meet the moon, the magic in the earth started to shudder. My own internal power felt like it was beating a bone drum against my soul.

The voices of the Memory Circle began to lull, and the Archivist, the most senior of the group, looked directly at me; her eyes were so dark they were almost black, the complete opposite of my stormy irises.

"No longer are you simply Zoryana, our princess and leader. From this moment on, if the land and the power of your ancestors see fit to choose you, you will be Zoryana Vekara, High Queen of the Dusklands, Keeper of the Last Hearth, The Nightblade Queen." No one outside the Memory Circle was privy to the process by which the titles were chosen; each queen had their own unique titles. Hearing mine made a shiver run through me as the magnitude of what was happening really hit me. While also the High Queen of the Dusklands, my mother's supplemental titles had been different. She was the Guardian of Unyielding Shadow and The Silent Crown. Compared to hers, I thought mine sounded more…hopeful? I prayed that that was a good omen. The Archivist turned to her sister and reached into the box the other female was holding, pulling out the symbol of my family's sovereignty, the Rooted Crown, created after the Breaking by Velastra—the first High Queen of the Dusklands—from the roots of the first tree that had broken ground in the Thornwood.

"Queen Zoryana, will you accept the Rooted Crown and your history?" the Archivist said, holding the crown up.

After another deep, steadying breath, I nodded. "I will. I, Zoryana Vekara, High Queen of the Dusklands, accept the titles bestowed upon me, and the Rooted Crown." My voice was strong, and I could feel Aris' pride emanating from him as he stood behind me.

"Ascend." I stepped forward to the very edge of the Thornwood and the Archivist placed the crown on my head. There was a moment in which no one breathed, waiting for the crown to accept me in return. It thrummed against my head, before the roots started to slide around my head, before they sunk into my temples.

A scream tore from my throat. My entire being was filled with grief and anguish, the power of the emotions taking over my body, joining with my already significant stores of magic. The ground beneath my feet rumbled, and I swore I could see a sliver of sunlight through the trees—there had not been sun in Nightfell since the Breaking. I had never seen the sun fully, but I was sure that was what it was. The moon bathed me in her light as words started to spill from my lips without my control. My soul's name, the histories that had been imprinted into my being. Like the other queens before me, the Thornwood and the land accepted me as the beacon, as the conduit for its power.

It felt like I was stuck in that moment for an age. When the torrent finally started to ebb, my soul assimilating the new power and memories, I hurt all over, but I also felt elated. I felt strong, like I could handle anything that came at me. Glancing at Aris, who had moved to stand beside me, I smiled, thankful for his support. Raising my hands, I half expected them to look different, but they were still the same, pale skin, long fingers. As I focused on my hands, darkness started to pool in my palms, before extending and solidifying into two swords. I heard a gasp and looked up at the Archivist, still standing in front of me…but it was not her that had made a sound. It was one of her sisters—the Armourer. "That power…that is Seravine's magic. No other Dusk Queen has inherited the shadows since the Breaking." Her voice was reverent, and my eyes widened further.

"She was born under the Quieting." The quiet, almost shy voice of the Astronomer came from the back of the group.

The Archivist nodded and smiled. "You may well be the one that we have been waiting for, my dear," she said fondly.

CHAPTER TWO
MY QUEEN

ARIS

SHE WAS BEAUTIFUL. ZORYANA HAD always been beautiful. Right from the moment my fool of a fourteen-year-old self had first laid eyes on her, I was smitten. It was only starling love, but I had been convinced I could have her to myself one day. The young female that would be Queen—I would not ever be enough for a female of her stature, a low-born soldier, an orphan. Even if I had been a favourite of her family—found in the Thornwood as a youngling, my parents having been killed by a dusk-wolf, though no one had believed me that was what had killed them, Queen Nyssara, Zoryana's mother had taken me in, giving me to the Oath-bound to train to one day be her daughter's protection. I did not meet Zoryana until years later when I went through my Shadowborne rite the same year as she had, but Nyssara kept an eye on me. Even with that favouritism, I could not ever wish to be anything more than a friend to the future queen. We had eventually given ourselves to each other, not permanently, not like my heart really wanted, but I would take what she was able to give. I would stand beside her, behind her, or in front of her as her shield, as was the oath I had taken all those years ago, and I would happily share her bed for as long as we could.

Standing with her in the Thornwood, as her chosen ceremonial companion tugged on a part of my soul that I found difficult to hide. As a people, we experienced and did not hide from emotion, but on this day, I had to keep it to myself. It would be inappropriate to show how much I loved her in the sacred setting we were in. Hearing her titles and watching the crown be placed on her head started to solidify just how much space was between us and growing.

As she screamed, her entire body engulfed in the light of the moon and the magic infusing itself into her, dark hair floating around her from the forces swirling around her, I had to hold back from grabbing her, to make it stop. She looked like she was in pain, and I had a primal urge to save her—part Shadowsworn oath, part love. The roots from the crown had pierced her temples, a trickle of dark blood coming from each spot. At the same time, she looked radiant, even more ethereal than usual. The light finally started to dim, and Zoryana quietened. She was breathing hard, like she had just been training; her pale skin was glowing. I shifted to the side, not enough to be in the way, but I wanted to be able to see her face. It wasn't only her skin that was glowing; when she flicked a glance to me, her eyes, those stormy grey eyes I had originally fallen for had changed—now looking like molten silver, like the moon's light she had just gained power from.

Beautiful was not enough to describe her now. There was not a word that seemed sufficient. I did not know if this increased etherealness would settle after the ceremony finished, but it did not matter. There was a moment where I could see in her the reason the Dusk Queens were so feared. Zoryana's mother had been formidable and terrifying; her grandmother had been the same. I could feel the power emanating from Zoryana in a way that frightened me a little, like she could explode at any moment. She had already been powerful, her mother had feared she would overflow, and now with the ancestral power, who knew what her limits were now. She looked away from me and raised her hands, looking down at them. Those thin hands with strong, long fingers that felt amazing sliding through my hair, or on my...

For Goddess' sake, Aris...not the time... I chastised myself.

Everyone's attention went to Zoryana's hands as darkness started to appear in her palms, spreading until she was holding two blades made of shadow, similar in shape and size to the veshkar that was strapped to my hip. The Memory Circle were looking at her in awe, and I was sure the same expression was on my face. The Armourer's words surprised me. Zoryana's mother had been the Guardian of Unyielding Shadow, but I had never actually seen her wield it. I was a soldier, not a scholar, so I did not know all the histories, but hearing that Zoryana was the first since Seravine to inherit the shadows...I would be lying if I was not thinking just how much harder my job as her Shadowsworn had just become. The King of Solnyr was not going to let her live if he believed she was Seravine reborn. Everyone knew she was destined for something great, but this was something else.

Their function served, the Memory Circle departed, and Zoryana turned to face me. Her eyes were still silver, but the glow was settling. I dropped to a knee in front of her, pulling my Shadowblade from its scabbard and presenting it to her.

"My Queen," I said, my head bowed. I had known this day would come when she would finally wear the Rooted Crown and all that entailed, but standing in front of her with the crown on her head, those silver eyes like mirrors reflecting my soul back at me, was a different experience. She was silent for a moment, and I was not sure whether to raise my head to look at her or stay where I was. I had joked about being disrespectful when she wanted me to, but in truth my oath to her meant everything to me.

A small huff that I could not quite tell if it was from amusement or frustration came from above my bowed head. "Oh, come on, Aris. You can stand," she chuckled. Lowering my sword, I looked up at her and smiled. That impish grin on her face was all Zoryana; the glow had settled completely now, the only thing different was her eyes. She held out a hand, and

I took it as I stood. "I hope you are not going to go all oath-bound on me and treat me differently." She was still smiling, but I knew her well enough to know that that was something she was actually worried about.

"I will treat you however you want me to," I assured her. "Until you say otherwise, we are still the same people…you just wear a crown now." I smiled and tapped the side of the crown that had finally released her from its hold, a little surprised it did not lash out at me; I did not know quite how sentient it was. She had small puncture marks on her temples, and her dark blood was still trickling down her face. "Come on, we should get you cleaned up. You are bleeding." I swiped the blood from her cheek. It looked…different. It was still dark, she was night-blooded, but it looked like it was full of starlight. The shimmer faded quickly, and I wondered if I was seeing things, all caught up in the moment, maybe. "Did you know the crown would pierce your head like that?"

She shook her head, reaching up to touch one of the bloody marks. "No. It makes sense, I suppose for it to take in the blood of the wearer, but no, I was not prepared."

Leading her over to where Sumerak was grazing, I helped her up onto my Dusk Stallion before pulling myself up behind her. Sumerak let out a huff and then took off towards the castle. Because we had not known how she would be after the ceremony, how she would feel, I had managed to convince her to ride with me. Vecheryn would have been fine going back on her own, but I also liked the feeling of her in my arms, and on the back of a steed was an acceptable place for that to happen in public.

As we rode through the land, her people came out to greet her, all excited to see her and the Rooted Crown. People looked hopeful for the first time in a long time. Zoryana was the youngest queen to ascend in a few generations—only twenty-seven, the youngest a High Queen could ascend, while Nyssara had been almost one hundred at her own ascension—unfortunately due to her mother leaving our plane much earlier than planned, but I knew she was capable, and her people knew as well. No one out on the streets looked worried or nervous; they looked happy. The younglings running alongside Sumerak giggled and waved. With her in front of me, I was unable to see Zoryana's face, but I could see her waving enthusiastically back to them. The Shadowborne and older looked up at her with reverence and adoration. The elders had watched her grow up into the female she had become, the queen she had become. I was happy they were pleased with who they saw before them. Zoryana's learning and sacrifice over the years was worth it if her people continued to love her as they did. We made it to the castle, and I slid off Sumerak, helping Zoryana off as well. She did not stop moving, greeting people, and accepting their congratulations on her way, until she was in her chambers and I had closed the door behind us. As soon as the door closed and the noise died down, Zoryana visibly relaxed. She let out a heavy sigh that sounded as if it came from the deepest depths of her soul and reached up to remove the crown from her head. It took a moment as her hair was caught in some of the roots from the ride, and she set it down on a stand that had been placed on her table.

"That... That was a long day," she said, sounding tired to her bones.

"It was," I replied, moving over to her and wetting a cloth from the basin that had been brought in before we got back. "Sit and I will clean your face." Surprising me, she sat without complaint or quip and raised her face to look at me. Evidence of how tired the public interactions had made her. Smiling, I knelt in front of her and softly wiped the blood from her face. The wounds on her temples were already starting to heal—I was not sure if it was some new power she had inherited, or if it was because they were caused by the crown, but it was impressive.

"I really do like it when you are kneeling in front of me," she said, almost like she had not meant to say it out loud. Chuckling, I shook my head. She was insatiable.

Reaching up to drop the cloth back in the basin, I grinned up at her. "I will always kneel for you...you know that. All you have to do is ask. What would my Queen like me to do now I am already on my knees?"

She giggled, then covered her mouth. That was not a sound she made all that often. "I think that can wait…I want…" She paused, looking like she was making one of the most important decisions of her life. "I want you to bend me over this table." She patted the tabletop beside her for good measure.

"That can be arranged." I stood, drawing her up with me. Pulling her to me, I dipped my head to capture her lips. Her responses to me, the way she kissed me back and pressed her lithe body to mine, were lifeblood to me.

I worked on the laces of her dress, the heavy material loosened, falling off her arms when she lowered them. Breaking the kiss, I looked down at her glorious body bared to me. Songs should be written about her body—not that I wanted anyone else to know what her clothes hid. She tugged my tunic up and I helped by taking it off the rest of the way while she unlaced my pants. Both of us naked, I encouraged her to turn, facing the table, right in front of the mirror. With a hand between her shoulder blades, I pushed, encouraging her to bend forward until her forearms rested on the tabletop. Our eyes met in the mirror as I stroked myself a couple of times. She licked her lips. With one foot, I parted her legs a little, my hands on her hips. Lining myself up with her entrance, I slowly pushed into her delicious heat. Both of my hands gripped her hips as I started to move, slowly and barely rocking to begin with. She was still watching in the mirror, so I made a point to lock eyes again as my movements increased. Her eyes were so different, but they were still her, especially as they started to cloud from pleasure.

Pulling almost all the way out, until only the tip of my length was still nestled inside her, I paused. Her muscles clenched like she was trying to pull me back in. Moving one hand from her hip, I caressed her butt cheek lightly. I was struggling, torn between trying to tease her and giving us both pleasure, but she was struggling too. She tried to push back but I kept her where she was. A soft groan came from her, and she dropped her head to the table in frustration. With a grin, my hand raised, then made sharp contact with her butt. The sound and the sharp pain made her head fly back up, looking at me with wide eyes in the mirror. It was far from the first time I had done that, but she reacted the same way each time, surprise and a hefty dose of arousal. Her muscles clenched again, tighter this time and I gave her what she wanted. Pushing my hips forward, I buried myself all the way into her. I loved the way she looked as she took me so completely like that. Reaching down, I managed to manoeuvre her leg so her knee was on the table, opening her up for me further.

"Goddess…yes… Oh, Aris!" The new angle made her flatten a little more to the table, but I could fill her even more completely. If the way her muscles were fluttering around my cock and her hands gripped the tabletop were any indication, I knew she was thoroughly enjoying the new angle and depth. Her moans were getting to me as I thrust into her repeatedly, the pleasure building in me almost to a breaking point. We both tipped over the edge together, her muscles clamping around my cock, milking me until I was spent. When I was able to move, I stepped back, pulling slowly out of her and helping her to straighten up. As soon as she was standing, she pulled me into a penetrating kiss.

"Now *that* is how you treat your Queen," she chuckled and moved past me to stretch out on the bed. I huffed out a laugh and shook my head. There was a knock on the door, and we looked at each other with wide eyes. It was more suitable for her to be in her room, answering the door in a robe, than it was for me. I moved into the dressing room. Sliding on the robe I threw to her, she opened the door. It was a server with her dinner. With the tray on the dining table, and the server gone, I re-entered the room. While our relationship was not completely a secret, it was better if we did not give the servers something to gossip about behind her back.

After a quick dinner, Zoryana fell asleep, and I was content to hold her. Our time together would be limited as her schedule was filled with more tasks, so I would take what I could get.

CHAPTER THREE
SUNRISE IN SOLNYR

AURELIAN

"IT IS TIME TO RISE, Prince Aurelian!" The shrill voice of Clanna, my housekeeper, jolted me into waking. As did the glaring sunlight that invaded my bedchamber when she pulled open the drapes covering the window.

"Sol, woman! You are evil," I grumbled. "What would you have done if I was unclothed, or with someone?" She had a habit of barging into my room if I slept past what she deemed acceptable and had walked in on me undressed or in throes of passion on multiple occasions, but it never stopped the blasted woman.

"Oh, my Prince. I have known you since your Firstfire years. Your state of dress is no matter to me, nor are your bedpartners," she replied, continuing to open the drapes of the many windows around the chamber.

It mattered to me. One memorable time was when she had walked in on me deep inside a daughter of one of my brother's courtiers; the woman had been making such a ridiculous amount of noise that I was surprised someone had not thought I was hurting her, not giving her pleasure that she had literally begged me for. It had been a little off-putting if I was to be honest. When Clanna had entered the room, the woman had screamed as if she was being brutally murdered and scrambled away from me to cover herself up, leaving me completely bare of any kind of cover. It honestly kind of hurt when she pulled herself off me without any care at all. I did not invite her back to finish off when Clanna had left and seeing her around the castle was always an awkward experience. There had been other instances, but that time was definitely a standout.

"Your brother the King has asked me to ensure you are up and ready for the council meeting in…" She paused to look at the time piece on the wall. "Oh my! In only twenty minutes!"

"Calm, Clanna. I will be ready, I promise you," I said, patting her shoulder as I ushered her out of the room. With her gone, I leaned against the door and took a few calming breaths. This council meeting was not planned, I did not remember seeing it in my calendar or hearing about it before…unless it *was* planned and my brother had not told me, so as to spring it on me later and make me look incompetent. My darling brother had a habit of forgetting to tell me about meetings—I generally found out in passing, annoying him greatly when I attended, despite his attempts to keep me away. I presumed he was trying to make me look inept so he could oust me somehow—though I was not entirely sure how he thought to make that happen, or who he would replace me with. As his heir I was required to be at all meetings to learn about the kingdom that I would inherit one day—unless my brother finally married and produced a legitimate Firstfire.

I was ready and on my way to the council chamber with plenty of time. I snagged a delicious Solfruit bun, my favourite food, from a server as they passed me with a tray—probably on the way to my brother's chambers. As much as I would hate if the server was to be reprimanded for my theft, I did hope they were going to Aurastes—having one missing would make him incensed. The Solfruit were particularly delicious this season, not as plentiful as usual, but the fruit was juicier and sweeter. Pushing open the door to the council chambers, I saw that some of the councillors were already there.

"Good morning, everyone," I greeted as I sat heavily in my chair. Pulling a goblet of water towards me, I nodded to the men as they returned my greeting. They continued to chatter around the table. Casually sipping on my water, I kept my face as neutral as I could while listening in on their conversations. You always got the best information when people thought you were not listening, and no one ever thought I was listening.

Considering I had been forced out of bed in such a rush, I was quite annoyed when my brother, in all his majesty, arrived late to the meeting. As usual, the, definitely not impromptu, meeting was a bore, full of the same nauseating drivel. Troop deployments, trade with the other kingdoms, the possibility of a match for one of the councillors' daughters. I looked up at that to see which daughter was destined to leave the court. Seeing how happy Councillor Graelor was, I deduced it was one of his. They were a little younger than me, pretty enough, but too young for me…and I would venture to guess they were much too young for whatever lord they were being sent to. I was starting to wish I was anywhere but in the meeting when Councillor Draven spoke up, mentioning the problems they were having with the harvest.

"My liege, the harvest is lower than expected. Our harvesters have reported a dark rot creeping through the crops nearest the Rift."

"What could cause something like that? We have had no troubles before," I enquired.

Everyone's head swung around to me—I usually stayed quiet in the meetings, preferring to listen—but before anyone could answer, my brother interjected, "The land beyond the Rift crowned their young new queen this past week. She evidently caused some of their evil to leak into our land." His voice was venomous.

I narrowed my eyes at him briefly. We knew nothing about the goings on beyond the Rift. The forest was impenetrable… that was what we had always been told. "How…how do you know about the new Dusk Queen?" I asked him. The look he gave me could have burned a lesser man alive.

"I have…my ways," he answered cryptically.

"Uh, I see," I replied, trying not to let on I actually did know what he meant. Spies, he had spies. I did not know why that made me feel uneasy. It meant somehow messages at least, or people, could get through for the first time in over a thousand years. I was not sure what to think about that. The rest of the meeting went on around me as I mulled over what it all meant. When it seemed like the meeting was over, I tried to slip out at the end before my brother was able to hold me back.

"Aurelian!" I sighed as my brother's voice called me back before I even made it to the door.

"Yes, brother," I replied, turning. He glowered at me, hating my casual use of the word 'brother' instead of calling him a title of some kind. He was nothing if not proud, my golden older brother. I realised then that no one else had left; I had been the only one to stand and try to leave. I slunk back to my chair and sat, waiting for whatever our resplendent King had to say.

"I want this statement on the record, in front of the council and my heir, that I do not acknowledge the new queen of the land beyond the Rift. Her lands have not been recognised as sovereign lands for generations. Their legitimate royal line died out long ago with the Witch Queen. The pretenders that have purported to rule since continue to perpetuate the lie they are still a part of our world, that their magic is anything other than a blight that threatens us all."

I was thankful no one was looking at me—I could not help the flinch I gave at my brother's words. Everything just felt…wrong. I did not know why. Generations ago, the Witch Queen had cursed the land and caused the Rift forest to emerge, killing the land around it, and the people that had been living at the border. The creatures that she created killed people stupid enough to attempt venturing into the forest before it closed itself off completely. The sun had died for a decade, until an ancestor of ours was able to revive it to bring light back to the land, and save Solnyr from ruin. At least, that was what we were taught. No one that had lived in those dark days was still alive, and all we had to look at were the history books, which had always felt too bright and sanitised for my liking.

My brother being the tyrant he was, forced us to acknowledge and accept his words before we were permitted to leave the council hall—which I did purely so I could leave. It felt too rehearsed, his speech. As a rule, Solnyr did not acknowledge the Dusklands as anything other than a wasteland. Why bother denouncing the new queen when her title meant nothing to our society? I supposed he would have had to say something due to the rot affecting the crops. If he did not, it could look to his people as though he supported the new queen—if she was indeed controlling the rot, then it would look like he supported killing his own people. He did—my brother was ruthless and not overly loved in the lower classes—but he did not need it to look that way so openly.

Some days I was beyond happy that I had been born second so I could hole up in the Archives with a book and a beverage or lock myself up in my chambers with a willing, warm body, and not have to deal with the goings on of the land beyond the Rift. Some days I thought I could do better—in reality, I would probably be a terrible king, but surely, I would be better than him. Over the years since he was crowned and I was named his heir, I had had many people come to me offering to *deal with him*, to put me in his place. I had obviously turned them all down—the thought of regicide, and fratricide on top of that made me feel ill. I was not my brother, who I was sure would not turn down someone's offer to get me out of the way permanently.

Wandering the hallways, I finally found Lorin, my 'assistant'. That was what he was employed to do—assist me and handle my appointments—but he was terrible at his job, mainly because he was being paid by my brother and was loyal to him, not me. Checking my schedule myself, I planned out my day. That morning's meeting was on my calendar. When I saw it, I gave the other man a look that I hoped clearly portrayed how annoyed at him I was. It looked like I had hours before my next engagement—a banquet my brother would use to strengthen his ties with the other smaller kingdoms and his admirers.

"I will be ready for the banquet at six…until then, I am going back to bed," I grumbled, stalking off to my room. On my way, I snagged a bottle of wine and another Solfruit bun from the kitchens. Closing the door, I stripped off my restrictive court clothing and relaxed on the lounger, picking at my bun and sipping the wine straight from the bottle.

A knock on my door made me jump, not expecting any visitors. With a grunt, I stood, looking down as myself. I was only in my underclothes; if it was Lorin, I did not particularly care if he was offended. If it was anyone else…I felt the same. With a shrug, I headed to the door, still holding the wine bottle. Ripping open the door, I was surprised to not find Lorin, or my brother, or anyone I thought it might be. Elaina, one of the only councillors' daughters that I could remember her name, was standing there.

"Apologies for my state of undress, you caught me unaware," I said. We had been born in the same year and had shared intimate moments regularly—which is why I remembered her name, I presumed—and she had seen me in much less. Her eyes raked over me, taking in my state of undress.

"Oh, no, please accept my apologies, Prince Aurelian." She simpered. Her voice had a syrupy quality to it, she could talk her way out of almost anything, or into anything she wanted. "I just showed up uninvited and unannounced. I am incredibly sorry." Oh, she was laying it on thick. It was a little refreshing, the overly obvious way she flirted. Opening the door further, I stepped aside, swiping my arm into the room to allow her access.

"I presume that is why you are here—surely not to just stand in the hall…dressed like that." I noticed her dress for the first time. It was one of her more risqué creations. I was curious to know how she convinced her parents to allow her out of their home with some of the dresses she had made. I personally thought it was perfectly acceptable; women's dress should not be as regulated as it was—men's clothing was not. This particular dress had parts cut out of it over her waist and was tight around her breasts, making them very enticing as they bloomed over the top. She smiled and walked into the room like she belonged there. The number of times she had been in my rooms compared to other women, I worried that she just might think that. She was incredible in bed, and a friend, but I had no intention to marry her. Marrying within Solnyr was not on the cards for me; I was destined for a princess from another kingdom chosen by my brother whenever he decided it served him most.

Reaching out, she took the bottle from me and took a sip. A small amount of the golden liquid escaped the side of her pouty lips, painted pink to emphasise them. I leaned in and kissed the wine from the side of her lips. I did not bother to ask why she was there or wait for confirmation. There was no other reason she would have visited or walked into my room with me being in such a state. She turned her head and captured my lips. Her kiss tasted sweet from the wine. My arm snaked around her, fingers sliding under the edge caused by the cut out. She sighed softly and moved her free hand up my exposed chest. Breaking the kiss, I took the bottle from her to get it out of the way. Spinning her around, I unlaced her dress with deft fingers, making it drop to the floor. She was not wearing anything underneath—yes, she had anticipated me allowing her in to fuck her. Leaning in, I took one of her nipples into my mouth, sucking and nipping the hard peak. Moving to the other, I shifted a little to help her remove my underclothes.

I was not really a soft and caring lover. I knew that could be considered a failing on my behalf, but it was who I was. I was not bedding women to get them to love me; it was a few moments of pleasure and fun. I had no need or want for love, knowing that even if it did happen it could never last. The women that shared my bed knew that, of course, they always thought they could be the one that changed me, but it had not happened yet. None of the golden-haired, sun-kissed beauties that shared my bed, who I used to lust over, were what I dreamed about at night. Even Elaina with her perfect body and skills in bed did not compare to my dreams. I pushed Elaina back onto the bed, spreading her thighs with mine. As I pushed into her, an image of the raven-haired enchantress that had been haunting my dreams swum across my vision. I could never see her face, but her body was breathtaking and her hair…I always wished I could run my hands through it. Gripping Elaina's thighs, my hips thrust into her over and over. She was one that I knew if her moans were real or not—they certainly were real at that moment. She was gasping, moaning, and practically screaming as I railed her, her hands rolling and squeezing her own breasts. She did have incredible breasts…her whole body was delicious. Thinking about my dream woman had increased my passion, my thrusts deep and fast. Elaina let out a particularly loud, passionate moan, her muscles gripping my cock like a vice. I was not quite ready to finish but I knew from experience that she did not expect me to stop just because she had climaxed.

I continued to push into her until I reached my own release with one final harsh thrust and a moan of my own. When I was done, I slumped forward onto my arms, hovering over her, still semi-hard inside her. "A pleasure, as always, Elaina," I said with a satisfied smile. Returning my smile, she propped herself up and kissed me.

"Mmmhm." She sighed softly and flopped backwards again. All the movement was starting to get me worked up again.

"Elaina…if you are not careful, you are going to have to stay a little longer."

"I have nowhere to be." Her grin was sinful as she clenched her muscles around me again.

"Sol, woman." I chuckled, but what she was doing was working. Along with the clenching, she wiggled her hips a little. "Flip," I grunted, sliding out of her. She did as she was told, flipping onto all fours on the bed. Pulling her closer to the edge, I entered her again from the back. This time, she used her hands and knees to push back against me, increasing the force of the movements.

"Yes, Aurelian. You fill me so good." Her dirty talk could use some work, but sometimes it was nice to hear that you filled someone, not that I was insecure about that. Our groans and moans were louder and more passionate this time, and it did not take long for either of us to climax. Both sated, I moved over to the bathing room to get a wet cloth to clean up.

Watching her leave, I smiled, thankful she understood the arrangement—or at least pretended to. Alone again, I stretched out on my back, staring at the ceiling, unable to get the vision of the woman who bewitched my dreams out of my mind.

CHAPTER FOUR
THE FIRST SEEDS OF DOUBT

AURELIAN

THE BANQUET WAS FULL OF my brother's stuffy friends, and even stuffier courtiers. I found myself caught in many conversations, each one more excruciating than the last. The food was exquisite though, and the wine flowed freely, so I could at least feed a few of my vices. In attendance was also some visiting dignitaries from other kingdoms—mostly just advisers, but the Kingdom of Alarinth had sent their prince, Renvir, and his wife. He was a little older than I was but he was interesting enough; I knew most of the kingdoms thought he was one of, if not the, most charming prince in the kingdoms, but I had always found him a little dull, but he at least knew some of the burden of being a prince next in line to a throne. He had also been raised mostly in Solnyr, so we crossed paths a lot—though I sometimes felt a little guilty over the fact he had been taken from his home at a young age by my own father as what was essentially a political prisoner. His wife was also gorgeous, and highly flirtatious, so that made talking to him even more enjoyable. I drew a boundary at bedding another man's wife, though I had heard they were not overly loyal to each other, but I was not above looking at her.

"Aurelian." My brother's voice called me from the other

side of the room.

"Please excuse me, I have been summoned," I said to the Prince of Alarinth and his wife apologetically and made my way over to where my brother was standing, surrounded by sycophants as always. "You called, brother." I did like that just calling him that annoyed him so much.

"Ah! Yes, Aurelian, I was just speaking to the duke here. He says his king, Hadros from Savrinn, is looking for a husband for his daughter, Irenn. Perhaps—" I cut him off, knowing where it was going but trying to steer the direction away from myself.

"She would be a great match for such fine a king as you? Oh, I agree, brother. She is young enough. She could give you heirs…" My brother looked like he wanted to strike me. I was not ready for a wife. It was true I was beyond the age most married—having turned thirty at my last name day—but my brother was five years older and also still unmarried. It made sense that he should be wed first. I also did not get along with Princess Irenn at all. She had spent a lot of time in Solnyr, and she was an unusually abrasive person. We clashed at every meeting—that would make for a horrific marriage.

"Perhaps," he grumbled.

"Please, excuse me, brother, I am afraid I have an early appointment in the morning and must try to get some sleep. Duke." I nodded to both of them, a little lower to my brother than the duke, and hurried as nonchalantly out of the room as I could. I did not have an appointment in the morning, but I could not be in that room any longer. Not one person in the room was able to keep my attention and watching people worship my brother as if he was Sol on earth was wearing on my nerves. Hiding in my room for the rest of the night sounded like a very good plan.

The next morning, Clanna woke me, shattering my head with her voice and the sunlight. Even when I swore at her, she just smiled.

"Here, please drink this," she said, putting a goblet of something that smelled terrible on the table beside the bed. With horror, I recognised it as the drink she had given me on numerous occasions after a long night of drinking made my head spin and my stomach roil.

"Why must you torture me so?" I grumbled. My sparkish tone made her chuckle. The older woman pushed my damp hair from my face and leaned in to press a kiss to my forehead. The motherly gesture tore at my heart.

"Because I love you, even though you make it difficult sometimes," she murmured, stroking my head again before leaving me alone. Clanna was the one woman I could confidently say I loved—even if it was just as a mother-figure.

I swallowed the horrible concoction she had left and let it settle. It was not long before my head cleared and my stomach settled. I did not know what was in the drink, I did not dare ask, but if I did not know better, I would suspect there was some magic involved. Clanna did not possess magic—much to her chagrin—but the drink had to have some magical properties to work so quickly. I had no appointments that day at all, so after a long bath, I dressed and headed out in search of my morning meal, deciding to spend the day in the Archives, where I felt most comfortable.

The walk to the Archives was long, up innumerable steps, some uneven and a little unsafe, but it was worth it. The scholars did not bother me there; they let me sit and study whatever caught my eye. As I was unlikely to become king—though my brother was yet to marry and produce a legitimate heir (though everyone knew there were a few illegitimate ones running around)—I had to begin deciding which faction or order I would choose. I was sure my brother hoped I would join the Golden Legion and die in a skirmish, but I was much more interested in books, so I was leaning towards the Order of Illumination or possibly the Archivists. As I finally entered the Archives, the archivists and scholars around nodded at me, acknowledging me as both their prince, but also as a fellow lover of knowledge, as I passed to find a quiet space to sit and mull over all I had heard over the past days.

As I continued through the winding maze of shelves and tables, I began wondering if I would find a space at all. There was an abundance of scholars about today, perhaps because of the Dusklands coronation. They would be updating history books, possibly looking for ways for my brother to do something nefarious, or to find out the implications of a new Dusk Queen. The last one—so far as I knew—had lived longer than any of us did. I had heard the Dusklanders lived hundreds of years, so this was the first new Dusk Queen anyone had experienced in their lifetime. Pushing open a random door that I thought led to a private study room, I found myself in a chamber I could not remember being in before. There were no shelves of books and scrolls, no tables, no scholars. Just another door. I knew I should leave but curiosity got the better of me—I had always been the adventurous one. Taking the torch off the wall, I tried the second door. It was locked. There did not seem to be a keyhole, or anything of the sort.

A memory came back to me from my early studies during my Dawnbreak years: ancient Solnyr vaults unlocked only for bloodline and intention. I did not think this was an ancient vault or anything; there was probably just a special key that was only held by certain people, but I spoke the formal, ancient phrase anyway, half joking, half curious. "By right of Sol's firstborn, I seek what is buried."

I expected nothing to happen. I expected to just laugh it off and leave like I did with most of my adventures. What I did not expect was for a sound like a latch opening, and the door to creak ajar. I gaped at the door in shock. I was not Sol's firstborn—that was technically my brother, as King, he was the Son of the Sun. Whatever magic was in this lock should have known that and never responded to a lie.

The door opened onto a staircase that ascended higher still into the tower. It looked like it was possibly built into the walls, so it was not overly visible from the inside or outside. Looking over my shoulder, I quickly slipped beyond the doorway and closed the door behind me. Sol, I prayed I had not just sealed myself inside forever. I climbed for what felt like forever until the stairs opened up in an open, slightly cavernous room. I suspected it sat on top of the Archives and was almost as big. It was filled with books, scrolls, even what looked like clay or stone tablets. Some looked like government documents and treaties. Everything smelled of dust and wax, making my nose itch. The air felt heavy…like it was carrying the weight of things that had been deliberately buried.

Infinitely curious, I found a sconce for the torch and chose a scroll at random. Sitting down at the dust-covered desk, I unrolled the scroll. It was labelled: *The Final Concord Between Sun and Shadow*. I expected to read the same words that I had been learning since I learned to read: Solnyr offered peace, the Dusklands refused, war began. But this scroll, this treaty, said the opposite. The Dusklands accepted peace and Solnyr betrayed it.

My entire world view shattered as I read. Line after line, clause after clause, it laid out the terms of the treaty—shared borders, mutual protection, no expansion of lightbound territory, and most importantly, no forced conversion by flame, shadow, or oath by either side. It laid out the terms of their marriage, including the titles they would hold and what their children would inherit.

It was signed by Caelen, the First Solar King, though he was titled Prince of the Sun on this treaty…and Seravine, the High Queen of Vesmor.

Vesmor. My pulse hammered in my chest. The history books I had grown up reading and learning from said no such treaty ever existed. None of them even listed Seravine as a *High Queen*, only a Queen, if they were being generous. And they did not mention Vesmor. As I read, I had discerned that Vesmor was the name of the unified land before the Breaking, and the Queens of the Dusklands were the supreme rulers, all the other kingdoms ultimately answering to them. These were the kind of records that could rewrite myth as truth and truth as threat to everything Solnyr stood for. I could not stop reading now I had started. I was enthralled in a way I had not been in a long time. I felt like I was under a spell…or that the one I had been under for my entire life was crumbling around me.

Standing, I chose another scroll that looked to be around the same age as the treaty. This one was even more damning. It was not another treaty, or government document, it was a confession. Scrawled across the scroll was a decree from the First Solar King, Caelen—my ancestor:

> *I break the oath made for the good of the realm of Solnyr.*
>
> *The Dusklands and their Queen will be painted as the aggressors and the truth will be sealed so as to save our lineage.*
>
> *Let Light be the only story that survives.*

I was pretty sure I had stopped breathing as I read. This was…this was wrong. I knew, every palace spark knew, that the official motto of Solnyr's founders, including Caelen, the First Solar King, was: *Let the truth burn bright*. This one scroll threw all that into the fires of Sol. What they should really have ended that motto with was: *Let the lie burn brighter*.

For the first time in my privileged, royal, obedient, gilded life, I was ashamed. Ashamed of my family, of my history… ashamed of the sun itself. We were the keepers of a gilded lie that had harmed so many and had caused the destruction of communities.

"We are not the righteous side… We are just the side that won first and wrote the history," I whispered to myself in the quiet room. It felt wrong to speak in such a space, but I could not hold the words inside.

I did not know how long I sat in that room, reading scroll after scroll, some innocent—their only failing was that they mentioned Vesmor—some damning for the Solar Kings. The more I read, the more I believed and understood. Caelen had wanted power to overthrow his father—to become more than just a Day King. By marrying High Queen Seravine, he had become the High King Consort—while that meant he was not a King in his own right, he was a High King, meaning he ruled over his own father. The power made him hungry for more, and he had somehow stolen or corrupted the power of his own wife, causing her control to fracture and explode, like a living, shadow version of a Sundrop.

When the light that rimmed the shuttered windows began to dim, I realised I had been reading all day. Someone would probably come looking for me at some point, and this room was the last place I wanted to be caught. I hurried out of the room and back down the stairs, managing to slip out without being seen, I hoped. I did not know what to do with all the new information I had discovered. I was highly distracted as I wandered the halls of the palace back to my chambers; I waved people off, not wanting to talk in case I somehow forgot everything in a conversation. Once I had locked myself in my chambers, I took a breath and looked around the room. The entire space was covered in what I now knew was propaganda—from the large sunburst sigils on the walls, drapes, and sheets, to the insignia on every surface, and the motto above my mirror. I wanted to cover it all up, but I did not think it was wise to let anyone know what I had found just yet.

CHAPTER FIVE
THE ENVOY

ZORYANA

The letter came a little over a week after my coronation. I was not even sure how it had been delivered. The sunburst seal in gold wax made my face screw up in confusion.

"Zorya?" Aris' voice sounded concerned as he called me by the name he had used during our starling years. The others around us looked at him, surprised at how casual he was with me. "Is something wrong?"

"Ari…it…it is a letter from Solnyr," I replied, turning the envelope to show him and those around us the seal. It was addressed simply to The Dusk Queen, my name or proper title was not there, but why would I have expected anything different? To be honest, it was much more diplomatic than expected.

"I should open it, in case it is a trick," Aris suggested. With the Shadowsworn oath he had taken, it made him harder to injure than anyone else in the room. He took the envelope I handed him and stood, walking away from the group before he broke the seal. Opening the envelope and taking out the letter, he waited a moment to make sure everything was safe, before walking back over and handing me the letter.

To Zoryana Vekara, the new Dusk Queen,

May your reign rise in calm shadow and end in lasting peace.

Word of your ascension has reached the Court of Solnyr, and in accordance with the ancient protocols between our realms, I extend formal recognition of your crown. Though our histories have walked divergent paths, the Sun Throne acknowledges the weight of your inheritance and the stability your rule may bring to the borderlands.

It is the judgement of my council—and my own will—that this moment offers a rare opportunity. The balance between our courts has endured long enough in tension, stalemate, and cold memory. Perhaps, under new sovereigns, there might be room for dialogue beyond the lingering echoes of war.

Thus, I propose a Conference of Accord to be established, to be held within your land as an extension of our good will, to re-establish diplomatic contact, explore terms of secured peace, and discuss matters of shared concern along our fractured boundary. To this end, I shall dispatch my blood and voice: His Highness Aurelian Solnyr, Prince of the Sun, Heir to the Light Throne, as my sworn envoy and representative.

He carries full authority to speak on my behalf, and I trust he will be received in the manner due his station—with the courtesy owed to one who bears his blood.

May the shadows of yesterday not dictate the shape of tomorrow.

In the Light's clarity,

Aurastes Solnyr IV, King of the Sun, Lord of the Dawnbound Court, Keeper of the Eternal Flame

My face must have been showing something concerning, as Aris once again said, "Zorya," but this time reached out to put a hand on my arm. "Zorya? What is it?"

I looked up at him, then to the crowd of advisers looking at me with the same curiosity. "The Light King congratulates me on my ascension, though he seems to refuse to use my full title while putting his on display, and proposes a...a conference to work out our issues. He is sending his brother as an envoy."

The room around me erupted with voices. No one in the room had expected a recognition of my coronation, let alone anything that may resemble peace talks. The noise around me was beating against my skull, making it difficult to think as everyone yelled and cursed.

"Quiet!" I said, raising my voice barely above my normal talking voice, but my confusion and worry sent a ripple of power through the room, stopping everyone and their words immediately. I took a deep breath and massaged my temples, right over the scars left from the Rooted Crown. "We have no choice in this. By the sounds of this letter, the prince may already be on his way, may be nearing the border and requiring passage through the Thornwood. Does anyone know how this letter got through in the first place?" I asked the room.

Everyone shook their heads. The Thornwood had been impenetrable for centuries. At the back of the room, the door opened and the Memory Circle stepped through, led as always by the Archivist. "My Queen, an opening has been discovered in the Thornwood. Sunlight... Sunlight has burned through the trees," she said.

I doubted the sun had caused the opening; Solnyr was not any stronger than they were over the past centuries. They were strongest in magic at the time of the Breaking. Since then, it was known that they had a very limited number of magic-wielders and they were highly regulated. I wondered if it had anything to do with the way the ancestral magic had reacted to my own power since my coronation. Maybe it had actually been sunlight I had seen that day.

"That must be how the messenger got through," I mused. Turning to Aris, I tapped the table lightly as I thought. "Can you send a few of your warriors to the opening to secure it?" He nodded and stood, a male of action. I looked around the group before me. "Serian, I am trusting you to go with the Oath-bound to the opening to meet Prince Aurelian and welcome him to the Dusklands. Take a retinue of people you can trust. Treat him well, but do not trust him. Light can be blinding." The male who had once loved my mother stood and nodded.

"It is my honour, my Queen," he said, bowing his head, his hands clasped over his chest in a ceremonial display of deference. We looked similar—my mother had never married, but there were rumours he was possibly my father, and he had treated me well my whole life. I trusted him with this task on the love he had for my mother, and possibly me.

I sat back in my chair and waved a hand to dismiss everyone else in the room, a little surprised when they all left without complaint. I had expected some resistance, but they all stood and left, leaving me in the room alone. I needed to prepare. How did I prepare for something like this? I had never had to deal with anything like this—no one had thought talks between Nightfell and Solnyr would ever happen, so I had never been advised on how to react, not even by my mother, who had covered many topics that others thought redundant. I felt lost. Did the Sun King think I was easily swayed because I was young? Because I was new and malleable? Well, Shadow could not be controlled, and I would show him I was as hard as the obsidian our weapons were forged from… But first, I needed to release some of my frustration before it started to cause issues.

When I was a youngling, I had trouble controlling my magic. No one had really been sure why; I did everything I was supposed to do in my lessons, I trained in weaponry, I screamed, I cried, everything. During my First Grief, I had caused a small blight that had lasted a week. When I passed from youngling to starling, I had cried for three days while my magic attempted to settle. After that, my mother had had a room built where I could practise in relative safety—for myself and those around me. Pushing open the door to the room, I made sure it was closed behind me. I centred myself in the room. Opening up a little, I tried to just breathe through everything. But once the gate was open, I was done for. My breaths turned to a frustrated yell and I let go. The room darkened around me until the candles were snuffed out, and I was essentially blind—this was new. Usually, it was just waves of power that escaped, but I had filled the room with shadow. Suddenly there was banging at the door.

"Zorya! Zorya! Are you okay?!" Aris' voice from the other side of the door sounded…well, he sounded scared, and frantic. Dropping to my knees, I tried to focus on bringing the shadow back into me, to get it under control. "Zorya… You… You are okay. We will get through this." Aris was still calling through the door, trying to calm me. It made me worried about what he could hear through the door, or whether my power had possibly leaked out of the room.

With his calming words, I finally felt like I could breathe again. I could barely see in the darkened room, but at least it was only because the candles were not alight, and not because of the shadows. "I… You can come in," I called out. As soon as I spoke, the door opened, Aris silhouetted in the doorway. He lit the nearest candle, then shut the door behind him, coming to sit on the floor with me.

"What happened?" he asked me, pulling me into his arms.

"I…I do not know. I came in here because I needed to let some of it out before I could focus on everything but it just… leaked out. I…the room filled with shadow," I replied, raising my face to look at him. He looked concerned.

"It was seeping under the door," he admitted. My eyes widened. That was why he had sounded so frantic, why he had changed from beating down the door to soothing me. The Memory Circle thought I was Seravine reborn… Did that mean I was destined to share in her fate? Groaning, I dropped my head to his shoulder. "Zorya…you are not dangerous. Neither was Seravine, not really. What happened was dangerous, but *she* was not. *You* are not. *You* are strong, and powerful. You are being faced with something no one could have prepared you for, prepared any of us for. Of course you are feeling a little out of control. Do not let the histories convince you that you are bad or anything other than incredible." He tightened his arms around me and pressed a kiss to my head.

"Aris…thank you," I murmured. He always knew how to change my mood. Aris pulled back slightly, moving a hand to the side of my face to tilt it so we were looking at each other.

"You are welcome," he said with a smile. I loved it when he smiled. The scar that sliced across his face just made him even more handsome, more roguish. I reached up and ran my fingers over the scar, and he closed his eyes briefly. Sometimes I felt bad that I had made our arrangement, essentially making him unavailable to anyone else. He deserved a great love that he could show to the world. Whatever female was shown the soft and loving Aris under the stoic Oath-bound warrior would be incredibly lucky. But other times, I was thankful that I had him as more than just my Shadowsworn warrior. We knew each other in a way that I was not sure I would find in anyone else. "How can I help right now, Zorya?" he asked. His tone was softer than would have been expected from a male in his position.

"Remind me…" I whispered. I was not even one hundred percent what that meant, so I would not have been surprised if he was confused. However, as usual, he took my sometimes-nonsensical words and made sense of them. His fingers stroked over my face, before he leaned in and pressed his lips to mine. My body instinctively arched towards him as I accepted his kiss and melted into his strong and familiar embrace. He made me feel safe, and I knew it wasn't fair on either of us, this arrangement, but he was the only person around me that treated me as Zoryana, not as the Queen. He loved me, or at least wanted me, and that made all the difference.

Aris shifted, sliding my legs around him, before laying me out on the floor of the room. I had avoided having anyone else in this room with me; it was essentially made to hold me if something bad happened. If I lost control, they would have somewhere to contain me…hopefully. In this moment, with my back against the stone floor, and Aris hovering above me…I was happy there was a different memory being made in the room that had always felt so negative to me. I reached up to help unlace his tunic and pull it over his head. His chest was crisscrossed with scars from sparring with sharp-edged weapons, a particularly vicious swipe over the upper left part, caused by a nasty bone-wolf in his Steelhands trail. I had spent many nights studying each mark…new ones appeared all the time, so there was always something new to discover.

It seemed Aris was not in the mood for exploration though. Now that he had established that I needed him to distract me, he was taking charge in the way he knew I loved. I did not break easily, thankfully, and he took advantage of that regularly. Without warning, and with no consideration to the fact I was laying on a stone floor, he took hold of my hips and flipped me. I managed to quickly move my hand up, narrowly avoiding smashing my face on the floor. That would have been difficult to explain… I shot him a look over my shoulder, rolling my eyes at how unapologetic he looked. His hands pulled at the laces of my dress, opening it to give his fingers room to trace my own scars—being royalty did not exclude me from the rituals our people endured to pass to the next stage of life, in fact mine had been worse.

I moaned softly as his fingers were replaced with his lips, kissing the long puckered line that ran from between my shoulder blades to the small of my back, right down my spine—the remnants of my Shadowborne ritual that had attempted to remove my shadow to bind it to the throne, the ritual had not worked as planned; instead a second shadow-beat was discovered so the slice was lengthened to accommodate. When it was clear my shadow was staying where it was, I was declared Shadowborne and wrapped up. Now the large scar marred my back like a second spine. It was still sensitive, and the way Aris' lips on the shiny skin felt was setting off little reactions inside me.

His hand slid into my dress and around to my front, palm flat to my body, just under my breasts, lifting me just enough so he could push my dress down my arms with his other hand. With my torso bare, he lowered me back to the floor, continuing to pull my dress off my body. The dress was pulled off my feet, and I looked over my shoulder to see him unlacing his pants, pushing them off his hips. My breath picked up as he moved between my legs, leaning over me to press a kiss to my neck.

"You might be my queen…but right now…I am in charge." His voice was almost guttural as he murmured in my ear.

"Yes…" I breathed as he straightened back up, his hands on my hips. He lifted my hips off the ground, until I was kneeling, rear in the air, torso still on the floor. "Oh…Gods!" A passionate moan left me as Aris entered me in one powerful thrust, his hips pressing against my rear. Raising myself up onto my forearms, I was able to participate as he began to move his hips, setting a punishing pace from the beginning. One large hand dug into my hip, the other slid over the small of my back, holding me to him as he pounded into me. Our moans and groans, the sounds of our coupling echoing off the stone all around us.

The hand on my back continued exploring, reaching my shoulder, where it tightened, forcing me to straighten up as well, until my back was against his front. His arm snaked around me, caging me against his body. The way he was holding me, like he was afraid of letting me go, told me I had scared him earlier with my explosion of power. And now he was taking out that fear on my body, if the intense pace he was somehow keeping up in this position was any indication.

"Aris…" I gasped as his hand travelled over my chest, giving attention to each breast, his other hand still hard on my hip—there would be a mark. I was starting to tremble as my release started to build.

"Zorya," he groaned in response. His thrusts were becoming stiffer. He suddenly moved his hand from my chest to grip my other hip, and I fell forward to my hands. He deepened his movements and my body clenched around him. "Yes…Gods yes…" He let out a series of expletives as I clenched again, my muscles starting to flutter as I neared my climax. I knew he was close too and I wanted to release together. At the thought, my body gave me no choice…my climax crashed over me, making my back arch more, pushing my hips back against his. The noise he released as he too reached his climax was animalistic and primal. Where my hands were braced against the floor, I could see shadows starting to seep out from under them. I was too far into my pleasure to care all that much.

Once we were both spent, Aris pulled out of me, much more tender than he had been, and helped me lower myself to the ground again. He rolled onto the floor beside me and turned his head to look at me. "You are so beautiful," he murmured. He lifted one of my hands that was still leaking shadow, running his fingers over my palm and fingers. The dark tendrils calmed and started weaving around his hand too. I huffed out a laugh.

"If all it takes to calm me is your touch, you are never allowed to leave me alone," I teased. He chuckled too. We both knew he was one of the only things that stopped me from following in the footsteps of my ancestors. We watched the shadows crawl over our hands for a moment longer before they dissipated. I did not know what was going to happen in the coming days, months, or years, but I knew I could count on Aris—his strength, his honour, body, and his heart.

CHAPTER SIX
SUN IN THE DARK

AURELIAN

THE NOTE FROM MY BROTHER was delivered as part of Clanna's morning ritual of waking me up in the most passively aggressive way possible. This time, the naked woman in my bed did not jump or try to scamper away, she just burrowed into the blankets and my side, like she was trying to go back to sleep, until the older woman had handed me the note and left. I recognised my brother's handwriting on the outside. While I decided what to do with it, considering throwing it out the window, my bed mate—I should really make an effort to learn these poor women's names—had disappeared under the covers completely.

"Sol!" I groaned as her mouth slid over my manhood. I threw the note on the table beside my bed and enjoyed the feeling of her very talented lips and tongue. My hand slipped under the blanket to find her head, fingers tangling in her thick hair. Her hair had been what had drawn me to her first—it was the darkest hair that I had seen on a Solnyrian woman, meaning she probably had blood from another kingdom, still golden, but closer to bronze. The darker hair had been the closest I knew I would get inside the castle to the woman that was still haunting my dreams—after a particularly vivid and frustrating dream the night before, I had needed to satiate myself somehow. She knew exactly how to bring me to the edge, and I was getting there quickly. Her attentions did not stop until I unloaded in her throat, a guttural moan leaving me in pleasure. I was not given the chance to offer to return the favour as she excused herself soon after, with a 'thank you' for her morning meal. I lay there stunned for a moment, before remembering the note. With a grumble, I reached for it and unfolded the parchment. My brother's loopy letters filled the page with damning instructions and an apparent attempt at staying anonymous.

Prince,

The time has come for your most important diplomatic mission that you have yet embarked on. I am sending a delegation of my most loyal advisers to the Dusklands.

You go as envoy, and you go as my brother. You go with two faces: the face the Dusklands may admire, and the face that must return the terms I require.

You will be received as a guest; accept the hospitality but never their leniency. Open every chest they offer closed. Let no page go unread without your eye. You will be my ear and my blade of ink.

Your orders, in plain:

- *Listen first. Let them speak until they tire. Truth reveals itself in what is repeated.*

- *Secure the clause on border passes. Insist on free merchant lanes in exchange for fixed patrol routes— always and only favourable to Solnyr.*

- *Probe their archives by friendly curiosity. If you find the old records, breathe nothing of it—but report immediately.*

- *Test their loyalties. Make them reveal who truly holds power—councillors, generals, or native magisters. The Queen is too new and young to hold main power.*

- *Leave a door open for those who will defect. Names.*

Promises. Safe passage. Bring me the names, Prince. Bring me the men who will trade land for gold.

- *If talks go well, return with a formal agreement. If they do not, return with names and weaknesses that we can exploit.*

You are more valuable alive than dead, yet you must remember that if they offer you a throne in exchange for silence, you burn the offer. We do not barter truth for comfort.

Bring counsel. Bring caution. Bring me the truth.

- A.

I read the note three more times. He was sending me into the Dusklands? He had publicly said he did not consider the new queen a threat. He very obviously did, and he was scrambling to gain the upper hand as quickly as possible.

"Sol..." I grumbled as I sat up. Did I want to go? What if the land really was full of monsters? Or the Queen took my head. However, after what I had found in that secret room in the Archives... Maybe I could gather more information. Try to work out exactly what happened...what *really* happened. Stretching, I finally forced myself to get out of bed, pulling on a pair of pants and walking over to my writing table. Stopping before I reached the chair, I changed direction and headed to my dressing room. I needed more time to think about my response.

Dressing did not take nearly enough time, and I was dreading the task ahead of me as I sat in the chair and found a piece of parchment and opened my ink pot. Dipping my quill in the ink, I let it hover over the page for a moment as I thought about what to write. I wanted to decline—I liked my life. Instead, I decided to write whatever came to me and see how it went.

Brother,

I will do as duty demands. But I will not do as fear demands. You say listen first. I have been listening all my life. I have heard whispers in archive dust and soldier tents and the pauses in every speech you give.

You say secure the passes. I know the passes are not what you want. You want advantage, not agreement.

You say probe their archives. I have already read enough in our own to know what lies buried there—and what we publicly burned from our own.

You ask for names of those who would defect. I will not bring you people to break. I am tired of being the hand that smiles while the knife is hidden.

You say I go with two faces. I have only one, and I will no longer wear it for you.

If the Dusklands are enemies, let me see it with my own eyes. If they are not—then I will not make them so for you.

And if I discover that the truth you fear is the truth they still remember...then I will not return as your weapon.

You signed your letter as A.

I sign mine as Aurelian.

When I was done, I could barely even look at the words on the page. Those words were treason. They were well written, if I said so myself, but they were treason, nonetheless. In a move that I was sure I would regret later, I did not dispose of the letter; I folded it and slipped it into the inside pocket of my jacket. The second letter I wrote was much more sanitised.

My King,

Thank you for the honour to be sent to the Dusklands as your envoy in these important talks. I will take your instruction and act as I am able.

I look forward to this charge and chance to make Solnyr proud.

Your steadfast brother,

Aurelian

It was short...much shorter, but it said what my brother

wanted to hear. He would not be bothered with any reservations or fears I had, and I could not let him know I had found the records above the Archives. I was sure my darling brother hoped I would get caught spying for him and that the Queen would have me killed, giving Aurastes even more reason to hate and denounce the Dusklands. I folded the second letter, wrote my brother's name on the front and headed to the door.

"Please take this to my brother, the King," I said to one of the guards standing sentry at my door. He nodded and took the note, walking off to deliver it. I wandered the halls in search of food; I had not had my morning meal yet and I already felt like I had worked a full day. I was eating an array of sweet buns when the official instructions arrived for my mission to the Dusklands.

My brother had been planning an invasion of the Dusklands for a long time. That was painfully evident in how quickly everything was pulled together. How had I not noticed? I made a point of looking uninterested, but I generally knew most of what was going on, but I had not noticed the efforts he was making to prepare. With great fanfare, I was leading a small retinue of attendants and soldiers out of the capital towards the Rift forest. We were heading for an opening that had appeared in the trees over the past tide, causing a bit of a problem for the border patrols who were having to deal with monsters coming through. According to reports, a lot of the creatures did not last long in the sunlight, but some of them did, and were taking out our troops with frightening frequency.

After two uncomfortable days atop my horse and sleeping in a tent that had not been provisioned for a prince, we finally reached the clearing. I had been to the border before, many times—as a Prince of the Sun it was one of my responsibilities to visit the garrisons to keep up morale and take grievances to my brother—I had even looked out over the forest from my window; it was so large that it could be seen from almost everywhere in the Five Kingdoms. The sunlight did not penetrate whatever the Witch Queen's magic had done to their lands, the whole land was in constant darkness. Lights from fires in what I presumed were villages and the Dusk Castle were the only light. Seeing the land through the trees, knowing I was about to cross through, was a different and unnerving experience. I was not ashamed to say I was terrified. No reasonable man would cross the border into a land so unknown without a small amount of apprehension. Everyone around me, even seasoned soldiers looked cautious at the very least.

What was waiting for us at the clearing was equally alarming. The men and women that stood on the other side were huge and imposing. I was not a small man, around six foot—tall for a Solnyrian and a full head and shoulders taller than my brother—but these people towered over me. I was looking at full-blooded High Fae for the first time in my life. No one I knew had ever seen High Fae in person. The Dusk people had not interbred with others since the Breaking, and it showed. The Solar bloodline had a small amount of High Fae blood, remnants from our ancestors being preferable as partners for the High Queens in the time before, but it was so diluted by now that we could barely be called more than lesser fae anymore. We were Solnyrian, that was all.

"Greetings," I said, hoping I did not sound like an insipid Firstfire. "I am Aurelian, Prince of the Sun, and I am here to meet with your Queen." Sol, I hoped one of them was not the Queen…that would be mortifying.

A slightly smaller, older man stepped forward. "Greetings, Prince Aurelian. I am Serian, adviser to High Queen Zoryana. She awaits your arrival at her home where we can begin talks."

"It will be my honour. Please, lead the way." I hoped there was not some ritual I needed to perform—from my illicit reading, and what we were taught about the Dusk people, they were still heavily into ritual and magic. Serian gave me a nod and instructed the giants to let us pass. I did not know if actual giants existed on their side of the Rift, but I was sure they would look like the warriors that flanked our group. Some stayed behind at the clearing to stop anyone else from coming through or anything from leaving I presumed.

For such a dark and obviously dying land, it was eerily beautiful. The landscape sprawled in front of us, dark soil and plants, twisted but thriving trees. It was very different to the vibrancy I was used to in Solnyr, but there was a muted wonder about the place. People came out of their homes to watch us pass, wary and suspicious, some ushering their Firstfires back inside as if we would hurt them. I supposed it was not far from the truth, if my brother had his way. We looked so different, suiting our surroundings—they were all mostly rather pale, with dark hair and light eyes, shades of blues and greens from what I could see, while my skin was darker, my hair was light, and my eyes were darker. I had the typical look of a Solnyrian, but my golden eyes marked me as royalty. One smaller Firstfire broke free from their parents and ran towards my horse. I had to call out to my attendants as they started to move towards the small being who was holding up a flower to me. Slowing my horse to a stop, I slid off and knelt down next to the Firstfire—did they call them 'Firstfires' in the Dusklands…I doubted it—and accepted the flower. It looked like a sunburst, but its petals were dark as onyx.

"Thank you," I said, making the little girl grin and run off towards her parents again. I heard her whisper to her mother that I was "pretty". The giggle that accompanied the compliment made me smile. Once I was back on my horse, the group began to move again.

The castle was colossal, especially compared to the Sun Palace. It looked like a mountain; it struck me that it possibly was or built around one at least. It looked like it had been carved from onyx or obsidian. Close up, as I walked through the doors, I could see it was stone, but it looked burnt, it was so dark. While the hallways were definitely tiled in onyx, the place was surprisingly warm, fires in every hearth and rugs and tapestries on the floors and walls. I did not know what to expect but it was not warmth and flowers.

I was led through the castle and into a cavernous throne room. The Obsidian Throne was situated at the other end of the room. The man that stood beside it made even the other warriors we had seen look small. He would have to be as wide as the throne, and he was taller than the back of the seat. Was the seat moving? I blinked a couple of times, thinking my eyes were playing tricks on me. It looked like the throne was not solid—it had to be, obsidian did not warp like that.

The woman sitting on the throne, High Queen Zoryana, was breathtaking. Her skin was the colour of the purest milk, her hair was as dark as the throne behind her, topped by a crown that looked like it was made from roots…roots that were alive. The crown shifted on its own atop her head. But it was her eyes that made her more than a little unnerving. They were silver—not grey, or light blue like most of her subjects—liquid silver, almost reflective like a mirror. And she was surrounded by shadows—so that was what was making the throne look alive. Magic was everywhere in the Dusklands, and it made me feel vulnerable. I was frighteningly ill-equipped to defend myself if something went wrong, we all were. It was something we had not prepared for, to our detriment.

"Prince Aurelian, welcome to Nightfell." Her voice was strong and rich, crackling with power. She had the potential to be highly dangerous, that much was obvious—I could see why the Kings of Solnyr and the other lands feared her, and her ancestors if they were anything like her.

I bowed my head. "I am honoured to be here, High Queen Zoryana. I thank you for accepting our offer to negotiate new accords."

A small, jaded smile turned up the edge of her plump lips. She had not had much of a choice in this situation either it seemed. She was much younger than I expected. We knew so little about the Dusk people that I had not even known her name until my brother had said it when he had denounced her coronation. Something I did know was the High Fae could live hundreds of years, but she looked younger than I was. I did not know how old she actually was, or anything but her name, and I certainly knew nothing about the man standing beside her, close but a respectful distance away. He looked like he could kill me before I had even registered that he had moved. Why they needed to be so highly trained, I did not know. That made me anxious—was the land itself that dangerous that they needed elite warriors?

"Indeed," she said, a hint of amusement in her tone. "I trust you are tired from your journey. Serian will show you and your retinue to your quarters. I have arranged for the north wing to be made ready for you all, I hope it is to your liking. We do not have sun for you, I am afraid, but the northern rooms are the closest I can get you to your own home." She had put thought into that. Her tone slipped slightly, showing a sliver of vulnerability under her confidence.

"I am sure we will be most comfortable," I assured her. When we were dismissed, following Serian through the castle again, to our rooms in the north wing. They were well-appointed and comfortable, with sleeping quarters and communal rooms for us to meet and eat in. As I retired for the night, unable to listen to my companions complain about everything, my mind was on overdrive. Everything I had been taught about these people felt so wrong.

CHAPTER SEVEN
SHADOWS AND SUNDROPS

ZORYANA

THE PRINCE OF THE SUN lived up to his name; he looked like he had been crafted from a Sundrop. His skin was a deep bronze, with light hair and those golden eyes that looked like what I presumed the sun looked like. His silky voice and demeanour set me a little on edge though, reminding me that he was not an ally. The Solar royalty knew how to spin tales and lies, as was evident in how successfully they turned the entire land against the Dusklands. When he and his people had left the hall, I finally relaxed, letting the shadows drop from around me. Everyone but Aris left the room, and he sat down on the smaller chair that looked comically small for him.

"How are you feeling?" he asked, voice soft and concerned.

"Tired and confused. I do not know what to think. He looked…uncomfortable, possibly a little frightened, but not… confrontational or superior, like I was expecting." I shrugged and reached up to pull the Rooted Crown off my head. It had been putting on a show, shifting on my head, but now my head was sore and a little itchy. "I think I will have my evening meal in my room tonight. You are welcome to join me. I just cannot handle being around too many people at the moment." Using the shadows to surround me had been effective, Prince

Aurelian's eyes had been drawn to them many times and his retinue had looked terrified, but I was still learning how to control them and after the outburst I had had when I had received the letter I would be lying if I said I was not a little afraid of them myself.

"Of course." Aris stood and held out a hand to me that I took and let him pull me up to standing. As I was straightening up, one of the guards entered. He acknowledged Aris with a nod and me with a bow.

"Apologies for the interruption, my Queen," he said, still in a bow.

"No apologies needed," I replied and he straightened up.

"I am taking the Queen back to her chambers where she will have her evening meal. Would you inform the kitchen while I escort the Queen? Due to our visitors from beyond the Thornwood, I will also be staying in her chambers tonight to ensure her safety, would you also ask that there is a plate for me?" Aris spoke up. He did not usually treat his soldiers as messengers, making both me and the guard look at him oddly. Though keeping me safe while our guests were in the castle was an acceptable reason for him to be there, he did not usually make it known when he was spending the night in my room.

"Yes, Commander," the guard replied, clapping a fist to his chest and leaving the room.

"So, you are staying in my room tonight, are you?" I teased as we left the throne room. I put the crown back on my head, thinking that it was best I did not walk around the castle with it simply in my hand like it was not an ancient icon of our people. "When were you going to ask if I approved?"

He let out a low chuckle. "Your safety is paramount, my Queen," he replied. "In cases such as this, if I believe there is a threat, my orders override yours." I knew he was reciting from an order, and that he was also being overly formal for the benefit of those around us, but it irked me a little that he could decide to sequester me without my consent if he thought the threat was high enough.

"I am gratified that you value my safety so highly," I replied, my tone unintentionally clipped. He looked down at me with a slightly confused look before he looked back up and we walked the rest of the way in silence. After a sweep of my rooms to make sure we were alone, Aris closed the door and watched me taking off the crown and my finery.

"Are you actually annoyed at me? Or was that just for show?" he asked, standing by the door, feet planted and his arms crossed. He was a ridiculously attractive male—even when he was being insolent.

"I am annoyed at the system. The thought that my autonomy could be denied like that simply because I am the queen vexes me," I admitted. "When the truth is, all I would have to do is let go of my magic and I would definitely be safer than if a skirmish broke out and I was stuck in my room."

Aris sighed and tightened his stance for a moment before relaxing, a nervous tick of his when he was stressed. "Zorya... you know I would never put you in danger. If you being a part of the fighting was the optimal option, of course I would let you unleash on them all." He moved up behind my chair and put his hands on my shoulders. Our eyes met in the mirror. "You are important—you have always been important to me, but now you are the single most important person in the realm. Being that significant and indispensable comes with its drawbacks, unfortunately."

I nodded, reaching up to put a hand over his. "I suppose," I agreed reluctantly. I had been unofficially ruling since my mother passed but it was not until my ascension that the people and the land itself truly accepted me and treated me as the Queen. A knock on the door made us both look at it. Aris walked over and opened it just enough that he could check who it was before opening it further. A server walked in with a tray of meats and various additions, placing it on the small dining table before leaving. Aris and I sat to begin eating. While we ate, we spoke about what we thought the plan forward should be. I knew my advisers had their own ideas, but in the end, any agreements with the Sun kingdom would have to be sanctioned by me and me alone. Our night continued with much of the same until we fell into bed a little after midnight.

Sitting across the table from the Sun Prince was a surreal experience. He and his advisers had been in the room when I arrived, which I was surprised to see, expecting them to keep me waiting out of spite. Perhaps these talks would not be as laborious as I predicted—I highly doubted it, but a female could hope.

"Before we begin," the Prince of the Sun stood with his goblet in hand, "I would like to formally congratulate you, High Queen Zoryana, on your coronation. I am privileged to be permitted entry into your lands to facilitate these talks between our lands and I sincerely hope we are able to come to mutually agreeable arrangements to begin mending the damage done to the once thriving relationship between the Dusklands and Solnyr."

The hall was silent for a moment. Shock—that was the general feeling around the table. Shock and a mite of scepticism. The Dusk side of the room was suspicious and looking for a flaw in the prince's words. The Solar side was looking at their prince like he had grown a second head. Those words had not been in their instructions—the prince was going rogue.

I too stood, causing a little havoc as everyone around me rushed to stand as well. I lifted my goblet in acceptance of his words. "Thank you, Prince Aurelian, for your kind and diplomatic words. I too hope we can achieve the previously unachievable."

AURELIAN

Without Clanna to wake me up, and no sun to tell me when it was morning, I had instructed one of my attendants to ensure I was up and ready in time. I wanted to be in the room before anyone else, to make sure I was coming in at a point of strength. I did not want to give anyone time to undermine me or my entourage. Dressed and fed, I was led to the room where the negotiations would take place. On my way, I made sure to take notice of all the details I could—exits, not that there were many I could identify, people that were around and how many guards were stationed in various areas; more guards generally meant something or someone important was behind the door.

We were seated at the long table when the Dusk advisers entered, followed by their Queen, her giant protector behind her as always, like a shadow. I had not seen her stand up the night before. She was easily the same height as I was, tall and strong. She was also not in a dress; she was wearing pants and a tunic like she was gearing for battle, her lithe, toned body easily noticeable in a way it had not been when she was sitting down in a dress. Dark leathers covered her torso like armour. The pattern on the leather looked like dragon scales—did they still have living dragons in the Dusklands? The Rooted Crown atop her head added to her height, making her seem like she could reach the sky. Her long dark hair was down but pulled away from her face, held there by a couple of tendrils from the crown—it was definitely alive. What kind of magic was used to craft it and maintain it that it was still so sentient after centuries? She also did not carry any weapons, despite everyone around her being armed to the teeth, including the councillors. The sight unnerved me further—the absence of weapons meant that she was so highly protected she did not need to carry her own, or she was the weapon. It could be both, but I was inclined to believe it was chiefly the second option.

My speech had not gone down well with my retinue. They were looking up at me like I had gone mad and I knew more than one of them was taking mental notes to report back to my brother that maybe I had been hoodwinked by the beautiful woman in front of me. She, however, looked amused.

Her advisers were understandably sceptical, but I meant the words. No matter what my actual directives were, or what my brother wanted, was peace not the best option for our land and people?

The way all her people scrambled to stand when she did was mildly amusing. Despite being the youngest person, I presumed, in the room, she was by far the highest-ranked person, but it looked like her people were still acclimatising to her new status. She accepted my congratulations with hopes of her own. *Achieve the previously unachievable.* Yes, that was the way to describe what any talks over the past one thousand years had yielded. Absolutely nothing more than more hate. The Queen sat and everyone joined her.

I looked down at the sheet in front of me, topics Solnyr wanted to raise. I had attempted to make it not seem like we were attacking them, but honestly, that was what my brother wanted. Taking a sip of my water to stall, I did not miss the kick from my brother's top councillor, Kirin, to prompt me to start speaking.

"Queen…sorry, would it be impertinent of me to ask if there is a shorter name I can call you?" As soon as the words were out of my mouth, I knew they were a mistake. The men and women around her glared and started to tell me exactly what they thought about that. Even her Shadow shot me a look that told me I was lucky she was in between us or I would be dead. The only one that did not speak was the Queen herself. A small smile tipped up the side of her mouth. She held up a hand; a small wave of power rippled from her palm, making everyone quieten.

"Zoryana is fine—"

"It is impertinent, no matter the outcome."

It was the first time I had heard her Shadow speak. He sounded as deadly as he looked, his voice more like a rumble. Zoryana sighed and reached out to touch the man's arm briefly, no more than a brush of her fingers over his arm but it was very familiar and surprising. My brother would never be so casual with someone below him. They looked around the same age, so perhaps they had known each other for a long time—who better to guard the most important woman in the land than someone who knew her so well.

"Zoryana is fine," she reiterated. "May I call you Aurelian?"

We were making progress. I could feel the disapproval emanating from both sides of the table, though the Dusk side was definitely less annoyed, trusting their monarch. I nodded with a grateful smile. "Yes, I would prefer that actually," I admitted. My title was useful sometimes to get me into areas that would otherwise be off limits or supply me with a steady stream of bed mates, but I much preferred to be less pretentious in conversation—especially when the other person I was talking to outranked me in a way that my brother could only dream of. With the name issue out of the way, I started.

"We discovered a rot in our recent harvest in the crops closest to the Rift—" At the word 'rift' she flinched, causing me to stop talking. I could not tell if it was due to guilt over her ancestor's actions, or if I had offended her somehow. "Is there another name for it?" Another kick under the table from Kirin, which I ignored for now. I would chastise him later for physically abusing his prince more than once.

"The Thornwood. We call her the Thornwood," Zoryana replied. Her voice was a little reverent. The crown on her head shifted slightly. I wondered if it was crafted from one of the apparently magical trees from the forest. She had also referred to the forest as a 'her', meaning they thought of the forest as living, possibly with a soul or at least sentient, not just a cluster of trees. That gave me pause—it made crossing much more dangerous than I had ever imagined.

"Apologies. We discovered a rot in the crops closest to the Thornwood," I continued. "It was tracked to the border where it looked as though everything was touched by blight." Again, she flinched. This was not a woman who was a cold and unfeeling monster that hated Solnyr and wanted it destroyed. She looked genuinely concerned and apologetic that the magic of her land might be causing anyone harm. She was silent though, they all were, like they knew there were issues and were not willing to divulge them. "Can anything be done to ensure this does not continue to happen, or be reversed?" My question was met with more silence. The Queen's Shadow shifted, his movement almost imperceptible and I might have missed it if I had not been looking at the Queen with him directly behind her. The man's hand appeared on her shoulder and she sat straighter.

"My sincerest apologies for the problems with your crops. Thank you for bringing it to our attention," she began, her words measured. "An effort will be made to discover the source of this supposed blight and bring it to an end to the best of our ability." Now that was an answer worthy of a courtier. It seemed my councillors thought the same thing.

"That does not ensure anything. Our crops are dying." Kirin's angry words drew the attention of the Queen. Her silver eyes flashed, and I was positive the ends of her hair raised off her body slightly as if lifted by a breeze.

"You presume to challenge me?" Her voice was deep, dark, and dangerous, and I was sure I was not the only one who was terrified. "You believe you can speak to me directly? Of all of you, your Prince is the only one with a position high enough to speak to me. He is the only one I will treat with—royal to royal. If you cannot refrain from voicing vacuous opinions, you will be removed and no longer included in these proceedings."

Kirin leaned forward and opened his mouth as if he was going to continue to argue, so I kicked *him* under the table this time. My brother would be irate if his number one adviser was omitted from the talks, and I would bear the brunt of his displeasure. The look the Queen was levelling at the older man would, on anyone else, be described as seething. On her—I did not even know the word. If looks could kill, and I was not sure if hers could or not, Kirin would be ash, the power simmering beneath the surface was wild.

"Apologies, Queen Zoryana," I spoke up, trying to dispel

the tension—or at least the additional tension that this had caused. She very slowly turned her mirror-gaze back to me. The warmth I could almost feel from her earlier was gone. "Kirin is passionate about helping our people—if the Blight expands and affects much more of our harvest, we will need to begin rationing." Mentioning the plight of my people did little to change her expression. She looked like she was trying to hold something back. Maybe what our books said about the power these queens held was true.

"My answer to your request has been given," she said simply and I knew it was time to move on. The mood of the room had changed, and I knew continuing to push the matter would not help. I just hoped my people would understand that too. I cleared my throat and started on the next point. I needed to steer this meeting back to a point where we could be productive. It was a fruitless endeavour—Kirin was sulking beside me and muttered occasionally, causing the Dusk people to look at him each time with a look that very clearly portrayed their annoyance. We were going to be banished from the land before we were able to do anything positive if he continued to be so obtuse.

The day was brought to an abrupt end without much having been negotiated when, after another mutter from Kirin, Zoryana stood and left the room without formally concluding the meeting. She was not going to suffer fools, it seemed, and the men with me were definitely being fools. Solnyr was a patriarchy, and it seemed like the old men in my retinue could not bear to take orders from a woman or even listen to her. When we were left alone, I turned to Kirin.

"You ruined this for us. We are lucky she did not send us home immediately," I said. "If you want to do my brother's bidding, you will be quiet and listen from this point on." I stood and left the room before he could argue. I just hoped I was able to salvage everything as we continued.

Aurelian's Ledger
Day One in the Dusklands

Day One of the Peace Accords, Nightfell Castle

Tenth day of Avaris, Year 1002 After the Breaking

The first council has concluded. If "concluded" is the correct word for a meeting that ended with the Queen walking out and my own advisers looking as though they had been flayed alive by a single glance. We are not off to a promising beginning.

I had hoped—foolishly, perhaps—that my brother's councillors would at least attempt diplomacy. But Kirin cannot help himself. The man has never stood before a woman with power and kept his tongue. The Dusklanders are cold, yes— but not cruel. And yet the way my people speak, you would think they were demons risen from the soil.

Zoryana Vekara is nothing like the monster I was told to expect. The legends said the Dusk Queens wear sorrow like armour and hatred like a crown. She wears neither. She listens, even if she does not answer. When I mentioned the Blight spreading across our border fields, I saw something real in her eyes. It was not guilt, but grief. It was like she already knew, and it cost her dearly to hear it spoken aloud.

The council chamber is a strange place. The air hums— heavy with old wards and older secrets. When she speaks, it feels like the room itself listens, not just the people within the walls. And yet, my own people cannot stop talking long enough to hear her.

Kirin's insolence nearly got him expelled—or killed, I would wager it was more likely the second. When she turned her gaze on him, I thought for a moment the air itself might crush him. Power rolled off her like a tide barely held in check. I do not think any of them noticed, but I did: the man behind her, her protector, the one I call her Shadow, steadied her with a hand on her shoulder, subtle but sure. Not fear. Control. Or maybe protection.

When the Queen's composure returned, her voice was hard but like glass. She offered to investigate the Blight but promised nothing, and though I wished she would promise to ensure its removal, she was right to respond as she did. How did one remove a blight. My councillors demanded certainty where there can be none. They treat her as if she were not even my equal in rank or power. She is superior in both, no matter what they believe. That thinking will end badly for us.

I tried to soothe it over, tried appealing to her empathy—reminding her that our people suffer, that was all I cared about. She looked at me as though I had said something indecent. I cannot tell if that was contempt or sorrow.

When the meeting finally dissolved, she left without ceremony. Kirin muttered again, and I nearly drew my sword to silence him. The Dusklands do not suffer fools—and we have brought a delegation full of them.

I find myself thinking not of the Queen's temper, but of her restraint. How much force must she hold in check every time she speaks to us? The Light Court has no language for that kind of strength.

If the rest of the Accords go like this, there will be no peace to bring home. And if I am honest with myself—though I should not write it—I am not sure which outcome I fear more: failure, or that I might begin to understand her.

- Aurelian, Prince of the Sun

CHAPTER EIGHT
FLAME

ZORYANA

LEAVING THE WAY I HAD had been petulant, I was aware of that, but that Dawn councillor...Kirin if I remembered correctly...had driven me to the edge of my tolerance. For at least the past hour, shadows had been swirling around my legs under the table, only calming slightly when Aris' hand touched my shoulder periodically. As I stalked from the room, shadows collected around my feet and the Rooted Crown pressed against my skull. I knew Aris was following me—I was not sure I even wanted to be around him at that moment, or if I *should* be around anyone. I did not know if I should go to my training room, or just to my chambers. Aris caught up to me, his hand appearing on the small of my back as we walked. The touch allowed me to breathe, and my wavering direction solidified towards my chambers.

With the door closed behind us, I unceremoniously ripped the crown off my head and put it away, muttering an apology to it for how I had handled it. My shadows were still moving around me as I looked at myself in the mirror. I looked terrifying. My eyes were like mirrors on their own, my hair was starting to flutter and dark tendrils were swirling all over me. Reaching to my sides, I clawed at the ties of my cuirass to remove it. Dropping it to the ground, I kicked off my boots and finally looked up to where Aris was still standing by the door. The look on his face was a mix of awe, fear, and concern. I closed the distance between us and started to remove his weapons. I usually let him do that, they were sacred to him, but I was not feeling all that caring at that moment. Though, I did make sure to put them down on the nearby table, not just drop them on the floor. With his weapons gone, I made quick work of his armour and tugged his tunic over his head. He had barely moved, only enough to make it easier for me to remove his clothing and to kick off his own boots. I pulled off my own tunic, then reached up to pull his mouth down to mine.

The kiss was hard and passionate as I worked out my frustrations against his lips. Aris seemed to wake up—his arms went around me and he lifted me, my legs wrapping around his hips as he moved towards the bed. His legs hit the edge, and he let go of me, making me fall to the mattress. Sitting up, I glared up at him before I reached out to unlace his pants, pushing them off his hips. Before he could react, my hand circled his manhood, eliciting a deep moan from him as my fist moved over his length. As I worked him up, my other hand went to work getting my own pants off. When we were both naked, I removed my hand from him, making him groan and look down at me in frustration.

"Am I not your Queen? On your knees, Shadowsworn," I commanded. His eyes brightened and he immediately dropped to his knees beside the bed, between my legs. "Now…show me what that means to you."

The grin that slid across his lips matched what I was feeling. Beginning to lose control during the meeting had turned me slightly feral, and he was matching my behaviour. He reached out, large strong hands splaying over my thighs before he pulled my hips to the edge of the bed. My legs were pulled over his shoulders, and he pressed a kiss to the inside of my thigh. I kept my eyes on him, propped up on my hands, as his head moved between my thighs. "Yes," I moaned as his tongue flicked over the centre of my pleasure. Shifting my weight to one arm, my other hand raised to the back of his head, sliding my fingers into his hair. He moaned against my flesh, the vibrations of the sound adding to the pleasure he was giving me. His lips moved over my clit and sucked on the sensitive nub, causing me to arch against him, my hand clenching in his hair, and a passionate moan left me. He knew every part of me, and I needed him to do what he did best—give me a climax that made me see stars, maybe multiple. His lips were replaced by his tongue, flat against my centre as he stroked my desire.

His hands came around my thighs, one staying there, the other travelled up my torso to my breasts. He palmed one, before pinching my nipple hard, making me gasp and push my hips against his face. He did the same to the other, eliciting the same response before he attempted to push me back. I allowed myself to fall back, but only to my elbow; I wanted to watch him as he worked on me. His hand moved downwards again until he slipped his thumb down to replace his tongue, circling and teasing my clit as he moved his mouth to my tunnel. He lapped at the entrance for a moment, before pushing his tongue inside me. The pleasure I was feeling, that was building in my belly, had me grinding my hips against his face. I was moaning with abandon, lost in my own pleasure. I was close to the edge. Usually, I would warn him when his face was between my thighs, but the climax crashed over me before I could say anything. My back arched and my thighs tightened on either side of his face. I would not be surprised if the moan that bordered on a scream that came from my lips was heard throughout the castle. He continued to move his tongue over me until I collapsed backwards.

Aris raised his head, his face glistening with my pleasure. He stood, and I could see his manhood was straining, ready for a release of his own. I considered making him wait until I had rested but it was likely he would retaliate at some point. Sitting up, I reached out for his hand and pulled him down onto the bed beside me. Rolling over, I moved astride his hips. His long, hard length pressed against my slick centre. "Lay back, so I can reward you for your loyal service…" Rolling my hips against his, I reached between us to position him at my entrance before lowering myself onto him. We both moaned and tipped our heads back as the pleasure of being joined took over us both. His hands gripped my hips as I started to move, my own hands braced on his chest.

Our movements were still filled with the same passion and heat, but we had slowed a little as the anger and frustration began to fizzle out. I did not feel like I was going to lose control anymore—unless it was passion-fuelled. With how hard Aris was, and how turned up I still was, I was sure we would reach our peaks soon, but I still wanted to make sure he experienced as much pleasure as he had given to me. His hands tightened on my hips, fingers pressing into my flesh, starting to control my movements, pulling me down onto him tighter, and making me grind harder on him to bring him to the edge quicker.

"Gods, Zorya…" he groaned as I picked up his desire and physical command. The way he said my name while we were intimate sounded so good that I felt it in my core. With the change in pace, it was not long before we were both tipping over the edge of our climaxes, moans from both of us filling the air until we were spent. Fully sated, I relaxed forward, his arms coming around me as I lay on his chest, both of us breathing hard. My anger at the insolence shown by the Dawn courtiers and their prince had not fully dissipated, but, thanks to Aris and the way he knew exactly what I needed and when I needed it, I was much calmer and felt like I was more under control.

We stayed like that for a while before I shifted off him to lay beside him. "Do you want to talk about it?" Aris asked, his hand running through my hair.

I sighed, tracing over the scars on his chest. "I did not expect diplomacy, not completely, not at first. I expected them to be disrespectful and contemptuous. I even expected cockiness, or rudeness. What I did not expect it to devolve into was backchat and muttering, like everything I said was below their notice." I supposed that growing up in a society that had always had a female monarch, I had not experienced males that thought they were naturally more important than the females in the room. "I knew Solnyr had always had a male monarch and does not seem to value their females beyond what they could do for the males, but seeing it, experiencing it, it made me furious. Maybe that makes me naive, I am not sure."

Aris was quiet for a moment and nodded. "They should all count themselves lucky that it is not your mother sitting across from them," he said, slightly amused.

I sat up a little in surprise and looked down at him. "What do you mean by that? Do you think I am weak?"

His eyes widened and he shook his head. "No, Zorya, I do not think you are weak. I just meant that you are much more diplomatic than she was. You want to find a way to possibly have peace. Your mother would have just had them all killed and be damned with the consequences. She was not known for her diplomacy," he clarified.

I chuckled. "That she was not," I agreed, lowering back down. I felt foolish for thinking he thought I was weak. Of course he had not. He was right, I did want peace. If I could achieve it during my reign, or at least put it in motion, I would consider my reign a success. I just hoped it did not cost too many innocent lives—or my sanity.

The next morning, seated across from the Dawn court representatives, I was determined to not let their muttering get to me. Aris was no longer a respectful distance away from me, but close enough that I could feel the heat from his body and his hand was planted on the back of my chair, fingers against my back. It did not start well with them making veiled taunts about the way I had left the day before, enquiring after my health. My hands resting on the table in front of me started to seethe with dark threads of shadow and the crown on my head shifted, an immature show of my power, sure, but they ceased their mocking comments quickly after.

"We would like to talk about opening up free trade

between our realms, now we have a way through the R—the Thornwood," Prince Aurelian started, stumbling over the word for the forest. That they called it the Rift angered me. The Thornwood was so much more than just a border—or a rift. It showed how much they did not care to understand, or they purposefully decided to demonise it. It did not surprise me that they jumped straight to trade routes—it made sense, of course, but it also showed that they just wanted a chance to get into the Dusklands without restrictions.

"So, you would like to take immediate advantage of a phenomenon we are not even sure how it occurred or if it will even stay open? What will happen if the clearing closes itself and Dawn merchants are caught on the Dusk side or our people are caught in your court? How will you treat them?" I would hope that if that did happen that my advisers would allow me to integrate anyone stuck on our side if they had good intentions.

Aurelian's eyes narrowed for a moment like he was trying to discern my intentions or meaning. "How they would be treated would be on a case-by-case basis," he replied. "If they have ill-intentions, surely you could not expect us to treat them like our own."

"No, of course. And if they do not have ill-intentions? If they are a merchant who is no longer able to see their family or go back to their home, that may never be able to go home? If their grief is so intense that they have difficulty controlling their magic, will your culture of emotional regulation see that as ill-intent? Will you attempt to suppress their magic like you have over the centuries to your own people?" A ripple went through the group in front of me. They did not like being called out for the way they repressed their citizens. They were silent for long enough that I knew I was not going to get an answer.

"How would this *free trade* be managed?" I continued. When they again did not answer, I smiled briefly. "This is not a subject we can resolve in one conversation. Which I see is what you and your people wanted... Perhaps your King thought he could outmanoeuvre me, because I am a new queen?" At least they had the decency to not hide that fact. "I did not wear the Rooted Crown, but I have been ruling for longer than you know. I became Queen the moment my mother joined the ancestors over two years ago. It shows how little you know of the Dusklands. How little you think of our competency—of my competency." I realised I had spoken a lot with no responses. I could almost see them thinking, trying to fit the information they had just found out into their story of us and of me specifically.

"If someone's magic is a threat to the citizens, they will of course be dealt with," one of the Dawn councillors spoke up. I watched Aurelian close his eyes and let out a sigh before I slowly turned my head to look at the man who had spoken. It felt like my own advisers were all holding their breath.

"Starting with myself, I presume," I said, my voice as calm as I could make it. I knew they thought the magic that I possessed was a danger to their court and people, especially now there was a way for us to cross from the darkness into the sun. "All magic is a threat to people who do not possess it or refuse to understand it. How will you determine the threat? Did they use their magic to cause harm? We too would not allow that. But just because someone has magic, it does not mean they are an automatic threat." I took a deep breath and turned my attention back to Aurelian. "We cannot allow *free* trade. Not to begin with. I am willing to table it for the future, but I cannot allow it now, until we know for sure what is happening. We will entertain negotiations for regulated trade routes. Trade of goods that either side may need to begin with, but no crossing of the border for simple curiosity—from either side—until we can ensure the safety of those who choose to cross." I had spoken to my advisers on this point before the prince had arrived, knowing infiltration under the guise of 'trade' was a real threat.

For a moment, I thought Aurelian would argue. He was looking at me like he was trying to figure something out that was vexing him. Then he nodded. "I will take that under advisement. I know my brother would like to establish free trade for both sides, however I can see your concerns, given how different our societies are and our approaches toward magic," he replied.

That was the only point we had remotely agreed on for the rest of the day. The men across the table were infuriating. They did not like that I was not giving them everything they asked for without discussion. Was that not what they were here for? To discuss terms for the possibility of peace? Or at least the semblance of it.

CHAPTER NINE
THE RITE OF THE SHADOWBORNE

AURELIAN

We had been at that table for almost two tides. The only point that we had remotely agreed on was the trade between Nightfell and Solnyr—and even that was not what I had been ordered to arrange. I thought Zoryana's points and concerns were valid, and the way she had handled it all was admirable, but I did not have an agreement for free trade to take back to my brother. I had highly regulated trade, restricted to goods only. It was agreed that the items would be brought to the border, inspected, and then taken through by the opposite side. Zoryana was reluctant to let Dawn traders through in case they were spies and did not want her own citizens to pass in case they were harmed in Solnyr. I could not deny that there was a large chance that the way magic was treated in my lands meant that the High Fae of Nightfell could be in danger. I hated to admit that, even to myself, but it was an unfortunate fact.

All other talks had derailed quickly, sometimes devolving into open arguments between my retinue and her advisers. Her side of the table stayed mostly quiet; I presumed they talked outside the room and she was given her own points to talk about—they were in the room to display the strength beside the crown. My side had no qualms about talking out of turn, especially if their words caused offence, which tended to set someone on her side off. Even when we entered the Days of Stillness, they did not even attempt diplomacy out of respect for the days, regardless of where we were. I was tired, and I missed the sun. I missed the Solfruit buns I loved. I missed having someone to warm my bed—I had not dared to attempt to find someone while I was there as a guest. I even missed Clanna and her fussing. Really…I missed Clanna the most, though I would never tell her.

We had been told that the Queen would not be attending negotiations on the Day of Shadows due to a ritual that required her attendance, so I was surprised when the note arrived, delivered by one of the guards that had been stationed outside our wing.

Aurelian,

I would like to show you a different side of our people and would appreciate it if you would accompany me to the Shadowborne rites taking place today. If you are amenable, someone will be by your rooms to collect you at nightfall.

As this is a sacred rite, this invitation is only extended to you as a visiting royal.

I look forward to your response.

Zoryana

The line about the invitation being for me alone made me grin. She did not like my councillors. It was smart to cover that by saying it was because I was royalty as well. I quickly penned an affirmative reply and sent it on its way with the guard. What did one wear to a Shadowborne rite? What was a Shadowborne rite? As someone who prided himself on his intelligence, I hated not knowing something. I knew that was what they called their next stage of life after their…starling years, I gathered it was similar to ageing from Dawnbreak to Brightborne in Solnyr, but the rite itself had been lost to

Solnyrian history. We had a version, but it painted the queen in a horrific and terrible way. Zoryana was extending this opportunity for me to see how she interacted with her people in a way anyone outside the Dusklands had not been privy to before. If it was truly horrific, I doubted she would let anyone from Solnyr bear witness. During the day, I met with my councillors, who told me to take notice of everything and how it could be exploited. I was really getting the true intentions behind this 'diplomatic' mission. I had not ever thought it was genuine, I had known it was not, but I had hoped we would get somewhere further than we had so far. The councillors had instructions from my brother that were different from my 'watch and gather' ones. I suddenly understood why we had not agreed on anything else in the negotiations—my own court was sabotaging them.

Nightfall came around—though I was not entirely sure how they kept time when there was no sun. I was escorted to a courtyard where my horse, Helios, had been brought out. The Queen was seated atop the most incredible horse, the colour of night. Her Shadow—Aris, so I had been told—was standing beside her. He was looking up at her, a hand on her thigh. I would have thought having his hand on her like that would be inappropriate, but they were very familiar with each other. I had heard a rumour they were lovers, and if it was true, all the casual touches and looks started to make sense. When my presence was made clear, they both looked up and Aris removed his hand from Zoryana's thigh quicker than was necessary. I had interrupted something—they both looked mildly annoyed, so I gathered they had been arguing. I realised then that there was no other horse in the courtyard.

Ah…he is not accompanying us, and he is not happy about it, I thought to myself. I could understand—if I was her protector I would not be happy to leave her alone with someone who was essentially the enemy. Zoryana schooled her features into a smile, Aris did not—he was looking at me with open hostility.

"Good evening, Zoryana, Aris," I said, bowing my head in her direction before walking up to the side of my horse, running my hand over his neck affectionately.

"Good evening, Aurelian. Thank you for agreeing to attend the rites with me. I believe it is time you saw more of our culture," Zoryana replied, straightening and arranging her dress over her legs.

Aris began to head back to the castle, leaving me alone with the Queen for the first time. "Your warrior is not coming with us?" I asked as she instructed her horse to start moving. I scrambled up onto my horse and followed.

"No. Unless they are family to one of the initiates, Oathbound are not usually permitted to attend a Shadowborne rite. As my Shadowsworn, he would usually be able to accompany me, however, I have asked you, and I can trust you…right?" She did not believe her own words for a moment. The look she gave me was a challenge.

"Yes, of course. I do not wish you harm," I said. And that was the truth. I knew what my objective was, coming to the Dusklands, or at least the one I was given, however I was not happy to cause harm to anyone if they were innocent, and so far, the people of the Dusklands did not look like villains. The ride was relatively easy, and it did not take too long to reach our destination. I would love to explore more of the realm—it was so intriguing how everything was still growing, determined, it seemed, to survive despite the sub-optimal conditions. Everything looked like it had evolved over the centuries to adapt to the changes.

"This is the Vale of Veils—I did not name it," she added with a small chuckle, though I could see she respected every part of her land, even if it had a ridiculous name.

Sliding off our horses, I tied Helios to a tree, a little surprised to see Zoryana did not do the same with her steed. "You do not tie up your horse?" I asked.

She smiled and ran her hand over the horse's mane. "Vecheryn is a Shadowmare, we are bonded. She will not leave." They bonded with their animals too. It made sense that their animals were magical as well, not just the fae. "Come."

She jerked her head towards the entrance of the cave we had stopped in front of. As we walked, the sounds of singing came from further in—low, rhythmic singing, that sounded a little sad.

"They sound as if they are grieving," I commented.

Zoryana nodded. "They are. To become Shadowborne, you must mourn the youngling and starling you were."

It sounded very intense. In the two tides I had been in the Dusklands, I had discovered that grief and mourning played a large part of their existence. They did not hold back emotions, and their funerals could last days as memories of the deceased were shared from everyone who knew them. The cave tunnel opened up into a cavern that was full of people, and a lot of emotion. Around the edge of the cavern, torches of blue fire ringed the area.

"The fire is called soul-fire. There is a well fuelled by the souls of our loved ones. The flames are only used for rites such as this," Zoryana explained quietly. I filed that information away and was conscious that she did not divulge where the well was, which was smart, really. In the centre of the cavern, a group of younger fae were clustered. They were all wearing the same dark cloaks and their feet were bare. They were also all holding a blade in their hands that looked like it was not made of steel, like it was some form of black glass or stone.

As we watched, each of the initiates knelt before another cloaked figure—"She is a Shadow-Seer," Zoryana whispered—who called out a name, the name of the one in front of them I presumed. Then a…spark or something escaped the kneeling initiate, and the Shadow-Seer plucked it out of the air, tossing it into the river beside her. The starling (I presumed they were still considered a starling at this point) stood and the Shadow-Seer whispered something to them.

"They are receiving part of their name they will take through the rest of their life. They will pick their second name themselves and declare it before the morning. One name is given by their lineage; the other is claimed by will. We believe in this duality of self, forged in the darkness of history. The dark does not erase," Zoryana murmured. "It transforms. We are not born of shadow—we choose it."

Their connection to everything around them was becoming clearer. A girl that could not be more than fifteen or sixteen stepped forward, trembling. She knelt and my gaze was drawn to the river, where I could see her reflection—I had not watched any of the other reflections before, focused on the fact that they were literally losing their names. At the moment her name was called out, the girl's reflection split into two, one staying with the girl, the other being swallowed by the water with her name. The more time I spent in this realm, the more I realised that their magic was not about domination or destruction like I had been taught. It was memory made solid, woven intricately into every facet of their existence. They were fuelled by their history, by their ancestors, in a way that I was having trouble comprehending. I was not sure I would ever truly understand, even with extensive study.

The line of starlings dwindled until each one had gone through the naming part of the rite. As a group, they moved through the cavern. Zoryana followed them, like she was helping to usher them through to the next stage of their lives. The group moved towards a glowing path…no, not glowing, smouldering. Zoryana moved to the front of the group, and I continued with the line of family members—I did not think I was permitted to participate, just witness. She stepped onto the path, and I realised for the first time that she too was barefoot. She did not flinch—I did, just watching her, let alone walking on the coals. One by one, the initiates followed her across the glowing embers, not one of them flinching either.

"You have done this before," I commented when Zoryana moved over to me.

She nodded. "Apart from during my own Shadowborne Rite…yes. Every queen does. So she remembers what it means to rise from ash."

As the last initiate reached the end of the ember path,

the crowd began to chant—low and sonorous, a single word repeated: *"Seryn."*

Zoryana leaned in to whisper, "It means *to carry the dark without letting it drown you.*" Everything was so profound. I supposed it was similar to our church services, where Sol was praised and revered. They were not praising a deity though; they were revering their ancestors and the memories of them…revering the land itself.

The initiates ringed a large fire in the middle of the clearing. As one, they plunged their swords into the fire, then they pressed the heated blades to their wrists. My eyes widened as they did it without hesitation—all but one smaller boy who was trembling. Zoryana stepped away from my side and knelt down next to him. Leaning into him, she whispered something I could not hear. Whatever she said gave the boy the courage to complete the rite. She ran an affectionate hand over his head and stood, coming back to stand next to me.

"Can I ask what you said to him? It worked."

"That bravery is not the absence of fear. Instead, it is feeling that fear and choosing to burn anyway," she replied. I felt that in my bones.

We followed the group through to another clearing where tables were set up, loaded with sweet-smelling cakes. The new Shadowbornes were handed cakes and found their families to celebrate with. Zoryana moved over to take two cakes from the table and handed one to me. "They are honey cakes, dusted with ash. They are sweet, but the ash adds a bitterness—as all life has two sides," Zoryana explained, leading me through the groups. She approached one group and asked them if we could join them. The way the faces of her subjects lit up at the fact their queen wanted to sit with them was beautiful.

"This is Aurelian, the Prince from Solnyr, visiting to celebrate with you all," she introduced me to the group. They were understandably apprehensive but accepted me as a part of their celebration. Sitting on the grass with the High Queen of the Dusklands, eating a cake with a group of her people was not something I had expected to experience on this visit. Her people loved her. The younger people in the group, new Shadowborne, the burns on their wrists red, asked me questions about life in Solnyr, some I did not know how to answer, but some were interesting and amusing:

"Does the sun really smell of spice?"—No, unless you are in a spice field, then the heat makes the smell stronger.

"Do the rivers there glitter gold?"—Sorry, no. The sun's reflection can make it seem that way sometimes though.

They accepted the answers I was able to give and soon we were telling stories and laughing together.

Something had shifted in my perception of the people. I had not ever felt that they wanted to harm me, they were suspicious, of course, but curious. After interacting so much with them over the evening, I now felt as if I was beginning to understand them and they me. As the fire started to die down, the groups began to dissipate, heading to their homes. Zoryana and I made our way through the cavern back to our horses. Her Shadowmare was indeed still standing beside Helios—who was also untethered now somehow.

The ride back to the castle was spent mostly in silence as I attempted to comprehend what I had witnessed. I appreciated Zoryana giving me space with my thoughts. She seemed to understand the power of contemplation.

"Thank you for agreeing to witness the Rite with me. I felt it was important for you to experience more of life here in the Dusklands—beyond bickering politics." Her voice brought me out of my reverie. She was looking at me, those silver eyes ardent.

"I appreciate the opportunity. Thank you. Being a part of something like that was…I do not have words to describe how I feel."

"I suppose they would call it sorcery in your tongue. But this is what your light destroyed all those years ago—the right to grieve openly and allow yourselves to feel." I had no reply, and I did not think I ever would.

We reached the Nightfell walls and were guided back to the courtyard we had left from. I slid down from Helios' back and moved over to assist her out of habit. She seemed surprised—as was I—but she allowed me to help her down. Her body slid against mine as she dismounted, making me more aware of my body than I ever had been in my life. My hands tingled where they had gripped her waist to steady her. For a moment that felt longer than it actually was, I had the High Queen of the Dusklands pinned between my body and her horse—both of us breathing hard, looking at each other with a mixture of emotions. I would be lying if I said I was not thrilled by the look of desire that flashed in her eyes. With her so close it was difficult to remember who we were and why I was there in the first place. I could forget that I was not back in Solnyr, one of my bed mates in my arms—though the fact I did not have to look down at her, her night-dark hair and pale skin, were a giveaway this was a very different situation.

Remembering where I was, I released her. I moved away, clearing my throat. Zoryana took a deep breath, running a thin hand through her hair. Keeping a respectful distance between us, we walked into the castle together as stable hands took the horses.

"You make even the dark seem holy," I commented, finally finding words but still in awe of everything that had happened.

Zoryana chuckled, shaking her head. "No. We only remember that holiness does not belong solely to the light." Her words could have sounded as if she was talking down to me or insulting my culture, but the look on her face showed she was just telling the truth, educating.

"Yes, we forget that often," I admitted. "Good night, High Queen Zoryana," I said as we reached the entrance to her wing of the castle.

"Good night, Prince Aurelian. I hope tomorrow brings us an easier time at the negotiation table," she replied, a slight chuckle in her tone like she did not really believe her words. I could not help but chuckle as well. We parted ways then and I walked back to my room smiling and wholly confused. This mission had been one I did not want to participate in, but it was proving to be interesting and awakening.

Solnyr called her a Heretic Queen. But tonight, I think the heresy may have been ours all along. We had built an empire on the lie that only light redeems. Yet here, in the heart of the shadow I was always taught to fear, I saw something purer— not worship of darkness, but reverence for survival. They do not beg the dawn to return. They are the dusk that never dies.

If I ever returned to Solnyr, I was not sure if I would repeat what I saw. Not because it must be hidden—but because it would be wasted on those who have forgotten what truth feels like or refused to remember.

The fire did not burn them. It had burned me though.

CHAPTER TEN
THE GARDEN OF OBSIDIAN ROSES

ZORYANA

After the night spent with Aurelian at the Shadowborne rite, I had been restless, unable to fall asleep. When he saw me alive and healthy, Aris, who had been waiting in my chambers to make sure I came back, visibly relaxed. I relayed the facts of the evening, and how Aurelian seemed to have taken it all in and that he had even interacted with some of the people. Aris looked surprised but accepted that the prince did seem to genuinely want to learn about life in the Dusklands. I had resisted the urge to tease him and ask him if he was softening towards the prince. He was, it was obvious to me, even if it was not to anyone else, or even himself. Though, I left out the weird moment between Aurelian and I when he had helped me off Vecheryn. I still did not know how to process the feeling of his body against mine, his hands warm on my waist as he held on a beat longer than propriety would allow. The thrum of desire that had rippled through me as our ragged breathing made our chests brush together. Aris and I had gone to bed, attempting to sleep until he got irritated with me as I moved around too much, trying to get comfortable. He let me go and rolled over, leaving me laying on my back, looking up at the ceiling until morning. I started my day tired, and without the patience to suffer fools.

It seemed the Solnyrian representatives had come to that day's meeting determined to make everything harder than it needed to be. I was on the edge of losing control again. The very edge. My entire legs were wrapped in shadow, and it was beginning to creep up my arms. The unintentional show of power helped briefly but they went back to being obtuse with such speed that would leave a dusk-wolf behind. I could see Aurelian was finding it difficult to pretend that he thought his companions were being reasonable, regularly closing his eyes and pinching the bridge of his nose when they spoke.

"We are getting nowhere," I said suddenly, making everyone stop talking. They all looked at me, some with alarm. It felt like I could barely see, like my eyes were covered by shadowcloth. I took a few deep breaths as I felt Aris' hand press hard between my shoulder blades. My vision began to clear, and I realised I had been closer to losing control than I thought. I stood but gestured to everyone to stay seated. "Prince Aurelian, I would like to talk to you alone. I believe we can talk more freely without the rabble," I said. His side of the table exploded in uproar—my advisers knew I was not talking about them, so they were content to sit and watch the Solnyrians complain, and to trust me to not sell off our lands to make a deal. I would be forever thankful for the trust they put in me during the talks. Aurelian stood and nodded.

"I believe you are correct, Queen Zoryana," he replied and started to move around the table, despite the protests of his companions. As I started to move towards the door, Aris stopped me.

"Alone?" he enquired.

"Alone does not mean without you. I will not do that to you again," I teased, knowing he had struggled the night before while I had been at the rite without him. Aurelian reached us and we headed out of the room. "I think a visit to the garden might help." The two males looked at me curiously, but I led the way out to one of my favourite places. The garden was full of roses that looked as though they were formed from obsidian. As they were dusk bloomed, they unfortunately would not survive outside of our lands. I did not know how they would endure if the sun returned to the Dusklands. I found a bench and sat, inviting Aurelian to join me. Aris took a seat on another chair close by.

"You are not here to make any agreements, are you?" I asked without a preamble. Distracted from admiring the unique flowers, Aurelian's head swung to look at me in shock. His face changed to shame after a moment.

"No. My brother does not want to allow the Dusklands to reintegrate with the rest of the land. He is afraid some of the other kingdoms may still harbour deep alliance to the Dusklands, despite the centuries and the narrative put forward by the Solar Kings since. His hate and fear run too deep to change his mind," Aurelian admitted. He continued to look at me, which impressed me. I was surprised to hear the possible view of the other kingdoms. The Breaking had cut them off from the Dusklands as well, leaving them to deal with Solnyr. I would not have been surprised if they all hated us as much as Solnyr did.

"And you? What do you want, Prince of the Sun?"

He took a deep breath and let it out in a heavy stream. "I-I do not know. I was raised to believe my people were in the right, that the Light was the only way. But I…before I left, I discovered a lot of information I cannot forget." He looked conflicted, as if he was wrestling with himself over what to disclose to me.

"Information?" I pressed.

"Old scrolls and tablets from ancient Vesmor." My eyes widened in surprise—not just from the knowledge that Solnyr had not burned everything relating to that time, but also at Aurelian's use of the name of the land before the Breaking. Out of the corner of my gaze I saw Aris lean forward a little. "One was the treaty between Seravine and Caelen. It—Our histories say that there was never a treaty, just that Seravine broke the world and Caelen barely escaped with his life. But the scroll I read—it was signed by them both and laid out everything, beneficial for both sides. I also found a note from Caelen explicitly saying he was breaking his oath and that the truth needed to stay buried." He took a breath and rubbed his hand over his golden hair. "I do not… Why keep it all? Why not completely destroy all the evidence? That was the plan, was it not? To eradicate any good will anyone held for the Dusklands. I have to presume my brother does not know of the room I stumbled upon as he does not spend time in the Archives like I do. If he did know about it, I would have thought he would have destroyed it. My brother is a sycophant… Devout to the Solnyrian histories and our version of the truth."

I was shocked. When I looked at Aris, his face was unreadable, but he was tense. He did not know what to believe. I understood that feeling. "Aurelian. Do you know if anyone else in your party knows of these documents?" I asked.

"I would not think so, but I cannot say for sure," he admitted. "I do not…I do not know what to think about it all. I have spent the past thirty years being told how the Breaking happened, being told that our version was the only truth. Being told that all people across the Rift were monsters, with the Queens being the worst." He at least looked a little embarrassed about admitting that point. "But everything I have seen about your people has been the complete opposite. The Shadowborne Rite was also in complete contrast to what our teachings say. I am having a difficult time reconciling it in my mind."

At least he was being honest. "And me? Am I different from what you have been taught?" I felt Aris, who had shifted his chair closer, so his knee touched mine, stiffen, anticipating a negative answer.

Aurelian looked up at me with conflict on his features. "You? Yes, you are definitely not like the teachings say. You have empathy for your people; you want to see them thrive. But I cannot deny—and neither can you—that you are dangerous or at least have the potential to be. I have sat through two tides of meetings watching you come so close to losing control, covering yourself in shadows. Even today, before we came out here, your eyes were glowing and looked like mirrors. Not to mention your physical Shadow—" He waved his hand in Aris' direction. "He is a giant and bred to kill. Am I supposed to say that I know for sure you would not be able to stage an invasion of Solnyr or the wider Five Kingdoms given provocation?"

Before I could speak, Aris cut across me. "Do not blame your insecurities on us." I let out a sigh. That was not the way to diffuse tension. It had the opposite reaction, of course. Aurelian's sundrop eyes flashed.

"Insecurities? Because I do not have magic? Because you are head and shoulders taller than me and twice as wide?" The Prince of the Sun was trying hard to pretend he did not feel lesser in Aris' presence. "Because I do not share the bed of a Queen?"

"Enough!" I flung out a hand in both directions, palm on each man's chest as the tension built to a point that they were both seething. "Who shares my bed is none of your concern, Prince." This conversation was declining into petty quarrels as well. I had hoped that speaking to Aurelian on his own would be simpler, less antagonistic. Maybe if it had just been us, without Aris, we could have, but I could not have left Aris behind again, not just because he would sulk, but though I had trusted that Aurelian would not try to hurt me surrounded by people, I did not trust him enough to be truly alone with him.

The reactions the two males had to my hand on their chest would have been comical if I was not so annoyed. Aris' hand appeared over mine on his own chest while he was still glared at Aurelian. The prince however had frozen and was looking down at my hand. He looked a little uncomfortable, like actually being touched by me was something he did not like, despite him touching me first by helping me off Vecheryn the night before, but there was also something else. Something I was not sure I knew what to do with. I also did not like that I was thinking about the fact that, despite his obvious misgivings about his own physique, I could feel he was not lacking in definition through the tunic he was wearing, remembering what it felt like to have him flush against me. He started to raise a hand like he was going to touch mine. I quickly pulled my hand away and it was like a spell was broken. Without a word, Aurelian stood and left the garden faster than I had seen him move since he arrived.

"I thought that would go better than it did," I grumbled, wiping my free hand over my face. Aris still had hold of the other one, though he had brought it down to his lap. "We need to be more careful. It is true that Aurelian is very observant, but it does not mean others from Solnyr have not noticed how close we are. I know our relationship is not a complete secret, but our people accept it, or at least seem to—Solnyr may try to use it against me." He quirked an eyebrow, a small grin on his face.

"I would like to see them attempt to take me and use me against you." I could not help it; I laughed. The thought of those small, physically weaker males trying to take down someone as highly trained as Aris was amusing. "Talking about sharing the Queen's bed…" That eyebrow rose again.

Chuckling, I shook my head. "You cannot just keep distracting me with intimacies," I scolded.

"It was worth a try." He shrugged. He was wicked and I loved him for it.

I needed a way forward. Aurelian confirming that the Solnyr delegation was not in Nightfell to negotiate a possible treaty or anything close was not a surprise, however, I had naively hoped it was true. Even without a 'treaty' I needed to avoid war. Solnyr now had a way to pass through the Thornwood—an opening that I had no doubt was caused by the events at my coronation. The opening was widening every day, despite our suspicions it would begin to close. It was taking a large contingent of the Oath-bound to cover the opening and patrol to make sure no other clearings appeared. A gap had been discovered but it was barely large enough for a small female to get through so it was watched but not guarded.

"Aris... What if my reign is the one in which we lose the Dusklands completely?" I looked up at him pleadingly, hoping I was wrong, that the feelings I was having were invalid. Reaching out, he cupped my face in his hands and leaned in, so we were eye-to-eye.

"Zoryana Vekara, High Queen of the Dusklands, Keeper of the Last Hearth, The Nightblade Queen... The Queen Who Would Not Bow. What if you are the Queen that brings us peace? What if your reign is the one in which we see the return of Vesmor." His voice...and the look he was giving me... That was reverence.

"The Queen Who Would Not Bow? Did you just come up with that?" I asked him.

"Yes—but you have proved it right. You have not conceded any point in these sham negotiations that will not benefit your people. You have thought of them and them only, even under pressure, when lesser beings have tried to pull you down." He leaned forward further to press a kiss to my lips. Though brief, the kiss said that he meant what he was saying, that he believed in me.

"Thank you," I murmured. "I am still not going straight to bed with you right now...no matter how many pretty words you say." He laughed at that, a full, rich laugh that I did not get to hear nearly often enough.

"Not exactly why I said all those things, but you are further proving my point...I cannot even get you into bed with pretty words, even though you need to let off steam and you know I can help with that in a very pleasurable way, there is no way Solnyr is going to make you bow to them." He let go of my face and stood. Holding out his hand, he helped me stand and we headed back inside to face my advisers who would not be happy to hear all that I had found out.

All of my advisers were looking at me in shocked silence. I

had called them all to my private meeting room and they had arrived quicker than I had thought. When I had explained what had happened with Aurelian, all he had admitted, even about the documents he had found, none of them spoke. I was expecting interruption and maybe an uproar and scepticism. However, they were all processing quietly.

"I suspected they were not being remotely genuine—apart from the fact they are from Solnyr—the way they talked around in circles like they were purposely trying to mislead us had me suspicious," Sura spoke. She was one of the younger advisers, not much older than Aris and me. She was my first appointee after my mother had passed. "And the information that Prince Aurelian discovered in the Dawn castle—I would love to see it all. I would presume the treaty matches the one we have here in our archives, but the letter from Caelen admitting his guilt...that is surprising. How did it survive the centuries?"

No one had an answer for that. Not one of us had ever expected there would be further proof of Solnyr's lies in their own castle. "We need a way forward. A way to not let the Solnyr delegation know we are aware—"

I was cut off by Serian, who added, "If Prince Aurelian has not already told them of your meeting." I nodded. "Yes, if Aurelian has not already let them know. We need time to build up our resources and our own proof of the Golden Lie."

After more planning, my advisers left for the night. I was again restless, pacing for a little longer, but once my head hit my pillow the exhaustion hit me and I was asleep.

CHAPTER ELEVEN
SOVEREIGN PROPOSITION

ZORYANA

Over the next few days, we greeted the Solnyrians and their bluster with more patience than before. Now that we had confirmed nothing we said had true stakes, we could be as casual as they had been the whole time. We were still not going to concede to anything, but we were no longer going to negotiate as if our lives and the lives of our people relied on it, saving us frustration, and the possibility that I lost control. Our new outlook to the negotiations obviously confused the other side of the table. They looked at each other regularly with bewildered expressions as we spoke. It did, however, make them change their focus, again attempting to appeal to our emotions. Trying to use our connection to everything around us against us. Because we knew for a fact they were being disingenuous, their comments did not affect us in the same way they had only a day before.

We were beginning to feel like we were getting ahead. My shadows had stayed under control for most of the session. They escaped my hands only once, when one of the Solnyrian councillors tried to insult me personally. If I was a king, I had no doubt they would not make personal attacks about my appearance or my abilities. It was all becoming very tiresome, the blatant disrespect, purely because I was female.

"It is remarkable how confidently you bear yourself, considering how differently the world beyond your borders measures beauty." Kirin's words may have been misconstrued as a compliment if he hadn't followed on with the comment about how beauty was perceived beyond the Thornwood.

"That was uncalled for." Everyone turned to Aurelian as he chastised his own councillor. "Whether the Queen would be considered attractive in Solnyr is not something we are negotiating. The answer to that is a resounding yes, and you know it. Stop being an idiot." I was unable to hold in the surprised but amused laugh that escaped me, causing everyone in the room to look at me.

"While I am thankful for the compliment, Aurelian, you are right. My appearance is a non-issue in these negotiations. As we seem to be at an impasse that we cannot get around, I would like to talk about the possibility of meeting the King in person." The entire room exploded with voices from both sides of the table, including from Aris, whose hand squeezed my shoulder in alarm. It was an option I had thought of as a last resort but had not spoken to anyone about as I had hoped it would not need to be invoked. "I am not talking about one of us going into the other's lands; we have a large clearing at the border, we can set up there. Neither monarch needs to cross the border or leave the relative safety of their own lands. Your beloved king does not need to step into the dark." I gave the other side a sweet smile. Aurelian's eyes were narrowed as he attempted to discern my motives. "I am happy to dismiss you all—go home, see your families and bask in the sun. You have been away long enough. Surely you did not anticipate spending this much time away from your homes. I just ask that you carry a letter from me to your king."

No one seemed sure of how to proceed. They had orders from their king, and I was certain they had not achieved them all, if any of them. Unless they had figured ways to leave their wing, they had not been permitted to wander the halls freely and the majority of the delegation had not made any efforts to see the lands or interact with the people. The Solnyrian side of the table merely nodded, shocked into silence for the first time since this all began, and stood, all leaving the room except their prince, who stayed seated, watching me closely. My own advisers also left, knowing I would explain my motives when I was able. I would have to discover a way to repay them all for the trust and respect they had shown me during the talks. When I was about to try—and probably fail—to dismiss Aris as well, one of the Oath-bound entered the room, requesting his commander's attention. Soon, Aurelian and I were alone in the room.

"Zoryana, what are you doing?" he asked, shoulders tense and eyes still narrowed.

"Your councillors will never let this happen, I am sure, but these negotiations are going nowhere. There is no point to you all staying here any longer. I am not some youngling that can be led along with platitudes. I am tired and I do not have the patience for this anymore. You are right, I am always on the edge of losing control. I know your people are purposefully trying to provoke me enough to make that happen, so they can prove that I am, in fact, dangerous. But I am not dangerous, and neither were my ancestors. We are misunderstood. We are provoked. We are needled until we retaliate. You and your people cannot understand us, cannot comprehend our magic and our customs. For over one thousand years, your country has actively tried to erase us. Light can blind, Prince. But you have a chance to make it illuminate instead."

He sighed and dropped his head into his hands for a moment. When he raised his head again, he too looked exhausted. "You are right—my brother will never agree. I will carry your letter back to him and be the liaison if you require." He paused again. "Though, I am trying to understand everything I have seen, I hope you know that."

"I would like to hope you are." I wanted to ask something I knew had the possibility of endangering his life and I did not know how he would take the request. "Aurelian—would you do something else for me?" When he nodded apprehensively,

I continued. "I need to see the scroll you spoke of—the one of Caelen saying he was to blame. We have a copy of the treaty here in our archives, I presume they are the same, but obviously we do not have a copy of that letter. That could help in so many ways. If you could find a way to get it here without endangering your life, I would be forever incredibly grateful."

His eyes were wide, and I would never shame him for the fear that he was unable to hide. "I—" he began. "That is a lot to ask but I…I will try."

I was surprised he did not ask for anything in return. "You do not want anything in return for doing this dangerous task for me?"

He looked down like he was thinking. "If I need it—I ask for sanctuary. If I am unable to stay in Solnyr because of this task you have given me, you will have a place for me here."

That was risky but then so was what I was asking of him. "Yes—if you require it, you will have a home here in the Dusklands," I agreed. He nodded.

"I should prepare for my journey home. Thank you for your time, Queen Zoryana." I just nodded to him as he stood and left the room. Rubbing my hand over my face, I sighed before I too stood. About to leave, the door opened, revealing Aris.

"How did that go?" he asked; he looked like he had been running.

"It went better than I could have hoped. Why did you have to rush off?" I asked, starting to walk towards my chambers. He explained the situation as we walked. Another clearing had opened up in the Thornwood, larger than the second one that had been found. Easily large enough for people to come through. We had thought they would begin to close but the opposite was happening. The magic of the Thornwood was changing, clearings opening up and widening, as though it was preparing to disappear altogether. There had been a small skirmish at the opening. The Oath-bound patrolling made it to the clearing just as Solnyrian soldiers were trying to cross the border. The Oath-bound received some injuries, but all of the Solnyrians were dead. By the time we reached my room, I was ready to scream.

"I would never want something like this to happen at any time, but the timing of this is terrible. I just asked Aurelian to get the scroll proving Caelen was to blame for the Breaking and try to bring it back here."

"You what?" Aris looked at me like I had gone mad. "The King will use that to start a war if he finds out."

"I know," I groaned. "I am hoping he does not get caught, of course. I do not want to be the cause of his death, of anyone's death. I do not want war. I do not want my people to have to endure that. But we need that scroll. If we are able to show the people of Solnyr and the other kingdoms the truth, I can only hope we can cause a change of perception and rebellion within their own lands. I cannot… Well, I can believe it…I just cannot believe the timing." My last words were barely a grumble. Sitting at my writing table, I pulled a sheet of parchment and my quill towards me. Dipping the quill in the ink, I started writing the letter to the Sun King requesting the meeting.

> *His Royal Majesty, King Aurastes IV of Solnyr, Lord of the Dawnbound Court, Keeper of the Eternal Flame,*
>
> *I wanted to extend my sincerest gratitude for your congratulations regarding my coronation. Your envoy relayed your good wishes, and your hope for an accord that you expressed in your letter.*
>
> *We, however, were unable to come to a mutually beneficial accord on any of the points raised. While all efforts were made, it seemed that your delegation was not able to make sufficient amendments to their directives to allow for real negotiation. I have dismissed them to allow them to return home to their families, and the sun I am sure they are beginning to miss.*
>
> *I would like to propose a meeting, in person, between the two of us where we may be able to speak frankly and make decisions that will improve life in both of our realms. I*

understand you may prefer to keep negotiation between myself and your envoy, however, I believe speaking without intermediaries, monarch to monarch, will be most beneficial.

No monarch will need to cross the border as the clearing your delegation crossed through is large enough to accommodate, meaning neither of us need to set foot on the other's land. I will allow you to choose the date and time.

I look forward to receiving your acceptance.

In memory and shadow,

Zoryana Vekara, High Queen of the Dusklands, Keeper of the Last Hearth, The Nightblade Queen

Looking it over, I sighed. I was not a great diplomat. I loved my people, and I loved being their queen, but these past few tides had drained me and pushed me to the edge of my patience with this side of my role. I went to sit back in my chair, and my head collided with Aris' chest as he was leaning over me to read the letter.

"Are you snooping?" I asked him, purposefully knocking my head against his chest.

"No—you would have asked me to read it over anyway; I was saving time." His reply made me laugh. It was true. He regularly read correspondence I sent out to make sure it sounded right, there were no mistakes, or I had not used too many words that might be misunderstood.

"Any notes?" I asked and he shook his head as he straightened up.

"No—Though, I would not have given him the honour of being addressed by all of his titles as he did not extend that honour to you, but I understand why you did it."

"I will not stoop to his level with petty moves like that—though I suppose including all his honorifics is petty, but it is a respectful petty." We both chuckled at that. With the letter written and folded, we sat down to make a plan for everything that we suspected was coming once Aurelian and the Solnyrian delegation returned home. We had no idea really how the King would react, only that we were sure he would reject the summons. I also very much hoped that I had not just signed Aurelian's death warrant.

AURELIAN'S LEDGER
THE QUEEN'S PROPOSITION

Third Tide of the Peace Accord, Nightfell Castle

Day Three of Solmera, Year 1003 After the Breaking

The Queen changed the tempo today. Until now, she has met the bluster of my companions with restraint, our arrogance with silence. But this morning, the rhythm of the negotiations shifted. She smiled. She laughed. She did not bend—but she refused to let the game remain ours to play. I think that is what unsettled the council most: the realisation that she had stopped fighting the way we expected her to and started controlling the field without ever raising her voice.

Kirin, predictably, embarrassed himself. He took offence to her patience and decided to test it. The words he used about her appearance were not just crude—they were sacrilege in a hall that answers to her presence as though it were a living thing. The air changed before she even spoke. Her shadows stirred—not as threat, but as instinct, the same way a bird of prey flexes its wings before striking. I was already halfway out of my chair when I told Kirin to shut his mouth. I might have gone further if she had not laughed. It startled everyone—me most of all. It was not the laughter of a monarch mocking her enemy. It was weary, almost self-deprecating.

And then she made her proposition. A meeting. Monarch to monarch. Zoryana Vekara was offering to face Aurastes IV on neutral ground.

The room erupted—as if she had thrown fire among us. Her own commander and advisers were startled. My councillors looked ready to faint. And yet she sat through it all, composed, deliberate, her silver gaze fixed on me. I could see what she was doing. She knows my brother will never agree to this. She knows the Kingdom of Solnyr cannot meet her as an equal without shattering a thousand years of propaganda. And still she offered it—not as plea, but as challenge. Smart, very smart.

When the others left, she spoke to me alone. No guards, no courtiers. Only the Queen and I, in a room heavy with the ghosts of every ruler before her. She said she was tired of being needled, provoked, and painted as the monster our scriptures have made her.

Her words have followed me all day. Light can blind, Prince. But you have a chance to make it illuminate instead. How long have I mistaken glare for guidance? How many shadows have I burned away because I could not bear to see what lived within them?

She asked me for something dangerous—to retrieve the scroll I had found in the Solnyrian archives, written by Caelen Solnyr, my ancestor, admitting guilt for the Breaking. I should have refused her. It would be treason to even think such a thing. I should not even write this in this ledger. But when I saw the way she looked at me—not as an enemy, not even as a diplomat, but as someone who still hoped for a world where the truth could matter—I agreed. She offered me asylum in return. I think she already knows what this will cost me. Maybe she even knows I will pay it willingly.

I do not know what she will write in her letter to my brother; she has yet to write it. But I know she expects war, even as she tries to prevent it. Perhaps we both do.

If Aurastes sees what I see here, he will call her defiant. Dangerous. If he sees what I feel, he will call me lost. Maybe he will be right.

For the first time since I left Solnyr, I am beginning to wonder if the light was never meant to be worshipped—only questioned.

- Aurelian

CHAPTER TWELVE
THE GOLDEN SPIRES

AURELIAN

Zoryana met us at the front of the castle, Aris at her side as always, to bid us farewell and good travels. Her letter to my brother was handed to me with much pomp and ceremony. Considering she had not shown that sort of affectionate behaviour the entire time we had been in the Dusklands, I realised she was making a show of it so my companions knew for sure she had given me the note.

"Thank you for your gracious hospitality these past tides, Queen Zoryana. It grieves me that we were unable to come to an acceptable accord, but I will carry your letter to my brother the King and I hope that will assist in bringing forward a resolution."

She nodded and reached out to put a hand on my shoulder. She then, surprising everyone including myself, leaned forward to press a kiss to my cheek. "I wish you luck when you return home," she whispered quietly before she straightened back up. Everyone was looking at her in shock, including her Shadow, though he had more of a look of contempt on his face, for me—I was sure she would explain to her people that the kiss had been a cover to hide her whispered words but still, it was slightly amusing.

With that, we were on our way back through the Dusklands to the border. Our exit was much different than our arrival. People still came out of their homes, but they did not keep their younglings inside, allowing them to run beside the horses to say goodbye. I liked to think I might have ingratiated myself to them in the time I had been there. At the border, the Oath-bound High Fae warriors let us pass through the clearing that had at least doubled in size since we had first come through. I had heard there were a few more openings that had appeared at other parts. It was odd to think that the Thornwood was opening up the clearings on its own—there was no interference from any fae, no one cutting down trees, just the magic in the trees and the ground starting to separate. I wondered what that meant for everything that was coming.

The ride from the Thornwood border to the Solnyrian capital was much longer than the one from Nightfell to the border. My companions complained the whole time, about the tents, the food, the weather, like any of us could control the weather. I did not know what they expected from Solmera, but like it did every year after the Days of Stillness, it started getting very warm. Though, the sun above us did seem determined to burn through us.

After two days of riding and listening to everyone complain, the golden spires of home came into view, glinting in the sunlight. We had all removed several layers of clothing on the way in order to cool down but also allow as much sun to touch our skin as possible while still being respectful. Riding through the gates of the castle, I realised that I had not come back the same person who had left a month prior. Trumpets sounded to announce us, the sound making me flinch. Everything was bright, so loud. The Dusklands had been softer—melancholy and dark, yes, but softer than the harsh light from the sun glinting off the gold-plated palace.

"Welcome home!" came my brother's voice from the castle entrance. He walked forward with arms outstretched and grasped my shoulders, pulling me in for a short, sharp hug. He had never hugged me in my life—not as Firstfires, not when our parents had died, not when I had left for the Dusklands and my possible death.

"Uhh…thank you, brother," I said, unable to keep the confusion and shock from my tone. "I have a letter from Queen Zoryana for you."

"That can wait—come in. I have arranged a meal for you. No doubt you have missed our superior, finer fare," he said, clapping me on the back and steering me inside the castle to the assembly room where there was in fact a buffet set up for myself and the others who had accompanied me.

"Thank you, Aurastes—this all looks delicious," I commented. I had actually enjoyed the food in the Dusklands, though my companions had not. Their fare tended to be heavier, focused on gamier meats and stews, but the flavours they had were so unique and I found I preferred the spiced meats and bitterness added to sweets, over the Solnyrian foods that were lighter and much sweeter. Though, I had missed Solfruit. I reached out and plucked a Solfruit bun from the tray, ripping a bite off and popping it into my mouth. Delicious. When I had a plate of food, my brother motioned for me to sit in the empty chair beside him.

"That you are back with naught but a letter, I presume that means you failed me?" he asked, all pretence of the loving brother gone. I almost choked on the bit of bun I had just put in my mouth.

"No," I started once I had swallowed. "Your directives were not to come home with a treaty—that was never the plan. So no, I did not fail. I watched, and I listened—that was what you asked me to do."

He glared at me. I had not missed my brother at all while I was in the Dusklands; in fact I had welcomed the distance. "And—what did you observe?"

I did not know what to say. I had not observed anything that he wanted to hear. "It is in my reports—I can give them to you to read through—"

"No, tell me now," he cut me off angrily.

So much for getting to eat first. I put my plate down to give him my attention, which was really what he wanted. "Queen Zoryana is young—only twenty-seven. Idealistic. Hopes to build a better world than the one she has inherited." I snuck a grape and popped it into my mouth. "The Dusk people love their queen. They run out to meet her in the streets, and she sits with them to learn about who they are. She literally sits on the ground with them." My brother frowned in obvious distaste at the thought of sitting on the ground at all, let alone with his subjects. "I attended one of their coming-of-age rites, their Shadowborne Rite. It was not at all like we are told. There was no bloodletting, no feeding of the young to the void. I am sure there are dissenters, all kingdoms have them, but I was unable to uncover any," I admitted. Which had been true; in my tides in the Dusklands, I had not come across anyone who spoke ill of the Queen. I had tried to speak to as many people as possible but not one person had missed an opportunity to praise their monarch with genuine, pure love. It was something I never saw at home when people spoke about Aurastes—they spoke with love and smiled, but the rot behind it all was evident, and sickly sweet.

I hesitated, not sure whether to continue. "She is powerful. They all are. I do not know if you have thought through what one thousand years of not diluting their fae blood might have created, brother. Full-blooded High Fae, is what that has created. Their everyday people are bigger, faster, and have magic they use like an everyday tool. Their warriors are giants—head and shoulders taller than me, and wider, both men and women. They may not be in skirmishes or wars consistently, but they are highly trained with weapons and magic. The Queen's personal warrior is only the same age as her but already a commander, scarred from training, and easily the biggest of the lot." I was talking a lot, but it was obviously what my brother wanted. "The Queen is..." I hesitated to use the word dangerous. I had thrown it at her in a moment of frustration, and I did believe it—she had a tenuous at best control over her well of magic—but saying it to my brother would just reinforce his views of Zoryana. "As I said—she is incredibly powerful. As far as I can work out, she draws her power and strength from the land. Or at least she was gifted it during her coronation. She has Shadows." My brother's eyebrows rose so high they were almost lost in his hair. "It does look like she is still learning control over her power. Which makes sense, considering she has been Queen for only a month. I did not see her lose control; she managed to pull herself back before she did, though she was heavily provoked." I gave up on pretending I did not want my plate of food and pulled it towards me again, starting to munch on the fruit.

We did not talk for a long time while I finished off my plate of food. I was beginning to think my brother might be finished with me, when he spoke again. "Did you find anything that we can use?"

I sighed. "No, not particularly. Their version of what happened during the Breaking comes from archives and direct accounts from Seravine and her daughter." I had not been able to visit the Archives, there had not been time, but Zoryana had explained it to me.

"There was a daughter?" my brother asked. I was surprised—I was further convinced he had not been in the room in our own Archives.

"Yes, Seravine had a daughter, born before her marriage to King Caelen. The woman was over two hundred years old by the time she married Caelen. The father is unknown, as seems to be a trend since, but she was Seravine's blood and the land accepted her as the queen. So, no matter how many times we call them pretenders...they are of the royal Dusklands blood. Plus—they are nightblooded; Zoryana's blood is black."

"Black blood..." My brother mused and I realised I had said one thing too many. "You saw her bleed?"

"Yes...she cut herself on something, I do not know what."

"Interesting..." I did not like how interested he was in that information. I could not discern what he could use about that.

"Would you like to see the letter she sent back with us?" I asked him, unable to hide my impatience. I was tired; I wanted to sleep in my bed. He nodded and moved his hand to take it from me. I watched as he broke the seal and read the contents. I did not know exactly what it said and I hoped it was actually what she said it would be and she had not turned me in. Aurastes was getting increasingly angry as he read until he threw the letter on the table. Zoryana's elegant script said exactly what she had said the letter would contain, with a few well-veiled barbs. One had to admire her finesse. Though I had deduced she hated being a diplomat, she was a fine one indeed.

"She wants to meet me. In person? This Firstfire thinks she can summon me?" I did not bother to correct him about her age—she was definitely not a Firstfire.

"Well, technically, her bloodline carries the title of 'High Queen'…meaning she can actually summon you…" I trailed off as he turned a furious glare at me. I held up my hands in surrender and sat back in my chair. "Are you finished with me? I would like to go and sleep in my own bed. While we were made comfortable, nothing can beat your own bed."

He was still glaring. "Yes, you may go." I took the dismissal and left the room as quickly as I could without making it too obvious. Heading for my chambers, I considered going to the Archives to get the scroll that Zoryana wanted, but I was tired from the ride, and I did not want to risk getting caught on my first night back. So, to bed it was and think about how I was going to steal such a dangerous piece of history and convince my brother to go to the meeting.

With a night of sleep in my own bed, and my customary wakeup call from Clanna—I had purposefully stayed in bed longer than necessary so she would feel obligated to come in—I was feeling much more refreshed and like myself. I could not deny I had missed Clanna. I had even given her a kiss on the cheek to say good morning, making her blush and giggle. Clanna had been the closest thing I had had to a mother for a large part of my life. As much as she frustrated me, I loved that woman. I wondered, if I needed to flee, could I get her out too?

After my morning meal, it had been my plan to head to the Archives to at least formulate a plan, or even just get it over with if I could manage it. Stealing from my own castle felt sacrilegious. Stealing that kind of information could be a death sentence. I was unable to start my mission, as I was pulled into meetings to talk about the reports we had brought back with us. Mine were very different to those of my companions. Mine, while they spoke about the love the people had for their queen and how she was with them, were more clinical and freer from bias—or so they sounded to me. The reports brought forward by my companions were full of bias, essentially pages of whining over how they were treated and that they were not given opportunities to spy. I wanted to yell at them—we had not been treated terribly at all. If the Dusklanders had visited us they would not have been given an entire wing with plush rooms and delicious food and servants. Their drivel made me sick, but my brother drank in every damning word.

CHAPTER THIRTEEN
THE TRAITOR PRINCE

AURELIAN

IT TOOK TWO DAYS TO have the time by myself to be able to head up to the Archives. It felt like my brother knew I had a pursuit that was against his motives. He kept me in meetings or attending useless parties. I had not even had time to fulfil other needs—Elaina had been hinting that she had missed me over the tides I had been gone. While I was tempted, I was starting to think Zoryana was the woman in my dreams and that was all I could think about. No Solnyrian woman was raising any interest in me enough to invite them to my bed.

On the morning of the third day back in Solnyr, I finally headed up to the Archives. I had no idea how I was going to steal the scroll. It was not overly large; I could put it into my tunic, possibly. Or could I get a book under the guise of borrowing it and put it between the pages? That was probably a better option. Greeting the archivists on my way through the room, I noted that there seemed to be less people in there than the day I had found the room. Would it be more obvious if I did not just choose a table? I had to stop looking so nervous. I was not just nervous, I was terrified. Walking through the rows of shelves like I was looking for something, I pulled a couple of books off the shelves and continued walking. Finding what I was sure was the door to the room, I pushed it open, trying to look as though I knew where I was going.

Thank Sol! I thought as the door opened to the empty room. Slipping in, I closed the door and walked up to the locked one. Saying the line I had the first time, I was happy when the door unlocked. Taking a torch from the wall, I headed up the staircase to the secret room. I was relieved to find it still full. Everything as I had left it. I found the scroll I needed on the table and folded it instead of it being rolled, slipping it in between the pages of one of the books. I was about to leave when I thought about how much other information was in the room. I could not bear to think I was leaving behind something critical. Could I spend a little more time without getting caught? If I looked quickly, just scanning things…

Deciding it was worth the risk—at least marginally—I started to rifle through the other scrolls. If something was remotely incriminating, I tucked it in the books I had taken from the shelves. There were more letters, decrees from my ancestors to bury the truth if it was uncovered. A scroll written by Caelen made me stop. The scroll outlined the use of an artefact that he had found that could…oh Sol…it could steal magic. Caelen wrote in detail how it worked—because he knew. He had used it—on Seravine.

> *The artefact did, unfortunately, cause Seravine's magic to fracture, leading to the explosion that created the Rift.*

I felt sick. This could not fall into my brother's hands. I hoped the artefact had been destroyed—it seemed that Caelen had escaped with enough power in the artefact to achieve his ends, but there was nothing I could see that said what had happened to it. Bundling up the bit of parchment into the books, including the one about the artefact, I hurried back down the stairs. Making sure the door was locked, I replaced the torch and headed for the outer door. What if someone saw me coming out. Coming up with a plan if I needed it, I pulled open the door, plastering a confused look on my face and looking around as if I was lost.

"Prince Aurelian—can I assist you with something?" one of the archivists was looking at me with a befuddled expression on his own face.

"Oh…I was sure this door led to a private study area, but it is empty. I must have the wrong door," I said, trying to still look confused, looking down the hallway and spotting the door to the private area. "One door too soon," I grumbled and then glanced up as my name was called out again.

"Prince Aurelian. I apologise for interrupting; the King has requested your presence at a meeting of the Council." I nodded at the messenger.

"No private study for me. I am going to take these with me though." I showed the archivist the titles, so someone knew where the books were and headed out. "I will take these books to my rooms and head to the council chamber." When the messenger was sure I was not going to run he left. I was terrified to have the books with me in my brother's presence, so I would have to put them in my room. Hiding them under my pillows, I then made my way to the council chambers.

I was met by everyone there already, including Aurastes. "My apologies, brother. I was in the Archives and only just received your message," I apologised as I sat in my chair. He nodded in acknowledgement, then started the meeting.

"The Dusk Queen has requested an in-person meeting between her and myself. Despite my misgivings, I have decided to accept her request." I could hardly hold back my shock. Others around the table were not as lucky. Murmurs began and people did not look happy. Aurastes held up his hand, and I had to smile a little as it took longer for him, a king for many more years, to silence the group than it had for Zoryana, Queen for merely tides. "This spark of a queen thinks she can summon me and be the one in front—I will go, however at a time that is convenient for us. I will march to the border tomorrow; however, we will not advise the Dusk Queen until we are less than a day away, not giving her time to properly prepare." The others at the table approved. I hated it. It was so underhanded, and not the actions of a man that thought he was in the right.

"Allow me to accompany you, brother. I know the Queen and her protector, it may make things easier," I suggested. It was possible that he would intend for me to stay back so there was still a royal in the castle, but I needed to go—I had to give the scrolls to Zoryana.

"Brilliant idea, brother," Aurastes replied, apparently keeping up the doting brother act from the night before. "You can be the mediator."

Perfect. "It would be my honour." We were immediately in full preparation mode, the councillors who had accompanied me to the Dusklands divulging everything they knew about the clearing in the border and the land around it on both sides, what we could expect to encounter there.

We did indeed begin to march the next day. With the King at the head, there was much more pomp and ceremony than when I had made this same journey. Gold banners and a full division of the Golden Legion in their burnished armour. The crown atop Aurastes' head was gleaming, and I was forced to wear my circlet across my brow. At least the accommodations were much more comfortable this time, with inns being chosen so the King did not have to sleep in a tent. When we were less than a day away, as planned, the notice was sent to Zoryana. I hated all of it. It was so disrespectful, but I did not voice anything or draw attention to myself. The pages in my satchel felt like they were shining like a beacon that would be discovered at any moment.

ZORYANA

We were already at the border clearing when the note came. The poor Solnyrian messenger looked terrified, coming face to face with the Oath-bound and myself at the border, rather than further into the Dusklands or handing the note to another messenger. He shook as he handed me the letter directly. The King was advising us of his arrival, in less than a day, an obvious tactic to make us flustered and arrive late. We could see the tops of the Solnyrian banners already, their gold glinting in the sunlight. My moon-light eyes were not made for the sun, even more so since my coronation, I would presume. I turned my back to the sun and faced my people.

"While the King of the Sun chooses to disrespect us with this note…" I held up the letter. "…And this show of force…" My hand then waved backwards to indicate the Solnyrian army coming towards us. "…We will not give him the satisfaction of showing him displeasure. We will not rise to his taunts, no matter what venom they hold. We are Dusklanders. The Shadow does not blind or hide as they say it does—it remembers, it protects, it observes, it endures. I believe in you all, and I am proud to be your Queen." Dusklands soldiers did not scream or holler, the Oath-bound that surrounded me clasped their hands over their hearts and bowed solemnly. We all knew this was not going to go well, but we had to endure.

As the Solnyrian hoard neared the border, I could see the King was incensed that his plan had not worked. We were already waiting for him, steady and firm. The legion stopped and Aurastes dismounted his horse first, followed by Aurelian and everyone else. He did not bow, not that I had expected him to. I decided on diplomacy and inclined my head, just the barest amount.

"King Aurastes," I said. "You honour the accords by coming in person."

"I honour nothing born of falsehood," he answered. "But I will give you this chance to repent." His voice made my blood boil, but I did not react.

There was a shift in the air as all the soldiers of Solnyr dropped to one knee, chanting under their breath, as if they were worshipping their king as a living god. The Dusklanders did not kneel—the only time they knelt was to take their oaths…and if their lover told them to.

My eyes flicked to Aurelian; his apologetic look told me he knew this was exactly how this was going to go. We all knew, I had to admit.

Aurastes raised his hand, and the priest behind him unfurled a scroll reading from what sounded like an edict—like the King of Solnyr could command anything of the High Queen.

"By order of King Aurastes IV of Solnyr, Lord of the Dawnbound Court, Keeper of the Eternal Flame, the Queen of the Dusklands has been found guilty of sacrilege, corruption, and blood sorcery. The sentence as passed down by His Royal Majesty is submission or sanctified death."

It took all of my strength not to lash out. Sacrilege? Of whose religion? Corruption? Of what and who? Blood sorcery? It showed how much he knew of our rituals. This was never going to be a negotiation, not that I expected one. But I had not expected a trap.

"So, this is peace in the language of Solnyr. Bow or burn." My voice carried over the border to the King and his troops.

"Your kind has poisoned this world long enough," Aurastes said. "Today, the light will cleanse what the dark defiled."

Aurelian stepped forward, standing in front of his brother. I could not see his face, but his body language was pleading. "Brother," he said, "do not do this."

"I warned you not to let her whisper into your heart," the King replied. "You have let her unmake you." I would have laughed if I was not concerned that I might have done just that.

"You have unmade yourself!" Aurelian shouted at his brother. "There is no light left in what you serve." The Prince of the Sun stepped back, away from his brother and towards the trees. The world erupted in movement as the small number of magic-wielders left in Solnyr were brought forward. They raised their hands, all number of runed items in their hands—stones, banners, cards. So, it was true—they could only channel through these objects and could not produce magic on their own. Sunfire shot towards us, and I threw up my hands, forming a shield of shadow, forcing the Sunfire to part around us, thankfully harming none of us. When magic did not work as planned, Solnyr sent forward soldiers. All around me, steel clashed with dusksteel, golden armour of the Solnyrians mixing with the dark armour of the Oath-bound. I was not able to shield my people as another wave of Sunfire came towards them with no consideration for collateral damage—both Dusklanders and Solnyrians fell victim to the fire, and to the explosions that followed.

"Zoryana!" My name caught my attention to see Aurelian running towards me. He collided into me at the same time Aris did and the three of us started to fall, just as something exploded by our feet, throwing us backwards. Incredibly dazed, I groaned, flattened underneath two males, and not in a good way ; the largest of the two was semi-unconscious and like a dead weight, having taken the brunt of the blow. I managed to roll Aris over, sliding out from under Aurelian as well, to make sure they were both okay. Once I was sure Aris was alive, I turned to Aurelian.

"You came back," I said.

"Too late," he answered.

I looked past him to see his brother's forces were starting to retreat, having done enough damage. "No," I said softly, a small smile on my face. "You are right on time."

Two Oath-bound soldiers ran up to us. "My Queen, you live. Thank the ancestors." The relief on their faces was tangible. They helped Aurelian and I to our feet, then leaned down to wedge Aris between them. I was relieved to hear him groan as they carried him. We followed them towards the camp, where the wounded were moaning and some screaming as their wounds were dressed.

"I did not know the small amount of magic your people possess could be so catastrophic," I admitted to Aurelian as we entered Aris' tent. He was being placed on his bedroll, a

Shadowhealer rushing in. The healer spotted me and moved to help me, but I waved him off. Aris needed him more.

"But, my Queen, you are bleeding!" the healer argued.

"And my Shadowsworn could be dying…he is your priority right now," I snapped, unable to keep the level of emotion in my voice to an acceptable level for a queen and her Shadowsworn. But I could not imagine a life without Aris in it. There was a deep bond between a queen and her Shadowsworn, but our emotional and physical relationship had amplified that bond—I was not sure what would happen to me if he did die. A cloth was pressed to the side of my head. I flinched away and saw Aurelian beside me, holding a compress with a streak of black blood on the side that had been pressed to my head. Conceding that I might need some sort of attention, I reached up to slide the crown off my head and reached out for the cloth.

"Please, Zoryana, sit, please let me help." Aurelian's pleading words softened me. I sat heavily in a chair and let him dab at the cut on my face. He was covered in dirt and blood, though it did not look like his—there was a decent amount of black smudges on his clothing and face. Was that my blood? His golden hair was mussed and his crown—

"Oh…your crown is cracked," I said apologetically. The gold circlet on his head had a large crack in it, holding on by the smallest amount. He reached up with his free hand, touching the circlet like he had forgotten he was wearing it, and pulled it off his head. Looking down at it in his hand, he dropped it at my feet.

"It is fitting. I do not think I will be welcomed back after running to you instead of him," he said with a rueful chuckle. He continued to clean the gash on my face until it stopped bleeding. When he could remove the compress without more blood leaking out of the cut, he sat down on the chair beside mine and reached into the satchel that was still slung across his body. "I have the scroll you asked for…and more."

"More?" I asked, taking the pages he handed to me. I spread

them out on the table in front of me. The scroll he had told me about was there: Caelen's admission he had betrayed his queen and that betrayal had caused her to erupt. I continued through them until I got to the one that I was sure was the cause of how loaded the word more had sounded. He...he had stolen her magic. And that made her unstable. Seravine had been nearly two hundred years old at the time of the Breaking; there was absolutely no way she just lost control, even after a betrayal. Hearing how it actually happened was heart-breaking.

I looked up at Aurelian. "Do you believe what you have given me?" I asked him seriously. His nod was enough, but he affirmed it with words as well. That was enough for me. Aurelian was guided out to an empty tent to clean up and change, given an Oath-bound uniform—all that was on hand. I sat by Aris' bed as he was slowly brought back to me. After making sure he was stable, we were left alone.

"You—you scared me for a moment there," I said to him through tears.

"I am sorry, my Queen. Please do not cry for me, I will not be leaving you today," he replied, reaching up to swipe a tear from my cheek. He slid his hand into my hair, thick with dirt and my own blood, and pulled me to him. Our lips met in a kiss that made me just add to my tears. We were both grateful he was still alive.

"May I enter?" came a voice from outside the tent. When I called out to say yes, Serian pulled back the flap. "My Queen, you need to rest and clean up. That shield you erected was a large show of magic, and then you were hit by the explosion from a Sunlance—Prince Aurelian confirmed what it was. You need to rest."

"I...I cannot leave," I admitted. The look that Serian gave me was not pity; it was something else. He saw the way Aris' arm was across my lap and the way I held onto his arm. I knew he did.

"Zoryana, come, my dear. Your Shadowsworn is healing, and he will not be alone in case anything is wrong. You need to regain your strength so you can be whole and healthy for everyone. It is hard, but it is your duty as queen. Your people look to you," Serian said, his tone soft and soothing. He moved further into the tent and reached out to push some of my hair behind my ear. "You look so much like your mother," he said, his voice so full of memory. It broke my heart. I did not look like my mother. She was fierce and strong—I did not feel that way in that moment. I felt like a youngling thrust into a situation she was not ready for.

"Zorya…Serian is correct. You need to at least clean up, if you are not going to rest. I will be here when you are ready," Aris said, shifting his hand off my lap. I leaned in to kiss him again quickly, and then straightened up, taking Serian's outstretched hand to help me stand. I allowed myself to be led to my own tent where a tub of water had been brought in.

"Do you need someone to help you? Do you need a Shadowhealer?" Serian asked, absentmindedly testing the water. It looked warm, and the way he removed his finger affirmed that.

"No, I will be fine. Thank you, Serian," I said, thankful for all his help.

"You are most welcome, my Queen," he said before leaving the tent. I started to strip off my battle leathers and washed myself with the cloth that was on the side of the tub. It was not long before the water was opaquer with my blood and dirt. I managed to clean my hair a little, getting the worst out before dressing in fresh clothes. The night was not over, I had no doubt this was not finished, and I needed to talk to my warriors. There was a plate of food on my table, so I sat down to eat, deciding that Serian was right, as always—I needed to refuel myself. While I ate, I wrote notes to all of the most important people, including Aris and Aurelian, asking them to meet me in Aris' tent in an hour. I did not want Aris straining himself to attend a meeting, so his tent was the most logical place.

CHAPTER FOURTEEN
THE OATH

AURELIAN

ZORYANA CALLED A HANDFUL OF her commanders, Aris, and I to a meeting. If any of the others were as surprised as I was to be included, they did not show it. Aris was out of bed, standing beside Zoryana, leaning against a pole. I predicted the leaning was to ensure he did not fall over, and that he refused to be lying in bed with all the soldiers and councillors around him. Being stubborn would be the death of him. Zoryana was standing behind the table in the tent, hands planted on the table as she watched everyone filing in with those quicksilver eyes. Her eyes flicked between each person, like she was counting. Straightening up, she looked directly at me.

"While back in Solnyr, Prince Aurelian risked his life to obtain and deliver a scroll from the Solnyrian archives. This scroll was written by Caelen, admitting his part in the Breaking. While on that mission, he also discovered other pieces of history that the Solnyrians have tried to extinguish. Letters from older kings demanding the eradication of truth." She sighed and picked up one of the pieces of parchment, her eyes starting to wander around the group. "The worst bit of history he discovered was a scroll, again written by Caelen, in which he outlines the discovery and use of an artefact. This artefact enabled him to siphon Seravine's magic from her, storing it in the artefact. The theft of her power caused her control to fracture—which in turn caused her explosion and the Breaking."

The room around us felt like it was holding its breath. No one spoke as they digested the information they received.

"My Queen," one of the female Oath-bound began. "Do we know anything about this artefact that may enable us to find it?" Zoryana shook her head and the group sighed, seemingly as one. Aris looked murderous, looking at the scroll in Zoryana's hand like he could kill Caelen through the page.

"We need a way to distribute this information to the people, preferably as far and wide as we can manage, but first we need to plan for the assault I am sure is coming sooner, rather than later." The scrolls were removed from the table, carefully put away, and maps were pulled out so battle plans could be made. I was not an avid student of military strategy, but what I could see from the way the Oath-bound studied the maps, pointing out where more openings had appeared in the Thornwood, possible places for the Solnyrians to try to breach the border, I knew that any education I did have was woefully lacking.

"I would just caution how many people are privy to your plans," I spoke up, making the attention of every one of the giant High Fae warriors swing to me.

"Continue, Sun Prince." The woman that spoke was more formidable than any of the generals in my brother's army.

"My brother has somehow managed to install spies in your court—even before the accords talks."

"Why have you said nothing on this before now?" Another warrior looked as though he would take joy in pummelling me into the dirt.

"Honestly? I was still unsure of my place here until now. I cannot go back to Solnyr—this is my home now, if your Queen sees fit to allow that." Zoryana nodded when attention briefly turned to her. "I do not know how he got them through the Thornwood, who they are, or how information is being delivered. I only know that he managed it."

The Dusklanders took my revelation and changed the way they planned. It was extraordinary to watch the way they pivoted and revised their strategies to accommodate new information. I had not seen anything like it.

With plans made, hours later, candles burning lower, flickering light making it difficult to see the details on the maps, the group left the tent, joining the rest of the army and citizens in the camp. The people reached for Zoryana as she passed them, and she took or touched every hand in her reach. That level of devotion would be tiring. My brother thought of himself as a living god. He was worshipped by some, but he did not have what she had—reverence and respect of all her people.

Zoryana stepped up onto a stool so her people could see her above the giant statures of the Oath-bound that surrounded her. Everyone quietened, looking up at her expectantly.

"Thank you. You all fought and defended the Dusklands with courage and love today. I am proud of every single one of you. Those of you helping tend to the wounded alongside the Shadowhealers, we salute you. Without you, we would be lost." Around the group, people clapped each other on shoulders and backs; Zoryana smiled at the display of camaraderie. "I wish I could say this is over; however, it is not. The Light will continue to try to erase me, erase us all. I do not say this to frighten you or convince you to continue fighting. I would never force this on you. If you need to, or just want to, leave, be with your families, look after your lands, look after yourself… You will receive no disdain, no anger. You will be who carries on our legacy and our truth." No one moved. She looked relieved, but sad at the same time. She had hoped they would all leave—and she would not have to watch more of her people die.

"We follow you, my Queen!" someone called from

somewhere in the group. The sentiment rose amongst the others, filling the air with their love and support. I could not take my eyes off Zoryana. She was on the verge of tears.

"I thank you for your support and belief. My hope, my wish, from the moment I was born, was to be a queen you could all be proud of. But you have all given me so much more." She clasped her hands over her heart and bent her head in the formal show of respect. It was usually directed at her. To see a monarch acknowledge their people in such a way made me love her more.

Love? Yes, that is what it was. She had shown me many times why her people loved her. Why Aris loved her. I was not ashamed to add my name to that long list.

A brazier was lit in the centre of camp, burning with violet flame drawn from the wards. Led by their queen, one by one, the Dusklanders who meant to keep fighting laid their hands above it and swore their ancient words. Their vows were not to a crown or a creed but to endurance itself—to remember, to protect, to stand firm.

When my turn came, I hesitated. The flame hissed at my hesitation, as though it could taste doubt. Zoryana stepped forward, her own palm blackened with soot and held out her hand. "As I have said before…Light blinds," she said softly. "But Shadow teaches sight. Choose what you want to see."

So, I did. I placed my hand over hers, the fire licking between our fingers, not burning but marking. It left a crescent scar across my wrist—the same shape as the one her wrist bore. Her people murmured a word then, half prayer, half welcome.

Oathfire.

The moment the flame faded, I knew I could not go back even if I wanted to. The mark on my wrist glowed faintly when I looked toward the east toward him—my brother. I am afraid of everything to come, but the fear is not consuming. It no longer smells of guilt. I feel clean and where I am supposed to be.

The war had begun. The world I used to call home will call me a traitor. Let them. If Solnyr burns the truth from its books, we will carve it into stone. Zoryana walked through the crowd again. I could hear her voice through the mass of people, giving orders and thanks in that low, calm tone that made people believe survival was possible. I think I finally understood why her people followed her: she never promised victory, only meaning and community.

After a celebration for those of us who swore their continuing, or new, oaths, people started to disperse, heading to their tents for some sleep before we marched in the morning. Zoryana, after a fond good night and thank you, followed Aris to his tent. I could not help but wish she was coming to mine.

ZORYANA

I had not expected so many to take the oath. I knew my people loved their home, but I would have understood if they wanted to leave, I would have preferred it. I did not want to see my people die. Aris held the flap of his tent open for me, and I led him in. Turning to watch him securing it, I smiled, happy that he was up and moving about. He was still sore; his burns from the Sunlance would take time to heal. But he was alive, and that was all that mattered.

"Do you want me to take my tunic off so you can have a better look?" His teasing words made me laugh and look up at his face. That scar that slashed across his gorgeous face from the first time he had ever saved my life, his crystal-blue eyes, strong features. I had fallen in love with him the day I had met him, a young fourteen-year-old princess, naive and not all that bright. Sure, it was starling love, never meant to last, but my life was not complete without him.

"You almost died today. Stupid—jumping in front of me like that. I cannot survive if you die—I cannot…" My words were foolish; it made no sense for a queen to speak like that.

He closed the distance, and his hands clasped my face.

I felt like I could breathe again—his touch always had the ability to ground me. "Zorya, why would I not shield you from death? Apart from the fact it is the basis of the oath I swore as your Shadowsworn, but also, you are the most important person on the field of battle—not just to your people, but to me. Zorya—I also cannot live if you join your ancestors."

Aris looked so earnest that I could not hold back the tears anymore, all the emotion for the past few days finally releasing. Moisture leaked from my eyes, and I tried to shake my head but his hands on my face stopped the movement. He pulled my face to his, kissing the tears from my cheeks before his lips met mine. The kiss we shared was something that should have songs written about it. His hands slid from my cheeks to the back of my head, my own hands slid over her chest, trying to avoid the areas covered by dressings, conscious of his injuries.

"Aris…you are injured," I murmured against his lips as he started to walk me back to his bed, intent clear in his body and kisses.

"Zorya…allow me to decide if I am too injured to worship you, or not ," he replied. Desire burned through me at his determination.

He took the last step, beginning to lower me down onto the bed. I was not entirely sure the flimsy structure would take both of us, it barely took his weight, but he did not seem concerned. We had both almost joined the ancestors today, he had been closer than I had, and it looked like Aris was making sure we both knew we were still there, both still alive and together. Raising the bottom of my tunic, he leaned in to press his lips to my abdomen, following the progression of the material up as he pulled the garment off me. The sounds of the camp around us reminded me of where we were and the need to be quiet. I was sure we were not the only ones giving in to the need to physically remind ourselves we survived, but I did not think my people needed to hear their queen in the throes of passion, brought on by her Shadowsworn warrior. Aris had other ideas—the way he gave dedicated and infuriating attention to each and every point on my body that brought pleasure was making it increasingly difficult to hold back my moans.

"You...I need you... Please..." I sighed. My body was starting to coil; I needed to feel him—needed to feel connected.

"What kind of male would I be if I refused such an enticing request—and from my Queen, no less." How could he tease like that? My thoughts were beginning to leave me, and he was still able to talk like that. He stood to remove his own clothing, and the rest of mine. Situating himself between my thighs, we both let out a moan of satisfaction, our bodies coming together as he pushed into me with slow, deliberate movements. Without his tunic, I could see all of the injuries from the day's fighting. His right side was covered in healing burns, covered in dressings designed to activate the fast-healing of the Oathbound, in addition to his already heightened healing ability from his Shadowsworn status. Nicks and scrapes covered the rest of him, likely from the explosion.

"Eyes up here," Aris said, tapping the underside of my chin to make me look up at his face. "My injuries are a brand of honour, not for pity, for me or yourself... Stop focusing on anything other than what we are doing." His voice was getting tight from the building pleasure. The sound sent a thrill through me.

My mission to stay quiet was failing as Aris' length filled me over and over, the tip hitting that spot inside me that sent Soulfire through my body. His own noises were increasing; the look on his face was one of pleasure, but also surprise.

"Zorya...how...how can I feel your touch...*everywhere*..." he groaned and shuddered, holding back a climax. Lowering my eyes, they widened as I saw what he meant. Tendrils of shadow were twined over our bodies, wrapping around his arms and legs, caressing parts of his body that my hands could not reach.

"Shadows..." I did not know how to explain but it seemed that an explanation was unnecessary. Whatever my shadows' plan had been, it was working. Aris' movements were becoming harder and faster as we both neared our peaks. I tipped over the edge first, muscles gripping and spasming as my peak crashed over me, making my shadows flare out.

"Gods!" His groan was explosive as he too reached his climax. As we lay, wrapped in each other, my shadows retreated, as sated as I was it seemed. "That was different," Aris mused as he stroked a hand over my arm. "Good different. Feeling like your hands were all over me all at once was…stimulating."

"I…I have no idea how I did it, so maybe do not expect a repeat performance any time soon," I chuckled. I could not decide whether I was impressed or concerned about the display of power. Impressed on the one hand because they had stayed controlled and very focused but concerned because I did not even know it was happening until he had spoken. I was not entirely sure whether that meant I was in control? Or woefully without it.

CHAPTER FIFTEEN
BATTLE WEARY

ZORYANA

The Solnyrians continued their assault on the Thornwood for another three days. While we thankfully were able to avoid civilian casualties, we had our first Oath-bound deaths on the second day when a device Aurelian called a Sundrop had exploded in front of the line of warriors. Five warriors met their ancestors, and fifteen were injured, some very unlikely to survive their injuries. When the Sundrop detonated, it was like the sun itself had been dropped on us. However, it was not just burns the ones hit suffered; the device was loaded with something that looked like molten gold. It covered those closest and solidified. It was horrific to watch. Both Aris and Aurelian had to physically hold me back to stop me running to assist. The grief of losing my people in such a terrible way—in any way really—set off an explosion of my own. Shadow erupted from my body, sweeping towards the Solnyrian forces. I did not know exactly what happened to the males it hit; in that moment I did not care. Their abominable creations had destroyed the lives not just of the ones who passed, or were injured, but their families and communities. The expulsion of my power on such a large scale exhausted me quickly. Before the shadows even began to dissipate, blackness overtook me.

I awoke atop a horse. Sumerak, I quickly realised, Aris' arms circling me as we rode. A storm was brewing in the dark sky. Tearing my eyes from the angry clouds, I saw Aurelian riding beside us atop Vecheryn. It was a surprising sight—since we had bonded, she barely let others touch her, let alone ride her, especially without me. I shifted slightly—now I was awake, the position I was in was a little uncomfortable. Aris and Aurelian both looked at me, relief etched on their faces.

"You are awake!" Aurelian exclaimed happily, words a little breathy.

"I…what happened? Where are we going?" I asked, voice small and tired. I did not like the sound of that. I sounded weak and vulnerable, a terrible position to be in as an embattled queen.

"We are going home. The Solnyrians have retreated—for now," Aris replied. He looked up ahead of us and I turned my head to see what had caught his gaze. Home. Nightfell Castle loomed ahead. Everything seemed so quiet, the normal activity reduced as so many of its inhabitants had been out at battle.

"The Light does not like to be caught in the dark…the storms hit and they retreated," Aurelian added. So, the clouds were not brewing storms then, it sounded as though they were finishing.

"How long?" I asked, fearing the answer.

"A day. I thought it would be best to get you back to the castle. The Well should help you recover." Aris' voice was tight. He knew I never wanted to tap into the well, or the Weave, as it was actually named.

"How can the Well help? I thought it was simply a place for the souls of your ancestors," Aurelian asked. To his credit, he looked like he had not wanted to seem eager for information considering his previous alliances, but he could not contain his curiosity.

"The Weave—or the Well colloquially—is the centre of everything. It is the reason Nightfell Castle is built where it is. The Weave connects us all. Each Oath-bound, when they take their oath, is gifted the link with another of their company. They can feel each other—not completely, they cannot read minds, or find them if they are missing, but spiritually, they know the other person is there. When one of them passes to meet their ancestors, that link stays, and the memory of that person is never forgotten. When they both pass, their memories are returned to the Weave. No one is truly forgotten." I rubbed the crescent scar on my wrist where my mother's memory link had been placed.

"That... That is beautiful," Aurelian said in awe after a moment.

Conversation lulled as we neared the gates. The gates opened and we started through them. As soon as Aurelian slid off Vecheryn, guards surrounded him, understandably overly cautious.

"He is here by my word," I called out to them. "And until he breaks it, his blood is his own." The guards lowered their weapons and stepped back. Aurelian hesitated slightly before he moved to Sumerak's side. Aris tightened his arms around me for a moment but relented, allowing Aurelian to help me to the ground. The golden prince held me tight, scared I would fall. I could stand on my own, I was sure, but I could not deny that I was not immune to his attentiveness and tenderness. Feet on the ground, Aris took over, swinging me up into his arms.

"I can walk," I grumbled. A laugh rumbled in his chest as he carried me inside.

"I know you think you can. However, there are a lot of steps between here and your chambers. You will get tired, and I will have to carry you anyway, I might as well just do it from the start," Aris replied. I slapped his chest but allowed him to keep me in his arms. A Shadowhealer rushed up to us, asking what had happened and what I needed. I was not able to dismiss them—Aris and Aurelian started answering the questions before I had a chance to say I was fine.

I was not sure how long the Shadowhealer fussed over me. It felt like hours. They finally determined it was an extreme case of magic depletion, and I would be fine with rest. They warned the two males with me about being distracting and not letting me rest. I had to laugh at that. It was more likely that they would have to sit on me to stop me from leaving the room—it was not a terrible thing to imagine. Finally, I was alone with Aris and Aurelian. The latter was looking around the room, trying not to make it obvious.

"Looking for something?" I asked him as I sat up. He jumped as if I had startled him.

"This is the first time I have been in your chambers...in this entire wing, actually," he replied. "I was...just taking it all in." I did not know what that meant exactly, apart from it being true—he had not been there before. Aris was also looking at Aurelian curiously.

"So...how much do you know about the Solnyrian army? What could you tell us that will help when they inevitably come back; I doubt your brother will let this lie," I said to change the subject. Aris sat on the side of the bed next to me. Aurelian looked like he considered sitting on the bed too, at my feet where he was standing, but thought better about it and reached for a chair, dragging it to the edge.

We settled in as Aurelian relayed everything he knew about the way the Solnyrian army—the Golden Legion—was structured. It sounded like having Aurastes at the head was a rarity; the King did not leave his castle all that often, especially not to go to war. Though I had apparently spent a day sleeping, I was still exhausted. Aurelian's voice was soothing and after a while I was struggling to stay awake. I stayed as present as I was able, knowing everything he was telling me cost him something, cost him everything. He could never go home. I had never asked him if he had anyone to go back to... A part of me cringed at the thought he had a family that we would need to recover, for selfish reasons only. I would go into the fire to get his family out of Solnyr if I needed to, he had earned that honour with everything he had done for us, but I hoped he did not have someone he loved. Why did that bother me so much?

We were all exhausted. Aurelian yawned between words and my eyes were starting to lower. Aurelian sighed. "They will underestimate you at every turn. My brother can never believe a woman could best him and his soldiers—your Oath-bound forces are full of women…and then of course, there is you. You are all your biggest weapon against them. He also believes he is righteous—he completely believes his path is holy—though it cannot be if you look at the true history."

"They think the dark cannot bear the weight of truth. But light runs from it faster than anything," I murmured. We all yawned again. "Rest, Aurelian. Thank you for your invaluable information. You will need your strength. We move again soon."

"Good night, my Queen," he replied. I was not sure he knew he had called me his Queen, but I noticed, I heard him. And I liked the sound of it coming from his lips.

"I will take you to a room," Aris said to Aurelian before turning back to me. "North Wing again?"

"No—a room in this wing will be fine. It will be quicker," I instructed. They both bent their heads to me and left. I did not know when it happened, but I was asleep before Aris returned, but I subconsciously felt him slide in and wrap his arms around me.

AURELIAN

Giving Zoryana every piece of information I knew about the Solnyrian army came easy. I told her everything, even the parts that could damn me if my brother's spies were nearby. I could see she was exhausted, but she continued to prompt me, asking questions and drinking in the answers. She was a leader like I had never met before. Even as battle weary as she was, suffering from depletion of her magic, she continued to learn, committing information to memory.

When she finally dismissed me, unable to continue the charade of not being tired, I had to fight the urge to reach out and touch her. Aris led me from the room, and down a hall that I presume led to a guest room. We did not speak for most of the walk; Aris did not talk much, I had noticed.

"Thank you," he murmured gruffly as we slowed to a stop in front of a door. "The information you have given us could give us a real, fighting chance."

"You are welcome. As much as I do not believe it is the soldiers' fault, there are some who believe in my brother's rhetoric so deeply that they are as dangerous as he is, more so maybe because they are trained. I do not want anyone hurt, but I-I think I feel more at home here than I ever did in Solnyr."

Aris was giving something serious thought; his brow wrinkled a little. "You will join the Oath-bound and I for training tomorrow. You need to be trained to fight with us. You did well, you have obviously had some training, but your movements are clunky—like the Solnyrian army. With some training I believe you could move like an Oath-bound if you put your mind to it."

That was the first and only compliment he had ever given me. "Thank you. I would be honoured to learn from you all." He gave me a stiff nod and opened the door to the room. It was more opulent than the one I had been given in the North Wing—I supposed because it was in the Queen's Wing, which made sense.

"I will collect you before moonfall. Be ready." With that, Aris left. Now I was alone, I was tired to my bones. Stripping off my clothes, I collapsed into the bed, groaning as I sunk into the comfortable mattress. As I drifted off to sleep, my brother's face jeered at me, chastising me, telling me I was a terrible brother, Prince of the Sun and heir. The face of my brother morphed into Zoryana's. She smiled and reversed everything Aurastes had said, barbs tuning to breaths of fresh air, jeers turning to soothing words, glares turning to smiles. I did not know what to make of that—I was exhausted. I would worry about it in the morning.

Aurelian's Ledger
The Return to Nightfell Castle

Four Days After the Border Confrontation

Nightfell Castle, Inner Courtyard

Day Sixteen of Solmera, Year 1003 After the Breaking

The ride back to Nightfell Castle was slow. The large group conscious they had something precious in their midst to protect. Zoryana continued to sleep in Aris' arms, not waking until the castle was in sight. She looked as beautiful as ever but tired in a way that I had never been, and I was sure I never would be. Zoryana and Aris told me about the well of power that connected everything and everyone in the Dusklands—the Weave, Zoryana said was its proper name. It was such a beautiful concept—that no one was ever really forgotten.

The gates opened without fanfare, but the moment I crossed the threshold, a dozen soldiers reached for their blades. It took only a glance from Zoryana to still them. Telling them I was there by her word was all she said, but it was enough. No one questioned her again—though they still look at me like I might sprout wings of flame at any moment.

They do not trust me. I cannot blame them.

It is strange how quiet a fortress can be after a battle. Not the silence of fear—the silence of endurance. The air itself feels heavy with exhaustion and power both—like the stones are remembering what they were built for.

I see the fatigue around Zoryana's eyes, usually so bright but now flat, but she carries it like armour—graceful, terrifying, inevitable. She asked me today about the state of Solnyr's armies. I told her everything I knew, even the parts that could damn me if my brother's spies are nearby.

When I finished, she told me to rest and offered a room in her wing of the castle. There was no warmth in it, no softness—just trust, given without demand. It is more mercy than I deserve.

The Dusklands are colder than Solnyr, but I find I sleep easier here. Maybe because the dark does not ask for purity. It just asks you to see.

Tomorrow, I will train with Aris and his guard. He told me their blades move like shadows—no wasted motion, no warning. He smiled when he said it, the first real smile I have seen from him. It looked almost like forgiveness.

The scar on my wrist still burns faintly when I touch it. Not pain—promise.

If the sun rises tomorrow, let it rise on something worth the light.

- Aurelian

> *Below the entry, is an annotation in Zoryana's hand:*
> *"The dark remembers those who choose to see."*

CHAPTER SIXTEEN
TRAINING

AURELIAN

IF I EVER DOUBTED THAT the Oath-bound were forged, not born, my first day of training with them removed the illusion. Aris woke me before moonfall—the Dusklands equivalent of dawn. He said the Oath-bound always train before sunrise: *We move before the light can find us.* I told him Solnyr's guards drilled with the morning bell. He laughed. He had a strong, deep laugh that changed his face. "That explains why they are so slow."

The Oath-bound are not like the Golden Legion. No uniforms of white and gold, no shouted cadence. They move in silence. Every motion is functional, precise, and deadly. Their style is more like a tide than a duel—fluid, patient, inevitable. You do not fight them; you drown in them. If you do not see them, you die.

Aris handed me a practice blade—a shorter, double-edged weapon than the ones held by the warriors around me. "If you can hold it for an hour, you can keep it," he said as he led me to the sparring circle. He took me through drill after drill, movement after movement to show me the fluid and deadly way they moved—like the shadows their Queen wielded. By the third hour my arms shook. By the fourth, my breath came ragged. By the fifth, I stopped thinking. There was only the rhythm of his strikes and the need not to fall again. I felt confidence in the fact I had lasted longer than the hour they obviously thought would be more than enough for me. The surrounding Oath-bound did not shout corrections. They did not mock. They simply watched. When I made a mistake, Aris repeated the move until I understood why it failed. He said nothing, but there was a strange patience in his eyes, as though he had been waiting a long time to see me stripped of ceremony. Put on an equal footing, or lower even. He was the commander, and I was but a warrior in training—at least I hoped.

When he finally called a halt, I dropped the blade and realised my palms were bleeding. Aris offered me a rag, jerking his head towards my hands. "Now you look like one of us." It might have been a joke. I am not sure. "You know—I expected your blood to be gold. I figured being royal you would not bleed red like the rest of us."

"You mean because Zoryana's blood is the colour of night?" I enquired. "So mine must be the colour of the sun?"

He shrugged. "It makes sense, no? Your people descend from the kings that the Dusklands Queens had a preference for, right? There had to be something special about your bloodline. I meant no offence; it was just an observation." He held up his hands as if he was surrendering.

"We are so far removed from those men, unfortunately—or fortunately, depending on how you look at it. We are not the same. The High Fae blood we used to have that made us preferable has been bred out of us…" I trailed off, a little embarrassed by that fact. While I was a prince, my blood was too lesser to ever be considered a match for a queen like Zoryana. The giant full-blooded High Fae around me were all better matches, despite their lower status.

"Come, Prince of the Sun. Let us continue." Outside a strategy meeting, this was the most I had ever heard him speak. We settled into positions, and I went through the motions and movements I had been learning all day, feeling stronger and more confident.

Zoryana came to the grounds near the end of the day. She stood at the edge and did not interrupt, did not speak, just watched. Her eyes moved between each group but lingered on myself and Aris. Every time I looked up at her, she was looking back. An hour later, when Aris dismissed us, she left without a word and before anyone could acknowledge her.

Aris led me back to my room and advised to have a bath. As we neared my room, there was a flask of dusk-wine and a small vial of balm left outside my door. No note. She did not need to leave a note to tell me who left it. "Use the balm as well—it will help your hands." With that advice, Aris turned and headed down the hall. I picked up the wine and balm, pushing open the door to my room. A steaming bath had already been drawn for me, and I thanked whoever it was that had made sure it was ready. Stripping off, I slid into the delightfully hot water. My muscles felt like they were on fire. I hurt everywhere. My hands were torn. I felt more alive than I had in years. Pain, it turns out, was the purest teacher. It asked no allegiance, just commitment.

I was sure tomorrow would bring another beating, but I would meet it gladly. If I could learn to move as they do, maybe the Dusklands will begin to believe that I belong.

I spent the evening bathing and drinking. I rubbed the balm on my hand, hissing as it made my torn skin burn. Binding them, I settled in bed to try to sleep to awaken with purpose in the morning, ready for more instruction and hurt.

Let the sun think me broken. The dusk was teaching me how to endure.

There was a certain kind of pain that stopped feeling like punishment and started feeling like purpose. The next morning, Aris decided that I was ready for what he called *real training*. I should have recognised the gleam in his eye as warning. It was not instruction he had in mind. It was reckoning. We faced each other at moonfall, the yard still slick with mist. The Oath-bound formed a loose circle around us—silent, watchful, and I suspected, taking bets.

Aris fought like the land itself: unyielding, deliberate, full of weight and grace. His blade—that strange half-curved weapon of the Dusklands—moved as though it has its own will. My moves were faster, more direct—the Solnyrian style built on precision and dominance, with a flair of what I had learnt the day before. For a while, it was like clashing philosophies made flesh. Light against shadow. Control against rhythm.

The first time he disarmed me, I reached out to catch the sword before it fell but caught the blade with my bare hand instead of the hilt. The cut was shallow, but it startled Aris enough that I got a hit in, kicking him in the thigh—not clean, but enough to bruise.

I expected a lecture about fighting dirty, but all he did was grin. Actually grinned. "Now you are learning," he said with what I took as approval. He swept my legs out a moment later. I hit the ground hard enough to knock the breath from my lungs.

By the end, neither of us was losing, but I was definitely not winning. We were simply there, two men burning off ghosts with every strike. Though, I suspected he was holding back for my sake. When he finally called a halt, both our tunics were soaked through with sweat. Blood had dried along the edge of my sleeve, and his shoulder was bleeding through a shallow gash.

We stared at each other for a long moment. Then, to my own surprise, I laughed. So did he. Not the laughter of victory—the kind that comes from remembering what it is like to feel alive.

Zoryana was watching again, this time from the battlements. When Aris noticed her, he raised his sword in salute. She inclined her head—nothing more—but even that was something to hope for. By the look on Aris' face, he drank in any attention she gave to him. If he reacted to her like that, the man who already had her, how was I acting? I was sure I looked like a fool.

We spent the rest of the day going over everything I had learned until I was moving smoother and more fluid, like the Dusklanders moved. I knew I still had a long way to go—I was still much too loud, I had been told—but I was improving already, and I would take that win. When we finally finished up, Aris handed me a goblet of dusk-wine. "You fight like a man who has spent his life trying to be forgiven," he said as we sat with the other warriors, unwinding at the end of the day.

"Maybe I have…there has always been something I felt was wrong with my life. I just did not know what, or how to fix it…" He did not argue or comment. He just poured me another cup.

The Oath-bound did not sneer when I passed them after that night. A few nodded. One even clapped my shoulder. Small gestures, but in the Dusklands, that was a declaration of acceptance. My hands ached. My ribs ached more. But for the first time in longer than I could remember, my heart did not.

"Tomorrow, Zoryana will ride to the front to survey the damage left by your brother's crusade. You should accompany us," Aris suggested. I took that as acceptance and agreed.

Around us, dusk had fallen. The dusk burns differently than the sun—quieter, slower—but it still burns. Maybe it was time I learned how to carry its fire.

ZORYANA

Watching Aurelian and Aris train had me truly wondering about the future for the first time. Seeing Aurelian's golden head moving amongst the dark hair of the other Oath-bound was an odd sight, but one I found I was beginning to get used to. He was already starting to move like them—a good student and surprisingly adaptable. It made me happy to see the others starting to accept him. He had sacrificed his life to help us, people who had been his enemy only a few months ago. He had been taught from birth that we were monsters, but he had accepted us and learned our ways to find the truth. He had thrown away everything. I was not sure I trusted him completely yet, decades of indoctrination were difficult to work through, but he was growing on me.

I left them to their training, and bonding, returning inside. I had spent the past days either in the Hall of Threads, trying to recharge, or in rooms pouring over documents, including the ones Aurelian had brought with him. My advisers and I were attempting to develop a plan to distribute the information we had found to the other kingdoms. If we could get them on our side, help them to understand and to break the propaganda they had been fed for over a thousand years, then we may be able to fight Solnyr on all sides.

When I finally retired for the night, Aris was waiting in my room. I could not help the smile that rose my lips at the sight of him sprawled on my bed, reading whatever book had been beside my bed. Since everyone had seen us interacting after the battle, we had decided not to hide our relationship any longer—not pulling away from physical contact or displays of affection in public. My chambers were also now his as long as he wanted them to be—his room in the barracks now sitting empty.

"This is filth ," he said, feigning disgust as he threw the book on the table.

"I need my books to be even more exciting than my real life," I teased. He looked affronted and sat up. He was bare-chested, and his soft sleep pants had rolled down slightly from the movement.

"More exciting? Our private life is pretty exciting," he countered, making me laugh. He was right. I changed and joined him in bed. "Oh, I asked Aurelian to join us tomorrow."

It made sense, though I was a little surprised he would think of that. "That is a great idea. The more he is a part of the better. The people and the Oath-bound will accept him faster if he is not kept out of sight."

CHAPTER SEVENTEEN
AFTERMATH AT THE FRONT

AURELIAN

I THOUGHT I HAD SEEN leadership before. I was wrong. We rode north at moonfall—Zoryana, Aris, and a small detachment of Oath-bound. The roads were half-choked with ash from the fires my brother's soldiers had left behind. In some parts we needed to cover our mouths and noses to breathe. The land still smouldered where the light had touched it—a white scar burned through the once lush, black soil.

By noon, we reached the edge of the Blight. This was different to the blight caused by Zoryana's magic. This felt... evil. Where the trees once felt alive, they were now grey—not dead, but also not living. Like the life had been taken out of them and replaced with silence. The air tasted of iron and frost.

The Dusklands people who had fled the nearby villages came out to meet us, thin and hollow-eyed. They bowed to Zoryana, but it was not fear that bent them. There was relief on their faces. The last they had seen her, she was unconscious, pale as death, and being rushed back to the castle. When she dismounted, safe and healthy, the entire crowd seemed to breathe again.

As she had on many occasions, she walked through

them slowly, unguarded, touching hands, calling names, remembering faces. Every gesture felt like an act of healing. Every word, a promise she meant to keep even if it killed her. And then—she did what no monarch in Solnyr would ever do. She kicked off her boots and stepped into the blighted soil barefoot. Aris tried to stop her. I did too. She gave us no chance.

"If my people bleed from this land, then I will too." Her voice was steady and determined.

Zoryana's magic rose around her—the deep, night-coloured shadows were not a show of force or proof of her power, she meant to heal. The ground trembled. The grey began to shift, faint veins of blue-green light threading through the roots. The Blight did not vanish, but it recoiled, like something alive and ashamed. I do not know what she gave the land in that moment—power, pain, certainly a part of herself—but she fell to one knee when it ended, and I swear I felt the pulse of her heart in the earth beneath us. When she stood again, her eyes were silver fire.

Her people watched her, silent, reverent, as though witnessing their own salvation, that she was their salvation. That was how gods were born. Aris helped her back to her horse, his expression caught somewhere between pride and fury. He loved her too—I saw it in the way his jaw tightened when she risked herself. I could not blame him. I felt it too.

Zoryana greeted her people with love and gratitude, despite the repeated efforts to push back the Blight beginning to drain her again. From what I could understand, we had not been back at the castle long enough for her internal well of power to recharge fully. Everywhere we stopped, she fed more of her magic into the ground. With each expulsion of power, she weakened, taking longer to rise, until she was forced to ride with Aris for the remainder of the day.

As we made camp that night, I found Zoryana sitting apart from the others, staring into the forest. I could not decipher her expression. It was a mixture of sadness and guilt. I went to her, foolishly, thinking to thank her for what she did.

"Please do not," she said quietly, before I could speak. "Gratitude makes it sound like a choice."

She looked at me then, and I understood: this was not faith, or duty, or even love. It was something older, harder—the covenant between a land and the soul bound to it. No prayer I ever learned in Solnyr could match that kind of devotion. I was starting to see what the Dusklands meant by endurance. It was not about surviving what had been done to you. It was about standing anyway, even when the world demanded that you fall. Zoryana Vekara was a different breed of ruler—selfless to a fault, and seemingly incorruptible by the immense power she held. She faced the world of hurt that had been presented to her with a balance of confidence and vulnerability.

"Can I just sit then?" I asked. She waved her hand at the empty space beside her and I joined her. "Zoryana—the way you love your people, the land, and the way they love you, it is something I have never seen. I know you think that means you need to give all of yourself but they…we need you to be healthy and whole."

"I have to do this, Aurelian. I have the means to help, to heal, and it would be remiss of me to keep it to myself. I would feel guilty if my people suffered because I was scared to push myself to the edge. Thank you for your advice…I just…this is who I am." She looked haunted, tired. Patting my hand lightly, she stood. "Good night, Aurelian."

I watched her walk towards her tent and disappear inside. I hoped we could show her balance before it was too late.

ARIS

Watching the easy way Aurelian could talk to Zoryana hurt sometimes. He knew what to say; he knew the burden of a crown. It was something I was never able to help her with. She needed someone who understood even a small part of what she was going through. I could calm her, relax her, give her pleasure, protect her—but he had the pretty words to make her see sense, I hoped. She needed him too—not just me. They looked *right* sitting together, opposites to each other in looks, but somehow complementary.

I could not hear what they were saying but I knew I should not interrupt. My place was at her side, as her shield, and, for now, in her bed. How much longer that would be my place, I did not know. I was determined to hold on as long as I could, but it was impossible to hold onto shadow…and the Queen who commanded it.

It was not long before she joined me in bed. She looked exhausted but she wore it well. I hated to watch her drain herself like she was doing. I could not do anything to help, to stop her, barring picking her up and hauling her away. She would hate me forever if I did that. I knew there was a part of her that resented me for not letting her go to those Oath-bound that had been killed by the Sundrop. She had exploded anyway, decimating the first few lines of the Solnyrian offence. They had died with her shadows choking and suffocating them. I was glad she had not seen what she had done. Despite them being enemy soldiers, she would hate herself for the pain and suffering she had caused. I was just thankful that it did not seem that the Sun King had seen directly. We had not heard of any new accusations of her being monstrous.

I held her until her breathing changed and then I held her tighter. I wished our bond allowed me to give her some of my strength to get her through her own duty.

We spent the next few days visiting the other sites where Blight was killing the Thornwood, Zoryana pushing power into the dying land at every point. While it looked like it was helping, she was deteriorating. The lustre was dimming in her hair and skin, and her eyes—usually so bright and alive—were beginning to look flat, like a mirror that has seen too many faces. I did not know how to help. All I could do was hold her while she slept and keep her upright in front of her people.

The other Oath-bound travelling with us were very obviously concerned, giving her sad and worried glances when she was not looking, always making sure someone was with her, even if I or Aurelian were there too. It was a testament to how much everyone cared for her.

The people could see it too, but they were beginning to look at her like a goddess. They touched her as she passed and said her name like something to worship. Zoryana never wanted to be treated like a goddess; she just wanted to be the best queen she could. Her power was immense, drawing directly from the well and the earth, but she always gave back—and that is what a god or goddess should do, give back to the land and the people. It had a downside though—I was scared it was killing her.

I left Zoryana in the care of two of my most loyal and trustworthy warriors, with strict instructions to at least attempt to keep her from using too much more of her magic and took Aurelian, looking a little ragged from the travelling and his worry, on a scouting ride to establish the extent of the damage in the area. If we could find places for her to visit that had less Blight, we might be able to save her, and we could find out a different way to fight the magic killing the land. It was a futile mission. The Blight was seeping into the Thornwood, and the trees could not fight back enough to stop it alone. Clearings were continuing to open up all along the tree line, making it impossible to patrol effectively. The enemy were taking full advantage, coming through and burning trees and farms—like they could cleanse the world with their righteous fire. My blood boiled as I looked around at the carnage.

"She cannot see this." Aurelian sighed as we sat on our horses looking over a particularly large patch of grey trees. He was right. A sudden burst of anger flared through me, directed at the Sun King and his assault against my home, my family. The righteous idiot would rather kill everyone and everything than accept that the Dusklands still thrive. He let the other kings keep their kingdoms, even their full sovereignty over said kingdoms. But he was determined to erase Zoryana and the people of her lands. I could not see the logic.

"No…but how do we keep her from continuing? I have a small amount of sway with her, but in the end, she is the Queen, and it is my duty to follow her. I cannot lie to her and tell her it is not worth her bother. Everything is worth it to her." My words made me sad, because they were true. Zorya would deplete herself completely before she gave up, because everything and everyone was precious and important.

"You are right," Aurelian replied. Leather cracked as his hands clenched on the reins he held. She was not just an idol to him; I could see that now. I had noticed the growing relationship between them, but I could see it plain as day that it was more than that for him.

"You love her, don't you?" My question made him look at me for the first time since we had stopped. It was clear on his face that I had it right.

"Is that not a common affliction?" I cocked an eyebrow. I did not believe at all that was it. "Yes…of course I do. It is almost impossible to not fall for a woman like her. From the moment I saw her, and the first time she took down Kirin, to the time I saw her with her people at the Rite…and now…I left my safe and admittedly cosy life, I became a traitor, all because she asked me to. She never promised me anything… Sure, she offered sanctuary if I needed it, but she never even hinted at anything beyond that, but how do you say no to someone so strong and selfless?" He sighed and rubbed his face. "But—she already has a great love, so I will be content to serve her in any way I can, and hopefully keep her alive." The pointed look he gave me when talking about Zorya's great love was confusing. I was the interim before she found that. We spoke about not being able to live without each other, but she would move on eventually, I knew that. Our arrangement was in place to keep us both from loneliness until we found someone else we wanted to spend our lives with. I was surprised I had had her as long as I had and I would cherish every moment. I was sure she was my 'great love', but I could not allow myself to believe that I could possibly be hers.

"Tell her—but tell her in a real way. Do not make it sound like it is just reverential or sycophantic—she has enough of that around her." The look on his face was surprised, confused, and maybe a little hopeful all at once. It would be comical if I had not been telling someone to move in on the woman I loved.

"I...thank you, Aris," he said, turning away. In silence, we rode back to camp. I could not deny my heart was breaking.

CHAPTER EIGHTEEN
FRACTURES

AURELIAN

HEALING THE LAND WAS KILLING Zoryana. Her power was draining, and her body was giving in. My talk with Aris on our scouting mission had my mind racing. No one was blind to the relationship between him and Zoryana, not that they were hiding it anymore—but Aris had told me to tell Zoryana how I felt. I was confused and sad—it sounded like he was resigned to losing her. I was not privy to the arrangement they had in place, but I did not think I could get between them. It would not be right.

When we arrived back at camp after dark fell, the fires were already burning low. The Oath-bound sat around, enjoying some downtime with a drink and a laugh while they played games or told stories. Aris and I found Zoryana in the central tent with the wartime council—half her commanders were arguing over ration lines, half trying to divine whether my brother's next strike will fall from the north or east. At our entrance, the voices in the tent quietened. I gave our report, telling them of the burned lands and the Blight—as Aris and I had both decided that lying to Zoryana would be wrong.

"Thank you for the report," Zoryana said, her tone formal and flat. Something inside me snapped at that tone—that careful distance she wore like armour, now worn tighter as she retreated inside herself.

"Zoryana—you cannot keep doing this. You have to stop bleeding yourself into the land, or there will not be anything left of you to save it." My words were not accusatory, just desperate to make her see what she was doing to herself.

Those eyes that were now so flat, flashed. She did not shout at me. Zoryana never shouted. Her voice just dropped—low, even lethal. "You think I have a choice?"

I was too far in to stop now. "Yes. Your people would follow you even if you stop destroying yourself to protect them… *I* would continue to follow you. You have nothing to prove." As soon as I spoke, I realised I had made a mistake; I had said too much. The words had come out louder than I meant, more personal than I wanted.

Everyone froze. The entire tent went silent. She rose then— every inch the Queen of Dusk. Power simmered at the edges of her hands, subtle but visible, the air warping faintly. Her exhaustion was evident in her face, and her tenuous grasp on her magic.

"You would lecture me about sacrifice?" she asked. "You, who has carried the sun's lies into other courts? Who willing turned a blind eye to truth over your pampered life so as not to upset the status quo?"

I did not flinch, though I wanted to. She was not being untruthful. My hands were not clean of blood. In my thirty years, I had taken part in things I was not proud of because my brother commanded me to. I dropped my voice—quiet and as calm as I could manage. "My previously pampered life, you mean, because I have been banished from my home to help you and your people. Yes, I will talk about sacrifice. Because I now know what it costs to believe obedience is the same as duty."

For a heartbeat, I thought she would strike me. She would have every right. Instead, she turned away, her shoulders rigid. "You do not get to save me, Aurelian."

"I am not trying to save you," I said. "I am trying to stand beside you."

That was when she looked at me again—and the look was pure wildfire, not anger alone but something older, hungrier. The kind of look that makes men ruin themselves willingly.

Then she left without another word. The tent emptied around me in silence. Even Aris did not speak. He just gave me that unreadable soldier's stare and followed her out. I stood in that empty tent going over everything, getting progressively annoyed and confused. I do not regret what I said. But I suppose I understood that standing beside her was not something you earned. It was something she allowed—or did not. And yet, gods help me, if she turned around right now and told me to follow her into fire, I would. Because she was right. I did not want to save her. I just wanted her to allow me to burn with her.

ZORYANA

Fury simmered beneath my tenuous control. As I walked back to my tent, the shadows caused by the flickering fire gathered around me, swishing around my feet.

"Zorya, please… He just cares about you," Aris pleaded, catching up with me as I was entering our tent. He secured the door, and I could feel him watching me as I moved around the space, obsessively moving things around.

"I do not need a lecture right now," I said without facing him. "And—you are defending him now? What happened to, *You cannot trust him, Zorya…he is still a Prince of the Sun…*? What happened to that?"

Behind me, he huffed out a laugh at my terrible impression of him. "Zorya…this is killing you. You know that. We all know that we can see it. We all love you and it is hard to watch you take yourself to the brink."

Leaning against a table, hands braced on the top, my head dropped at his words. I was just so tired. "I…I can feel it all the time. The magic. I…I cannot refuse it. I want to help, I want to save my people and my land, but also the magic wants to return and needs to help." There was a consistent thrumming beneath my skin—my land was dying and the ancestral magic that I had inherited needed to help. Everything started to calm as Aris' hand pressed to my back. The pressure was firm, and I took a deep breath, trying to calm the storm inside me.

"I do not know what that feels like," he admitted. "But I need—we all need you to know you have support. You do not have to do all this on your own. Okay?" Sighing, I nodded and his arms snaked around me, pulling me back against his chest. "I know you know I love you…so let me, please."

Tears leaked from my eyes as the emotion and pain from the past months crashed into me. I had only been Queen for a little over a tide before the King's letter had arrived; even now, after everything had happened it had only been a matter of months. I did not know how anyone could follow me—the land was falling apart under my watch. I was devastated.

The storm came fast out of the Thornwood, wind and rain cutting through the camp like a blade. I was alone in the central tent, maps scattered, the lanterns guttering. The land was angry. I had been forced to rest for a few days. My body shut down, and I slept for two days, and spent an extra one recovering. The Blight had spread further, and I was feeling the call, like a rope around my heart being pulled to help. Though I had rested, I was still exhausted, and my nerves were frayed. I felt terrible but every conversation turned into an argument, and I was irritable at best, mean at worst. Everyone around me just took it and looked at me with pity, making my mood worse.

"Zoryana?" Aurelian's voice behind me caused my body to tense—a myriad of annoying feelings running through me.

"You still think this is about you and what you have done or can do to help," I said cruelly, turning to face him. It was not true, I knew that, but I was not always able to stop myself.

He had done nothing but say my name to provoke this. To his credit, he did not lash back.

"I think it is about the world," he answered, words measured and steady. "And you cannot continue to carry it alone."

He was right. I could not. They had all been telling me that for tides. But I froze, anger rising inside me, no longer simmering, but boiling. Lightning tore across the sky then, bright enough to illuminate the tent through the canvas, and the wind threw the tent-flap wide. My every instinct told me to lash out, chastise him for daring to talk to me like that. Go against every thought or desire I had to just be like everyone else.

Instead, I stepped forward. The space between us vanished like breath on glass. Neither of us spoke, both of us shocked at the closeness. When my hand found his collar, it was not gentle. His hand caught my wrist but did not try to move my hand; instead it was like he was keeping it there.

The world narrowed to breath and heartbeat—to the taste of thunder in the air, the salt of sweat, the tremor that runs through two people who have been at war with themselves for too long. There was no tenderness in the way our lips crashed together . It was surrender—not to peace, but to truth and what we had been holding back from the moment we first saw each other, from the first time he had helped me down from Vecheryn and held me. It was a battle fought with lips, tongues, and teeth. A kiss that had my insides melting and aflame. When we finally pulled apart, lips swollen, both of us were shaking and breathing deeply.

"Now you understand what it means to stand beside me." My words were ridiculous and on the edge of rude. Is that what he could expect? Kisses fuelled by anger and cruelty as I slowly turned into the monster his culture had said I was?

Before he could reply and say something beautiful, or hateful, I released him and stalked out of the tent into the raging wind and rain. My heart was racing—the cold rain shocked me into consciousness, and I almost ran back to him.

Instead, I let the rain hide my tears as I took the long way back to the tent I shared with Aris...having just kissed someone else.

He was not mad. The quiet way in which he started to pack his possessions broke my heart. I had to physically hold his hands to stop him; calling his name fell on deaf ears.

"Aris, stop. What are you doing? Why are you packing?" My voice was shaking slightly.

He barely looked at me, but he did stop and drop his bag. "I have been waiting for this to happen since he arrived for the accord talks," he admitted and I knew his heart was breaking. "Dreading it, but waiting, nonetheless. I have watched you get closer; I even told him to let you know his declarations of love were not just worship. I know what our arrangement is, Zoryana. I...I will do my duty."

My heart shattered. He was resigned to give me up after one kiss. "No...no, Aris." Tears started to well in my eyes, starting to blur my vision. "No...I was not lying when I said I cannot live without you. I do not want you to be just my Shadowsworn. You are so much more to me. I love you. I do not know what is going on with Aurelian—whether it happened because I am so tired, and I was so angry. Please, Aris...don't...I cannot lose you..." His gorgeous blue eyes were wild, like a tempest in the sea that was described in so many books from before the Breaking. "Just...just let me work out what is going on..."

"Zorya, I—" His voice was thick, and I wanted to cry. It sounded like he was going to reject me. I did not think I could take that with everything else. "I-I understand you cannot understand why you kissed him, even though everyone else knows why, but what are you saying? Are you saying that you want both of us?"

"I—" I stopped, on the verge of a denial. For as long as I have known what desire was, I had wanted Aris and no one else. I had never been attracted to anyone else, male or female. Aris had been the only one that stirred anything within me. That changed when Aurelian had arrived, looking like sunlight in human form with his bronze skin, and golden hair and eyes. I was fooling myself if Aris' question did not intrigue me. Could that even be an option? Would either of them be amenable to that? I doubted it, the two males were very dominant, I did not think that they would be happy to share a female between them. My eyes locked with Aris. His gaze was unreadable. "Aris…I…would you be unhappy if that was the case?" Those tempest eyes widened. I assumed he had not thought I would agree.

"Well, I—You…" He trailed off and rubbed his hand over his face. Sitting heavily on the edge of the bed, he looked up at me like he was trying to decide if I was joking. Letting out a groan, he was on his feet in a moment and closed the distance. Our lips met with a lot more tenderness than his movements would have indicated, and so much more than I had kissed Aurelian with. His hands caged my face as he controlled the kiss, taking what he needed, and I willingly gave. Pulling away, he sighed and rested his forehead against mine. "Zorya…if that is what you want, what you truly want, I will stay, of course I will. He is not a bad male, and I know he loves you and he has proven he will put his own life on the line for you. If it was going to be anyone, I suppose I can deal with it being him."

I had to admit I was surprised he agreed at all, and so quickly. That air of resignation had left him, and he looked… happier somehow. Releasing my face, he picked up his bag and started to replace the items that he had packed to where they had been before. Standing in shock, I just watched him. "Are you sure, Ari? I do not want to make you uncomfortable or do anything that you do not want to do just to please me."

The grin he threw over his shoulder hit me in the chest. "My mission in life is to please you, Zoryana. It always has been, you know that. I might ask for a few more…rewards than I do currently, but I promise, I am not mad. If I have to share you with anyone, Aurelian is the best option." His reiterated words about him being happy it was Aurelian made me wonder if he was harbouring a bit of fondness for the Sun

Prince. His request for more rewards made me roll my eyes. He just laughed at me.

I could not deny the conversation had me feeling lighter, stronger. I could feel the pull from my magic to go out and fix more of the land, but it was not as overwhelming. The power simmered under my skin, but I felt more in control than I had in tides.

Aurelian's Ledger
The Night of the Storm

Nightfell Encampment

Day Twenty-Six of Solmera, Year 1003 After the Breaking

I do not know whether tonight began as an argument or an ending to something. The storm came fast out of the Thornwood, wind cutting through the camp like a blade. She was alone in the tent, maps scattered, the lanterns guttering. I meant to speak of strategy. I said her name instead.

She turned, and every trace of restraint from last night was gone. The mask of control had cracked. The woman beneath it was all edge and fury. Out of nowhere, she blamed me for thinking everything that was happening was about me. I did not know where that had come from, but I did not agree. I believe everything we were experiencing had everything to do with saving the world, but she could no longer carry it alone.

Lightning tore across the sky then, bright enough to paint her in silver and shadow both. The wind threw the tent-flap wide. Her hair flew across her face for a moment and my heart lurched. It was her. Zoryana was, without a doubt, the woman I had been dreaming of before visiting the Dusklands had even become a possibility. My raven-haired enchantress. I did not anticipate that when I discovered her that she would be furious with me, no matter how gorgeous she was when she simmered. For a heartbeat she looked like she might strike me—and perhaps she should have.

Instead, she stepped forward. The space between us vanished like breath on glass. No words. Just heat, and fury, and the sound of rain hammering on canvas. When her hand found my collar, it was not gentle; when I caught her wrist, it was not resistance. It was recognition.

The world narrowed to breath and heartbeat—to the taste of thunder in the air, the salt of sweat, the tremor that runs through two people who have been at war with themselves for too long.

When our lips finally came together, it was not tenderness. It was surrender. Not to peace, but to truth. When she finally pulled back, both of us shaking, she spoke quietly to tell me that was what it was like to stand beside her.

Before I could fully comprehend what she had meant, she was gone—leaving me with the storm still raging inside the tent and inside myself.

I can still feel her heartbeat against mine, as if the mark on my wrist answered it.

If this is the fire we have lit, it will either forge us or destroy us. Maybe both.

- Aurelian

CHAPTER NINETEEN
RECEDING BLIGHT

AURELIAN

THE RAIN STOPPED BEFORE SUNRISE. The camp smelled of wet canvas and smoke. The world, however, looked washed clean, though I know better—mud only hides the blood for a while. I had woken before the watch change. Habit? Or guilt? I was not sure. Zoryana's tent was still dark; only the guards outside moved.

After a soldier's ration of the morning meal, I found myself in the central tent, trying to compose a report on the state of the Dusklands' army and people who stayed with us, but all I accomplished was a piece of parchment with ink dropped on the page, but no words. I am unable to think of anything other than the night before. The sound of thunder cracking the horizon. The way Zoryana's hand trembled—not from fear, but from restraint breaking.

There is a kind of silence between two people after a moment like that; it is almost sacred, almost unbearable. I told myself that nothing had changed—that we were still two leaders on opposite ends of a dying world.

A small commotion outside caught my attention. Leaving the tent, I saw Zoryana leaving hers. She looked different, renewed somehow.

"We march at moonfall," she called out, spurring everyone around her into action. Her tone was even, her expression composed.

No mention of the night, no trace of it in her bearing. But when she passed me on her way to the central tent, her hand brushed mine—just a fraction, accidental to anyone watching. To me, it felt like an oath renewed.

I knew better than to speak of it. The Dusklands had no use for romance in war. They had oaths, and battle, and the quiet understanding that some bonds are forged only in the moments before they break. I could not name what the night before had been—mercy, anger, need, or something carved out of all three. I only knew that when she had said *stand beside me*, I finally understood she did not mean as a soldier. She meant as equal. And I was willing. Even if it killed me.

Aris exited the tent a moment later, running his fingers through his hair. I wondered why he kept his longer than the other Oath-bound—perhaps he was not required to shave it as a Shadowsworn. A quick nod and a clap of my shoulder heightened my confusion. Frozen to the spot, it took a moment for me to be able to move again. Either Zoryana had not even told him, or he did not care. I was not sure how that made me feel beyond the confusion. Shaking my head, I joined everyone in the tent in time to hear the instructions.

Before long, we were atop horses again and on the road. People came out to see their Queen, calling out her name in love and reverence. She looked strong, her Shadowmare, Vecheryn, walking smoothly, though swishing her head every now and again, looking happy to be out and about again and having Zoryana astride her. As we neared our destination, Zoryana's smile started to droop, even as she sat taller and Vecheryn started to walk faster. Her feet were on the ground before the horse even stopped, heading to the enlarged area of Blight. Aris and I shared a concerned look—the area was much bigger than it had been during our scouting mission.

Before anyone could stop her, Zoryana had dropped to her knees, hands pressed to the dying land. The scream she let out as the power surged through her had both of us running to her side. Without thinking, I laid a hand on her back, looking up as Aris did the same. She was hot to the touch, the power inside her warming her up like an ember.

As she pushed her magic into the ground, blue lines wove through the dying soil. Colour followed and the Blight began to recoil like it had before but this time it looked like she might push it back completely. Soon though, her magic sputtered and she slumped against me. All around us, the ground was coming back to life. A small huff that might have been a laugh made me shift to look down at the queen in my arms. "I told you two I could do it," she teased. "You two worry too much." Aris and I shared an incredulous look over her head. He still had his hand on her back as she burrowed into my arms further, reaching up to grip Aris' arm to hold it there. "This is nice." Her smile was tired as she looked up at us. "We...when we get back, we need to talk about something..."

"When you have rested, heart," Aris chuckled, shaking his head. I was so beyond confused about the situation I could not even speculate in my own head about what the conversation would be about.

We convinced Zoryana to rest for at least a small while, though she fought us until she collapsed with exhaustion. Leaving her to sleep, I followed Aris out to the fire, joining the other Oath-bound. My hands clasped around an offered mug of dusk-wine, my mind racing as I tried to keep up with conversations around me. The amount of power Zoryana had just expelled was more than she had done when she had decimated the Solnyrian army and she had slept for a day, and never really recovered. She had literally revived the earth under her hands this time—how would she recover from this?

"Drink, Prince. You are going to need it." Aris sounded amused.

"What do you mean?"

The Shadow shook his head. "No—this is her conversation. But you are going to want to have finished that mug." I immediately lifted the mug to my lips. Dusk-wine had an interesting quality that wine from Solnyr did not have. The golden wine I had been brought up on was sweet and syrupy, made to taste and feel like you were drinking the sun. Dusk-wine felt light when you drank it, like it turned to smoke in your mouth—I presumed that was why people drank so much of it.

Everyone turned their gazes up as Zoryana emerged from her tent a lot sooner than anyone could have predicted. She looked rejuvenated in a way she had not in weeks. Waving her hand to make everyone sit, she stood behind Aris and I, taking the mug he handed her. I drained the rest of mine, my head brushing her body as I tipped it back. I had not realised she was standing quite that close. One by one, the Oath-bound excused themselves for the night, leaving the three of us by the fire.

"Aurelian—would you join us in my tent? I would prefer to not have this conversation by the fire." Her voice was soft, not at all sounding as though I did not have an option to turn down the conversation.

"Yes." I nodded and stood, following her inside, Aris bringing up the rear, securing the tent-flaps. Zoryana sat on the edge of the bed and patted the space beside her. I looked at Aris, not sure if she meant for me to sit or him. He motioned with a hand towards the bed, indicating that I should sit.

"I…" She looked a little nervous now we were here. I had never seen her nervous, not like that. "I need to apologise to you for how I kissed you last night." Oh no…she regrets it… That would devastate me. "You did not deserve the anger I had directed towards you. Nothing that has happened is your fault. You have been nothing but supportive, even when I did not deserve it, when you did not know me, and did not know if I would be any different than what you had been taught about my people, and I treated you so badly."

"Zoryana—really, it is okay. You do not have to apologise," I tried to assure her.

"Thank you," she murmured and looked up at Aris. He nodded from where he leaned against a tent pole. "Aurelian. I apologise for the manner by which I kissed you, not that I kissed you in the first place. I am sure you will agree—that has been building for a while." The chuckle she released sounded more self-deprecating than I had ever heard from a monarch.

"I would agree with that." My reply was halting, curious. "Zoryana—why am I here? What do you need to say?" I cringed slightly. My words sounded harsher than I had intended. She did not look offended.

"I—We—I do not want to—I would like to see where this attraction goes...but I...I cannot choose between you and Aris." Her words spilled out of her lips like she thought they would disappear if she did not say them so quickly. My mouth dropped open as any response I might have had died on my own lips. She... She wanted both of us. I looked up to her Shadowsworn warrior, who just shrugged. They had definitely spoken about it. And he was onboard?

"Well—uhhh—I—How does that work?"

"We have not worked out the logistics," Zoryana admitted.

"She wanted to make sure you would not completely dismiss the idea before she thought about it too much," Aris added. The look Zoryana gave him was comical—like she was annoyed he had outed her insecurities.

"I am not one hundred percent saying no...I just want to know how it will work."

She perked up a little at that. "I...I suppose for my part—I am very attracted to both of you. Aris and I have been together for years and I cannot let him go, as cruel as that is. And then you sauntered into my throne room looking like the sun, standing up for me even though you had every reason not to...and I do not know... You intrigued me. As much as I am sorry it was anger that fuelled our kiss, it was a really lovely kiss." Her smile lit up her eyes; their lustre was back. "How the three of us work as a unit—I will leave that up to you two, you are the ones this is the oddest for. I would never ask you to do anything you were uncomfortable with." I looked up at Aris again. Never would I have thought this would happen. I could guarantee Aris felt the same.

"For my part—if I would have ever thought about it, I probably would have suggested you," Aris admitted. He straightened up away from the pole and moved towards the bed, sitting on the other side of Zoryana. She sat back, resting on her hands so the three of us could still see each other. I did not know how to take all this in. It was not the first time I had been propositioned by two partners, but they had both been women.

"I have never entertained the idea of being in a relationship with a woman and a man." This conversation was changing the way I thought about everything. It made sense though. We both loved her, and I would never tell her to choose—I would lose, there was no doubt about that. I was not so arrogant as to think I held so much as a sputtering candle flame to the bond she had with Aris. I let my eyes take in Zoryana's figure as she reclined on her hands. She was giving me a chance to be with her. While it was different to what I could have imagined, I did not think I could turn it down. "Okay. Yes. Let's give this a try."

Zoryana's entire body seemed to light up with joy. She straightened up, flinging her arms around me. "Thank you," she murmured into my ear. Her breath on my skin made a shiver run through me. Yes, I was not going to turn down the chance to be with her in whatever capacity she allowed it. She pulled back and smiled all the way to her eyes. "Do you think we could try that kiss again?" Her innocent question made me laugh.

Meeting Aris' eye over her shoulder, he nodded. If this was truly going to be the three of us, I wanted to make sure he was in fact fine with everything as well. It was all the permission I needed. Reaching up, I ran my fingers over her cheek, touching her face for the very first time. Her skin was soft and warm, the flush under her skin heating her cheeks. With my hands cupping her face, we came together again. This time, it did not feel like a fight, an explosion of desire; it felt like a dance. The way her soft lips felt against mine was indescribable. A moan muffled in our mouths as her tongue slid against mine. This kiss was passionate, heated by our desire for each other, nothing else. The bed shifted slightly, then Zoryana let out a moan of her own. The kiss broke and I could see what—apart from the kiss—had made her moan. Aris' hand was under her tunic, caressing her body. I could work with him to worship the woman between us. He knew the most about her and what she liked—but I liked to learn and explore.

"That was…much nicer," Zoryana said, breathless. She licked her lips slightly. The glimpse of the tip of her tongue was enough to make me want to kiss her again. She had other ideas. Zoryana faced Aris and leaned in to press her lips to his. Her hand went up to slide into his hair. The giant man let out what could only be described as a growl. Now I understood why his hair was longer. I also understood why he had been unable to stop himself from touching her. It was surprisingly arousing to watch them. I hesitated—the closest I had been to touching her was helping her on and off horses or holding her after the Blight cleansing. But she would not have asked for this if she did not want me to touch her. Sliding my hand over her leather-clad thigh, I was gratified to feel the muscles clench under my touch. I had never felt so much like a Dawnbreak with his first lover before—not even when I actually had been a Dawnbreak with my first lover. Zoryana's hand appeared on mine on her leg, encouraging my hand higher. Taking her cue, my hand slipped under her tunic, fingers brushing her skin. I was not ashamed to admit that I too moaned at the touch. She was smooth and perfect. With my other hand, I moved her hair aside, revealing a strip of milky skin. Leaning in, I pressed my lips to her neck. The sound she let out was the most erotic thing I had ever heard.

"Oh…Goddess…" Her moaned words were not muffled.

Flicking my eyes up, I realised Aris was kissing the other side of her neck. Zoryana's hands began to roam, one going to Aris' legs. Her other hand found my thigh and squeezed. That was enough for me, but she did not stop, her hand soon found its way between my legs. Having her hand on me over my pants was more than I could have imagined. I had determinedly tried to not imagine what being intimate with her would be like, but I would not have imagined it like it was unfolding.

CHAPTER TWENTY
THE THREE

ZORYANA

I WAS IN AWE OF how Aris and Aurelian had not only accepted the proposition, but they were both quite enthusiastic about it. Their lips on my neck and hands on my body were assaulting my senses from all over. I did not know anything about Aurelian's history, but I knew this was the first time I had been in a situation like this, and unless he had done it before we started our relationship, I was sure it was Aris' first too. I did not know the mechanics of it all, but I knew the feelings this was bringing up inside me were overwhelming in the best way. My hands on the males' legs roamed until I found my goal. Moans vibrated against my neck from both sides as my hands massaged them through their pants.

My hips rolled a little, trying to cause much needed friction to alleviate the growing passion in my core. The movement caught both of their attention. Aurelian's long fingers progressed upwards, goosebumps rising on my skin as he teased and stroked my chest. Aris' large hand slid between my legs, giving me that friction I needed. Rolling my hips against his hand, with Aurelian fondling my breasts…I could already feel pleasure building in my core.

"I-I… Oh…" I was trying to say I needed more…needed

one of them inside me…but I could not get the words out. Their attentions were becoming so distracting I was losing the ability to speak.

Always acutely aware of my needs, Aris took the hint and started to unlace my pants, sliding his hand into them as soon as they were open enough. His calloused fingers moved against my centre, making the feeling worse, not better. My core was on fire in the most pleasurable way. Both males raised their heads and stood, taking me with them. I did not know what kind of communication they were doing behind my back, but it was effective. I knew they could work together—they had proven that on scouting missions and in skirmishes—it was one of the reasons why I had even entertained this idea, but I did not realise how that cooperation would translate into an intimate setting. Aris removed his hand from my pants and stayed standing, his hands caressing each bit of skin as he raised my tunic until it was off and he had unrestricted access to my upper body. Aurelian dropped to his knees in front of me—he sight was incredibly alluring—and removed my boots. His hands slid up my legs, gripping the top of my pants to peel them down. I did not miss the way he looked at me, or the quick lip lick. This was torture. My pants removed, I saw Aurelian's eyes flick up, past my face and I had to smile. It was kind of arousing that they were communicating so much. This was Aurelian's first time as part of our dynamic, and he was constantly making sure he was not stepping over any of Aris' boundaries. It was a little endearing. He then looked up at me like he was asking for my permission as well. My slight nod was all he needed. Raising my leg over his shoulder, he pressed a kiss to my thigh, as his fingers made light contact with my centre. The tentativeness in his touches was adorable, and it struck me in a way I did not expect. My heart tugged as he started to explore what made me moan or shudder. His inquisitive nature was a boon in an intimate setting, it would seem. Fingers, lips, and tongue moved over my centre, extracting every ounce of pleasure he could. Aris was never one to be left behind either. His rough palms encompassed my breasts, squeezing and rolling, before focusing on my nipples, making pleasure shoot through me. An embarrassingly loud moan left me as Aurelian pushed a finger inside me.

"Yes...oh gods...I...I am... Gods I am close." My words were punctuated by moans. I always tried to warn Aris, so I was happy I still had some mental capacity to do the same with Aurelian, not knowing his preference for these things. He did not change tack, just delved in further; his fingers replaced his tongue, fingers moving to my clit. I went over the edge of my climax in a huge way—if Aris was not holding me upright, my legs would have given out, I was sure. When my shudders began to ebb, Aurelian raised his head. Looking down at him, face slick, my leg still thrown over his shoulder, my lingering aftershocks felt like the beginnings of another climax. "That...mmmm." I had no real words to describe how good everything felt.

Sure I could stand on my own, Aurelian lowered my leg and Aris moved from behind me. Both males were so aroused they had to have been in pain, enclosed in their pants. Reaching out, I unlaced Aris' pants, then Aurelian's. Catching on that I wanted them as naked as I was, they both helped me unclothe them until we were all naked. Softly, I encouraged them to sit on the bed and dropped to my knees between them. Their eyes widened, looking at me, then at each other. It would have been comical if I was not so turned on. It was interesting how different they were—Aris was just a huge male in general, very well proportioned. His pale skin was covered in scars—large ones from wounds that should have killed him, and smaller ones from training—his gorgeous blue eyes had that tempest look about them again in his arousal. Aurelian—also impressively built but leaner from his softer life, though bulking up from the training he had had in the Dusklands, bronze skin smooth and basically free from blemish. His sunlit eyes were molten, like the heat inside him had melted them. Running my hands over them both, I would be lying if I did not enjoy the way they both reacted. Though they looked so different, their reactions were the same—both groaned and dropped their heads back.

"Gods, Zorya…" Aris moaned as my fist moved over him. Aurelian made an agreeable noise as I also worked him. Leaning in, my tongue flicked over the head of Aris' dick. Before he could do more than groan, I moved away. He gave me an incredulous look when our eyes met, shaking his head at my grin.

Raising my eyes to watch Aurelian, I lowered my head and swirled my tongue around his tip. The look of pleasure on his face was so erotic, I wanted more of it. Sliding my lips over him, I heard both males take in a breath as I took him into my mouth. A hand that I was sure was Aurelian's, tangled in my hair briefly before letting go. It returned, this time with Aris' hand guiding him, giving him permission and letting him know that I liked it. With renewed confidence, his fingers twined in my hair at the back of my head as I moved my mouth over his cock. My other hand was still moving over Aris as well. His hand ran over my arm, stopping at my shoulder for a moment, before finally resting at the point my shoulder met my neck.

A shudder ran through Aurelian and his hips bucked, forcing his cock further into my throat. The hand on the back of my head and my neck—mainly the one on my neck—held me in place. Aris was naturally dominant—it made him an effective leader—and he had manhandled me in intimate situations many times, but he did not usually hold me in place like that. I did not mind, it was hot, but it was a little surprising when I was not able to move my head back. Aurelian's fingers tightened in my hair. A moan vibrated around my mouthful as I started to feel pleasure building within me again.

"Yeah…" It was the first time he had actually spoken more than simply a moan or groan. My eyes flicked up to see his eyes were closed. He was beautiful in the throes of passion—beautiful all the time, really. "Fuck, Zoryana…yeah." The curse made me suck harder, causing his hips to jerk again. Both hands at the back of my head tightened, making me gag slightly as Aurelian's cock hit the back of my throat. Neither male released their hold, like they were feeding off each other, which was what I had hoped would happen, when they were caught up in the moment. "Zor—I—fuck…I-I am close…" Aurelian was struggling to string words together, which I took as a good sign. When I did not try to pull away, his eyes opened and looked down at me, eyes wide, half in surprise, half in intense pleasure. He groaned again, deep and guttural. His hips bucked again, and his hot load coated my throat. Swallowing around him, I took everything he had to give.

"Gods…. That was… Damn, I did not think I would like to watch so much…." Aris let out a breathy chuckle that trailed off as he too succumbed to the pleasure my hand was giving him, his cum exploding over this belly.

I looked up at them both—living gods really—sitting on the bed, both looking down at me. I was hot again, but I knew they would need some recovery time before anything else happened. Both males looked incredibly sated. Aris reached down and pulled me up onto his lap, engaging me in a deep, fiery kiss, surprising me a little—he would be able to taste Aurelian on my tongue. He did not seem to mind. Aurelian shifted closer and pulled my legs over his. Gods! I moaned into the kiss as Aurelian's lips closed around my nipple, sucking on the hardening peak. As he sucked and nipped at my breasts, his hand was moving over my legs until it slipped between them, moving over my centre. I was wound up from sucking his dick, and I needed another release. My head tipped back, breaking the kiss with Aris as my pleasure skyrocketed again.

"Goddess…that…that feels so good," I moaned. My eyes found Aris' face. He was looking down at Aurelian's hand between my legs, his tempest eyes intrigued. That was interesting. *Very* interesting.

CHAPTER TWENTY-ONE
COMING TOGETHER

ARIS

LOOKING DOWN AT ZORYANA, SHE was radiant… even with another male's cock in her mouth. I did not have much experience with other females, except a few in my starling years and early Shadowborne days when I did not think I could have what I really wanted, but in my limited experience, the sight of Zorya going down on someone—usually me—was exceptionally erotic. I did not know what possessed me to do it, but when Aurelian's hips bucked, I tightened my hand on Zorya's shoulder, restricting her ability to lift her head off the other male. While I had no objection to moving her around to give us both the highest level of pleasure, I usually refrained from forcing anything. We had never had that kind of dynamic. The sight of her sucking Aurelian's dick, along with her fist pumping my own cock like she was born to do it, was doing something to me, bringing out some baser nature. She did not protest, I would have released her the moment that happened—in fact, she moaned around her mouthful. Fuck, she was gorgeous.

Kissing her with another male's cum on her tongue was an experience. I was unsure what it meant that I was not feeling territorial, or disgusted. It felt like it was supposed to be that way. I knew she had asked for this new arrangement, so she did not have to choose between us and break one of our hearts, but it was already more than that. Beside me, I felt Aurelian shift closer. Our sides were not quite touching, but we were close—even that I did not mind. What was happening to me? Same-sex relationships were not unheard of in the Dusklands, in fact they were quite common, but I had personally never found another male attractive. There was something about the Sun Prince though… Perhaps it was his uniqueness, or the way he loved Zoryana as I did. It did not really matter why.

Aurelian lifted Zoryana's legs up over his. She moaned slightly into the kiss. I had no idea what he was doing, but whatever he was doing, she liked it. The other male's hair brushed my chest. He must be kissing her chest. Zoryana let out a stronger moan, breaking the kiss for a moment. Looking down to see what had caused that, Aurelian did not just have his lips around her nipples, his hand was between her legs. I knew from experience that she got very wound up from giving pleasure—he had picked up on that very quickly, which solidified my thought that this was how it was supposed to be. Watching Aurelian giving Zoryana pleasure was weirdly arousing and I was surprised to feel my cock stirring again. I was going to need to be inside Zoryana before the end of the night. As soon as I was hard again, unless she was already being fucked by Aurelian, I was going to need her.

She was moaning and her hips began to buck against Aurelian's hand, brushing against my cock with each movement. Her arm snaked around my shoulders to steady herself and I tightened my arm around her back, allowing her something to lean against to help her movements. The scene was intensely arousing—I was definitely on the way to being hard again. My other hand palmed my own cock as I watched the other male bringing our Queen to another climax.

"Oh Goddess…yes…" Her words trailed off as she came. Aurelian's eyes, molten gold, met mine as she rode out her climax on his fingers. The look that passed between us was one of camaraderie—two males working together to serve our

Queen. His eyes flicked away, down to where I was moving my fist over my own cock. I was sure I did not miss the brief flicker of desire in his face, gone quickly and replaced with confusion before he focused back on Zoryana. Now, that was very interesting.

Zoryana came down from her high and one of her legs fell off Aurelian's, opening her up. Aurelian grinned, removing his fingers from her and bringing them to his lips, sucking her pleasure from them. Both Zoryana and I watched him, intrigued…and very much turned on. I was hard again. Zorya was looking pretty sated and leaned against me.

"Sorry, star…no sleeping yet," I murmured. She looked up at me in surprise, then looked down at my straining cock. With some assistance from Aurelian, I lifted her enough that she could split her legs around me, so she was straddling my legs. "Ready?" I asked her to make sure she was not sore or something. With her nod, I lifted her again and lowered her onto my cock.

AURELIAN

Being with Zoryana was more than I could have imagined. Being with her and Aris was opening up some curious and confusing feelings inside me. Seeing Aris stroking himself had made my own cock twitch. I had never found another man attractive, but Aris was different somehow. I did not think I wanted to do anything with him personally but seeing him naked and aroused was stimulating to say the least. Helping him lift and turn Zoryana so he could fuck her was different too—helping another man give a woman pleasure was not how I thought I would be spending my nights. He lowered her down onto him and her body arched as he filled her. It was one of the most languid and true moments I had seen from a woman in bed. She was so genuine and innately sensual on a level that I had not seen before—the women I usually had in my bed were purely there for a good time and to say they had slept with a Prince. Zoryana on the other hand, she took and gave pleasure like it was her lifeblood.

She started to roll her hips, grinding on Aris' cock, his hands gripping her hips. Both of them were already moaning, worked up. Her ability to stay turned on was legendary. I could not deny that everything was getting me hard again too. Aris moved his hand from her hip to fondle her breast, so my hand replaced it. Her ass was firm as my hand gave it a light squeeze.

"Fuck," Aris groaned and started to rock his hips as well. The angle that I was at gave me a view between their bodies, the vision of Zoryana being impaled again and again by Aris' dick…far out I was a goner. I could not help but wrap my hand around my own cock as well to get myself hard again—it was not going to take much and honestly, I was more than happy to get myself off at this point, not thinking that Zoryana would be able to take another…especially after the pounding she was getting from Aris.

Suddenly, Aris let out a loud moan, and he slammed Zoryana down onto his cock. She stilled as he climaxed. She moaned but it sounded more like she was experiencing second-hand pleasure, not another climax of her own. When his eyes reopened, Aris looked down at my lap, seeing that I was hard again. He looked up to catch my eye, his hand dropping from Zoryana's breast to her hip again. Clenching on her hips, he lifted her off him, making her grasp his shoulders at the sudden movement. A moment passed between them and she nodded. She allowed herself to be passed between us until she was sitting on my legs. Looking up at her face, I could not help but once again be struck by how beautiful she was. She smiled and leaned in to kiss me as she rose her hips, her hand between us, lining up my cock with her entrance. Our moans muffled in the kiss as she engulfed me for the first time. She felt better around me than I could have hoped. The kiss broke and we moved together, grinding and thrusting. I was conscious that she had just had Aris come inside her, her slickness partly her own arousal, but partly his cum. The thought, which probably should have turned me off, wound me up further. My hands tightened on her hips, helping her move on me harder and faster. Aris' hand—larger than mine I noticed—appeared on her butt. There was a sharp sound and Zoryana let out a sound that I could not identify—it sounded like a mix between a squeak and an intense moan. Her muscles clenched around my cock, fluttering. The sharp sound happened again, and Aris' hand brushed mine. He had slapped her ass. It turned her right up and soon her grinding became writhing. The difference in movement set me off. Our moans erupted together as our climaxes crashed at the same time. Having her muscles choking my cock while I was coming was the ultimate feeling.

All of us sated, Aris stretched out on the bed. He reached out to take Zoryana from me. She looked exhausted in the best way. She snuggled up to him, and I suddenly was not sure whether this arrangement included me sharing their bed for more than fucking. Zoryana turned her head and smiled at me, extending her arm to me. Aris nodded as well. We manoeuvred to all fit on the bed, Zoryana between us, her backside pressed against my front, my and Aris' arms around her. I did not know when it happened, but I fell asleep, feeling the best I had in my entire life.

ZORYANA

I woke up pressed between two males, deliciously naked and the memories of the night before fresh in my mind. When something so out of the ordinary and incredible happened, sometimes I convinced myself I had imagined it… The immediate confirmation had me smiling. I had fallen asleep with my back to Aurelian but somehow, I had woken facing him. He was still asleep, eyes closed—he looked even more beautiful somehow. Perhaps feeling my eyes on him, his fluttered open. The sleepy smile that graced his lips lit up his face.

"Good morning, Zoryana…" he murmured, voice full of sleep.

"Good morning, Aurelian," I replied, leaning in to kiss him.

From behind me, Aris' arm tightened around me. I chuckled as the kiss broke. "And good morning to you too."

"Morning," he said gruffly, raising himself slightly so he could lean over to kiss me.

I hoped no one regretted everything we had done…I certainly did not. I wanted to let the world burn around us and never leave the tent. I was very un-Queen-like and the magic inside me would never allow that but the way they had made me feel was something I had never experienced. I had caught a couple of moments where both males looked aroused by each other's anatomy too… I hoped one day they would love each other as well, but I was happy they were willing to work together for now. My body was pressed between them—they were both semi-hard, Aurelian against my front, and Aris against my backside. They both shifted slightly, and I could feel hands moving over my skin.

"No…you are not going to convince me to go again…the world is awake…do you want everyone to hear us?" I chuckled, trying to extract myself from the bed. How Aurelian and Aris became a unit so quickly, I was not sure. They both reached out to pull me back, but I was quicker and managed to scramble off the bed. I was so glad no one else saw my undignified way of leaving the bed. Straightening up and attempting to recover some of my dignity, I planted my feet in a defiant stance. The sight of them both still laying on the bed, lower halves regrettably hidden by the blanket, but chests on full display… it was distracting to say the least. The way they were looking at me like I was their morning meal reminded me I too was naked.

"I did not think I would be awakening fiends with this agreement." I laughed and looked around for my clothes.

Finally, all cleaned up and dressed, Aurelian in his clothes from the day before—thankfully identical to the other uniforms he had been wearing recently, we left the tent. The knowing looks from the Oath-bound having their morning meals or preparing for the day that met us made my skin flush.

I had not intended on keeping everything a complete secret but having my people look at me like that. I was not sure it was especially dignified. Though, it was nice that they felt I was part of them enough that they did not exclude me from that. No one actually said anything, which I was thankful for as they handed us bowls. Sitting between Aris and Aurelian felt more charged than usual, with casual brushes that made my skin light up. When Aurelian got up to change, he touched my shoulder as he passed me—it was such a small gesture, but it made my heart flutter. Aris leaned in to press a kiss to my temple and took my bowl to give to the people washing up. I watched his retreating form in surprise—he had touched my arm, or back in public before, but never kissed me, not even a kiss on the cheek. Feeling eyes on me, I looked around at the others sitting around. They all looked away quickly and continued on with what they had been doing before.

CHAPTER TWENTY-TWO
THE SILENCE NEVER LASTS

ZORYANA

WE HAD SPENT THE NEXT tide fighting off invaders into our lands. The Solnyrian army was getting bolder, and I was not sure how much longer we could hold them off as well as we had. As we tired, our ranks were starting to take major injuries and more losses. Each Oath-bound or citizen who was called by their ancestors tore at my heart. Every pyre we lit, every memory jar that was filled with a shadow, taken home by a family member who would cherish the memory of their fallen loved one, chipped away at my resolve, at my control. The Blight was continuing to spread in places I had not made a visit to yet—thankfully the magic I was pouring back into the land was holding it back in those places. But I had not been able to travel the entire Thornwood border, and it hurt me to know my land was hurting and I could not help fast enough.

The only solace I had were the nights I spent wrapped up between Aris and Aurelian—whether that was simply sleeping after an exhausting day or continuing to explore and enjoy our new relationship dynamic. The males were becoming closer night after night as well, caressing each other's bodies, and coming close to kisses, caught up in the moment—memorably as they loomed above me, as I had my lips around Aurelian's cock, and Aris filled me from behind. Having both males with me was helping to keep me grounded, though they regularly made me see stars, and I recovered from the magic drain quicker. I thanked the ancestors every day and night for bringing them into my life and allowing me to be with both of them. I would not have been able to choose, even if I was forced.

We heard about the advancing Solnyrian army a little before moonfall. An Oath-bound, young and newly blooded, burst into our tent, thankfully pretending he did not see the three of us in bed, or at least that he did not care. The frantic way in which he was speaking spurred us all into action and the poor young male had to pretend he was not seeing a lot of naked skin—of his commander, and his queen—as we scrambled to dress. Joining the rest of the camp, the information was given in a much more succinct way from one of the older Oath-bound. They would be at the border by morning, and the King was with them, though it looked like he was staying in the back, protected.

Everyone heard it then, the beating of drums. War drums. We were thankfully camped at the most northern part of the Dusklands, closest to Solnyr, and where the army was marching from. It meant we had more time to prepare as we did not have to travel to where they would attack. Oath-bound started to move around the camp, saying goodbye to loved ones who had come to stay with them and gathering weapons and supplies. Turning to Aris and Aurelian, I kissed them both, not caring that there were people that would see. I was no longer hiding. Hiding had not helped the Dusklands for the past one thousand years, hiding my relationship with Aris had not helped us to be happy for the past almost ten years. And hiding this new relationship with Aurelian was not going to help anyone—except the enemy. I needed my strength, we all did, and our teachings were so clear on what hiding emotion can do—stunting growth and diminishing magic…and we needed all we could muster right now.

"I want you both to know that I love you. I do not think this battle will go wrong for the three of us, or for the Dusklands as a whole, but I just…I wanted you both to know that." My voice cracked though I tried to keep it together. I honestly believed what I had said—the three of us would be fine, but it did feel significant.

Aurelian smiled. "I love you too, Zoryana," he replied, reaching up to stroke the side of my face softly. "And even you…I suppose." His tone took on a teasing edge as he looked up at Aris.

My Shadowsworn grinned and clapped Aurelian on the shoulder. "You too, Sun Prince." His whole face softened as he turned to me. "And I love you too, Zorya." Leaning in, he pressed a kiss to my forehead, then, surprising everyone, did the same to Aurelian. The little smile on the Sun Prince's face was adorable. We parted ways to prepare, collecting our own weapons and supplies. Meeting back at the horses, I swung up onto Vecheryn before either male was able to help me as they liked to do and rode up to the front of our host. Vecheryn turned to allow me to face them, Aurelian and Aris coming up behind me. I did not have a speech, I did not think I was one of those rulers that needed pretty words to whip my warriors into a frenzy—they were already ferocious and furious. This was not the time. Instead, I just clasped my hands over my heart and bowed my head. The ceremonial gesture of respect was repeated by everyone around.

As a unit, we rode and marched forward. We did not have banners or horns, or gleaming armour. The Dusklands did not need pageantry to defend our land. Being at the head of an army was risky for a ruler, I knew that—as did the Sun King, that kept him protected at the back—but I would not force my people into a battle I was not willing to lead them into myself. As the Solnyrian army closed in, the sun reflected off their armour, filling the air with light and very briefly blinding me. My damn eyes were not made for such brightness, worse since my coronation. Their channelers came forward, runes already alight.

"Channelers!" Aurelian called back to give the rest of our army time to prepare. It was enough, as the Oath-bound were able to raise shields and I was able to lift my hands just as the Sunfire raced towards us. Shadow exploded from my hands, engulfing most of the fire. Some sparks got through and thankfully hit shields instead of people. I was determined to only use my magic as defence—Aris had finally admitted what had happened to the Solnyrian soldiers I had killed after the Sundrop attack. That destruction of life weighed on me—they had killed my people, but no one deserved to die like that, choking and suffocating.

"Hold the line!" I called to Aurelian, sliding off Vecheryn, sending her off to safety. Aris did the same with Sumerak. Together, we moved ahead with his chosen first wave. I hung back, letting them go forward without worrying about defending me too, and knelt on the ground, hands planted in the ground. The blue ley lines that webbed the world lit up. Everywhere a Dusk warrior stood, it flared, and I hoped the magic was telling me the right thing—they should get a boost to support their magic as they became the silent lethal weapons they had trained to be.

Aris dropped back, his shoulder bleeding—it looked like he was lucky it was even still attached. I started to stand to go to him, but a short shake of his head stopped me. Aurelian and the wave that had agreed to follow him stepped forward to take Aris' place. Continuing to pour my magic in the ground, I watched Aurelian fight—he still did not move as rhythmically and quietly as the Oath-bound around him, but he had lost the clunkiness of his Solnyrian training. His sword glinted and I was sure I saw it light for a moment—it might have been a trick of the light, but I wondered if it could be possible that my magic may heighten any latent threads inside him. The ley line had flared very slightly under his feet. He was struggling a little against a Solnyrian soldier—his insignia made him a commander if I remembered correctly. They looked as if they were talking, it was possible they knew each other, but

Aurelian ultimately cut him down.

I did not know how long we fought for; I did not know how to tell the time using the sun. Wave after wave of soldiers came down on our unit. Being the more well-trained and deadly soldiers, the Oath-bound cut down more Solnyrians than we lost, but the sheer numbers the Solnyrians had on their side was overwhelming. I was exhausted, unsure of how much longer I could continue to feed the well and support my people magically. Finally, the horns of retreat sounded from the Solnyrians, and I was able to withdraw my magic. Falling back onto my butt on the ground, I sighed heavily. A nearby Oath-bound held out a hand, which I took and allowed them to pull me up to standing. They held onto me, making sure I could walk, as we also pulled back. Thanking them, I allowed myself to be passed to a Shadowhealer. There was not anything physically wrong with me, but they were able to do something that revived me enough that I could walk alone and they could move on to others that needed their expertise more.

Walking through the lines of the dead and injured, I made a point to lay a hand on each of the fallen as I passed them, wishing them a smooth journey to the realm of the ancestors. I reached the area the injured had been moved to so the Shadowhealers could work effectively. I moved through them, allowing them to touch me as I passed, allowing them to take whatever strength they needed from me. Reaching one male who looked particularly bad, I looked up at a nearby Shadowhealer. The small shake of her head told me everything I needed to know—he was not going to make it. He had been one of the ones that had agreed to serve under Aurelian, despite him being Solnyrian. Kneeling beside him, I took his hand and laid his hand, and my own over his heart. Leaning in, I whispered words in our ancient tongue that would help his passage beyond this realm. I stayed there until he breathed no more. Taking the memory jar from the Shadowhealer, I captured his shadow so it could be given to his family—his mate and their three young ones.

I helped to light pyres for the fallen and said the sacred

rites, my heart breaking with each name I condemned to the realm beyond. Everyone moved on to drink and celebrate the lives of the fallen. I stayed on the ridge, looking out over the fires. Two figures came to stand on either side of me, both putting an arm around me. Aurelian on one side, no longer a Prince of the Sun but a Dusklands warrior, and Aris, my Shadowsworn, his shoulder no longer bleeding I was happy to see. We stood together in silence, grieving for the lives lost that day, and the ones we will lose in battles to come.

AURELIAN

Entering our tent, I realised just how exhausted I was. Aris had been called aside by one of the warriors, so I was alone with Zoryana. She sat heavily at the table, her armour still bore the marks of the fight, the silver filigree blackened from her expulsion of power.

"The dark never promised to spare us. Only to remember us." I wondered sometimes whether she was the one speaking when she spoke so poetically. She had so many lives inside her—from what had been explained to me, she carried the magic and memories of all the Queens that had come before her, though she was the first to receive Seravine's shadows as well.

Sitting beside her, I reached out to lay a hand on her arm. "Do you ever grow tired of carrying so much memory?"

She smiled—a small, sharp curve of the mouth. "Every day. But I would rather remember than forget." There was nothing I could say to that. So I poured us each a cup of dusk-wine. We drank in silence. At some point she leaned back, eyes half-closed. I thought she was starting to fall asleep until she spoke. "What does Solnyr teach its princes about mercy?"

Her question made me pause. After a moment, I replied, "In Solnyr, mercy is considered a weakness; that forgiveness is something you earn by surviving."

She looked at me then—really looked—and said, "Then

maybe that is why you left." I did not know if it was kindness or accusation. Maybe both. She fell asleep soon after, right there at the table, her head on her arm. I covered her with my cloak and left the lamp burning low.

Outside, Aris was waiting. He did not ask questions, just nodded once and walked with me until we reached the outer fire.

He said, quietly, "She will keep fighting until she breaks. We need to make sure she does not."

"I will try," I promised.

He looked sad. "I fear trying will not be enough."

He was right, of course. Nothing ever was enough. But tonight, for the first time, I thought the dark felt almost gentle. And for now, that was all the mercy we were allowed. We drank with the others until the fire started to die down, and everyone parted. As a second tent had not been erected for me at this camp, I followed Aris into the tent we all shared. Zoryana was still asleep at the table. It felt a little odd to get into bed with Aris without Zoryana between us. Neither of us spoke and just let our exhausted bodies relax. Zoryana joined us not long after, stirring me briefly as she crawled onto the bed between us, pressing a kiss to my cheek before she too settled.

AURELIAN'S LEDGER
THE BATTLE AT THE THORNED VALE

The Thorned Vale, Western Front

Day Ten of Threvos (Thren in the Dusklands), Year 1003 After the Breaking

The first battle changes you. The next one just reminds you what you have already lost.

At dawn, the sky looked like polished iron. The light never truly came. Even the birds were silent. We rode out before the mists lifted, our armour dulled with ash, no banners or ceremony.

Zoryana rode at the head—black hair unbound, silver eyes bright against the storm-dark sky. Her presence steadied the line. No shouting, no theatrics; only quiet command and respect for the people who followed her. The Oath-bound followed her as though she were gravity itself.

I rode at her flank, Aris on the other. Three figures in the midst of an army that should not have had the courage to stand against Solnyr's legions—but did.

When the enemy came over the ridge, the world filled with light. Channelers threw everything they had at us. They had turned the sun into a weapon. The air itself burned. Zoryana raised her hand, and the shadows rose with it—great veils of night, catching and folding the fire until it hissed and split. I saw it then, clearly: her power is not destruction. It was defiance made manifest.

She turned to me once, mid-chaos, and told me to hold the line. And gods help me, I did. The Oath-bound fought like echoes of her will. Aris moved ahead of us, a blur of dusksteel and fury, cutting down the zealots who had broken through. When he fell back, bleeding from the shoulder, I took his place.

The Solnyrian commander called me traitor. I told him he was right. Then I showed him what the light had taught me—and what the dark had perfected.

The battle lasted hours. When it ended, the Vale was nothing but smoke and the scent of rain on blood. We had driven them back, but at a cost too high to count. The Dusklands had held. Barely.

Zoryana walked the field after, silent, touching the fallen one by one. When she reached a dying soldier who had fought under my command, she knelt beside him, whispered something in the old tongue, and pressed her hand to his chest until his breathing eased. Not a queen. Not a deity. Just a woman giving mercy in a world that has forgotten what that means.

Later, as the fires burned low, she stood beside me and Aris on the ridge overlooking the valley. None of us spoke. There was no need to.

For the first time, I understood the strange peace that lives inside her fury. Victory does not feel like triumph. It feels like survival. And survival, in this world, is sacred enough.

- Aurelian

CHAPTER TWENTY-THREE
THE SUMMONS

AURELIAN

PEACE, IT SEEMED, WAS ONLY the pause between storms. After only a couple of days back at Nightfell Castle, Solnyrian couriers reached us at midday—two half-broken horses and a scroll sealed in the wax of Solnyr. The riders would not cross the gates. They left the message in the dust and fled before the guards could ask their names. When it was brought to her, Zoryana took the scroll, her fingers steady as she broke the golden seal. Only her eyes betrayed her—that flicker of cold rage, gone in an instant as she read the scroll in silence.

"It seems the sun has declared war on the night." She held up the scroll to read it aloud for all around her to hear. "By decree of the Throne of Light, the lands of Dusk are declared heretical, their ruler apostate. A crusade shall cleanse the stain and restore the balance of the world. It shall be called The Dawn Reclaiming."

Aurastes' words were brief, sanctified, and venomous, nothing I would not have expected from my brother. There was no irony left in him. Having read the decree, Zoryana took deep breaths to calm herself. They only worked halfway, as she suddenly tore the scroll in half and dropped it into the brazier. The wax hissed; the parchment curled. It smelled of incense and blood.

"Zorya, what should we do about this?" Aris asked. There would be plans to be made, but as always, deference was given to her as the Queen, and the one loved and adored by everyone around her.

Her answer was the same as it always was. "Endure."

The council convened that evening. Every lord, every commander, every Oath-bound captain within riding distance crowded into the main hall of the castle. I sat at Zoryana's right hand, the mark of my oath faintly visible beneath the sleeve of my tunic, while Aris took his place at the table as the lead commander of the Oath-bound. Some of them still looked at me with mistrust, others with calculation. I did not blame them; they saw my face, so different to theirs, and thought of the enemy.

Zoryana let them argue until the room ran out of air. Then she spoke. Quietly. So quietly that everyone had to stop to hear her. "We will not fight for vengeance," she said. "We fight because this is our home, and because no light that demands blindness deserves to rule the sky."

There was no applause as there would have been in my brother's court. Only the sound of a hundred people exhaling at once—the sound of conviction taking root. Conversations became more focused after that; plans and strategies were laid out and debated over their efficacy. I offered to give over all the knowledge I had about Solnyr's legions, their routes, their supply lines. The commanders looked at me with renewed respect, my offer hopefully finally giving them the proof that I did not mean the Dusklands any harm.

Afterwards, when the hall emptied, she moved to the window overlooking the valley. The storm had passed, and the night was clear, the stars sharp as glass.

"Zoryana…do you believe we can win this?" I asked her.

I did not doubt the Dusklands could hold their own but the numbers the Solnyrians had on their side were an asset.

"Winning is not the point," she replied without looking up. "Surviving with meaning and truth is."

The war we had all tried to prevent was now a certainty. But for the first time, I did not feel helpless. I felt ready.

Let the sun march. We would meet it in the dark.

The Dusklands prepared for war unlike any nation I had ever seen. Solnyr drilled in open fields beneath hymns and banners. The Dusklands moved in silence. No proclamations, no spectacle—just the sound of steel being honed in shadow. Every day, the Oath-bound gathered in the lower hall, and every day, I learned something new about what "oath" truly means here. It was not rank or contract; it was integration.

Each Oath-bound carried a fragment of another's vow—blood-mixed, spell-bound, memory-anchored. When one falls, the others remember what they saw and felt in their final breath. It was horrifying. It was beautiful. It meant that no death in the Dusklands was ever alone.

Zoryana said it was all part of the Weave, reminding me of the time she had told me about it after she had dangerously depleted herself. It was how the Dusklands survived the centuries Solnyr tried to erase them: a network of memory stronger than any archive. Every shadow remembers the one before it.

I began working with her archivists and tacticians. The maps in the Dusklands were not drawn with borders—they were drawn with threads. Lines of magic, ley crossings, forgotten bloodlines, sleeping wards. The Dusklands were not defending territory; they were defending an entire living system. It humbled me and terrified me.

Solnyr had no idea what they were walking into. Light burned bright, but it burned straight. The dark bended, adapted, endured. Aris oversaw the Oath-bound's deployments. We began a series of manoeuvres along the western ridge—guerrilla tactics meant to bleed the crusade before it reached open ground. He was efficient, severe, but there was a kind of weary pride in the way he watched his soldiers.

Though we had become much closer in a personal setting, I asked if he still doubted me on the field of battle. He said, "Doubt makes us better. Trust makes us careless. But I am starting to think you might manage both." High praise from him.

Zoryana, meanwhile, was drawing too deeply again. The Blight ate at her still, and I could see the strain when she thought no one's looking, everyone could. Her fingers shook when she signed the decrees and her eyes were losing their brightness again.

I tried to tell her. She said, "I have no luxury of rest. Rest is what the dead take." She smiled after she said it. That smile will haunt me.

I spent my days between maps and reports, trying to predict my brother's next move. But a part of me wondered if that is what he had always feared—not corruption, but comprehension. That I would see the dark not as an enemy, but as a mirror. Every day, I lost a little more of the man I was in Solnyr. Every day, I found I did not miss him.

"We need to take her mind off it, even just for a little while," I said to Aris desperately. The grim nod he gave me increased my worry. Sitting in Zoryana's room, waiting for her to return from her meeting with the Memory Circle—the incredibly important group of spiritual leaders who kept records and memories from every branch of the Dusklands society, so I had been told—was making both Aris and I restless. I had started pacing, Aris watching me, tense and stressed. He was accustomed to going everywhere with Zoryana as her protection; however, the Memory Circle had insisted that she came alone and that she would be safe. I started to list off ways to distract Zoryana from everything; nothing really would make a difference, and I was really just talking to fill the time.

"Would you please stop pacing?" Aris grumbled from the bed. "And stop talking?" I barely heard him, so I did neither. Suddenly, Aris was in front of me, like a wall stopping the progression of my pacing. "Stop!" Any response I might have had was lost as he gripped the front of my tunic, capturing my lips in a rough kiss. It was the first time we had kissed. The kiss was full of frustration, tension, and a little bit of anxiety. Like my first kiss with Zoryana, this was not tender. We pulled apart, panting, looking at each other in shock, hot desire in our gazes.

"I am sensing a theme in the way you Dusklanders show affection for the first time," I said, trying to make light of what had just happened. Aris looked at me like I had gone mad. "You and Zoryana both like to start with those rage-filled kisses, I have noticed." Aris still looked confused. "My first kiss with Zoryana was anything but tender, and this one was the same."

"This is not the same. I was trying to make you shut up." He was adorable when he was grumpy. I was tempted to tell him just that.

The door opened before I could and we both looked in that direction, finding Zoryana standing there looking at us, a little confused.

"Did I interrupt something?" she said, a little chuckle following her words. Hurriedly, she closed the door and leaned against it. "Do continue." That broke the moment and Aris and I laughed.

"He has been pacing and talking the entire time you were away. I had to stop him," Aris said, stalking over to Zoryana and caging her against the door.

"And how did you do that?" Her question sounded innocent, but the look on her face was anything but.

"He got in my face," I answered. Her gaze turned to me as I moved in as well.

"Oh... Got in your face?" She looked up at Aris. "With your face?"

"Mmmm...perhaps." Aris ducked his head to kiss her neck—an obvious attempt to distract her.

"Oh yeah? You...you want to re-enact the situation for me? I might be able to give you more ideas on how to handle it..." Her voice was becoming breathy as Aris' lips moved over her throat.

She looked relaxed and happy. Whatever the Memory Circle had done had rejuvenated her somewhat...not just her magic and health...but apparently her desire as well. I took her hand as she reached out to me and moved in. She pulled me in, making me press my body to Aris', not hers, then engaged me in a kiss. We were leaning over Aris' bulk of a body so both of us ended up with an arm around the other man. Aris dropped a hand to Zoryana's hip, brushing against my front, causing a twitch. It was an accident, of course, but it felt a little like a continuation of earlier. He shifted, making the kiss break, and glanced at me with a short jerk of his head upwards. I was not sure what he meant but I moved out of his way. Zoryana let out a squeal as Aris hefted her over his shoulder. The look she gave me over his shoulder was comical; she was a mix of angry, frightened, and very aroused. I just shrugged. There was nothing I could do to stop him. He dumped her rather unceremoniously onto the bed, making her bounce slightly. I thought he would immediately join her, but he turned, wrapping a hand around my wrist, pulling me closer until I too fell onto the bed, lying beside Zoryana. We turned our heads to look at each other, both confused as to where this was going.

He was looking down at us like he was torn, trying to decide what to do or who to do it to. I did not know what had changed—maybe it was the impending battle that could be the end. Neither Zoryana nor I moved. Ultimately, he decided to focus on Zoryana—which was fine with me. He reached for her hips, pulling her closer, pushing her dress up to her hips before delving between her legs. She let out the most sensual sound and her eyes closed as she enjoyed what Aris was doing to her, hidden under the skirt of her dress. Leaning over, I loosened the front of Zoryana's dress, sliding a hand in to caress her breasts. I tried to shift to be able to bring my mouth to them as well. As I started to move, Aris' hand shot up, landing on the top of my thigh, stopping me. His hand was so close to my cock, already straining in my pants, I wondered what he would have done if he had landed any closer. My answer came quickly as his hand moved, tentatively moving over my bulge until his entire hand was over me. I had frozen so as not to spook him, the other man had not lifted his head from pleasuring Zoryana, but it was clear he knew what he was doing. My stillness made Zoryana look up, her eyes already clouding over from pleasure. She noticed what was happening. The sight seemed to turn her up even more. Her moans increased, moving her hand to her own exposed breast to take over where I had frozen. The pressure Aris used as he palmed me through my pants was almost perfect; I suppose he would know what he liked and figured that it would be the same for me—apparently correct. I moaned softly and my hips rolled a little against his hand. The additional pressure had me painfully hard.

My attention was drawn away from Aris' hand by the earth-shattering moan that Zoryana let out, both hands going down to clasp on the back of Aris' head. A muffled groan came from between her legs, making her hips buck again. Her orgasm, and the way it was affecting Aris, made his hand clench on my dick.

"Fuck…" I groaned, almost on the verge of coming in my pants. I had thought he might stop when Zoryana released him—I was pleasantly surprised when he did not. Hand still on my crotch, he stood. We locked eyes and I was struck—he was a handsome man, I had never said any different, but obviously aroused, his face slick with Zoryana's pleasure, his hand on my crotch, and how bold he was being…he had taken on a different level of attractiveness. Zoryana sat up on the bed beside me, looking thoroughly intrigued. Aris started to unlace my pants, pulling out my cock. His hands were rough with calluses from handling weapons most of his life as he wrapped his hand around my length. I moaned deep in my chest as his fist moved over me. Beside me, Zoryana was palming and squeezing her own breasts, enjoying the view. I did not know what to with myself. Looking up at Zoryana, I smiled.

"Dress off…" I commanded. Shuffling off the bed, she let the dress fall and stepped out of it. "Sit…here…" I pointed to my own face. Her eyes widened in surprise—as did Aris'. Was this not something they had done before? I was starting to unravel—I decided I wanted her on my face when I came. She climbed back onto the bed and looked confused as to what she should do. Generally, I'd like her to be facing my head, but I was conscious that there was nothing for her to hold onto as I was laying across the bed there was no wall for her to face. Reaching up, I guided her to straddle my face, with her front towards Aris. She seemed hesitant, so I gripped her hips and made her sit properly. My tongue swiped over her centre, making her jump a little. "When I said sit, I meant it… Sit…" I said, perhaps a little stronger than I would usually speak to her. Taking the guidance, she sat like I wanted her to. I moved my tongue again, thankful that she stayed. My own hips were starting to buck under Aris' hand as I licked and sucked at Zoryana's centre. She leaned forward and her hands appeared on my chest. The feeling of the material of my tunic between her hands and my chest reminded me I was still basically fully dressed, as was Ari—Zoryana was the only one that was naked. Zoryana let out a moan that sounded intrigued. I could not see anything with her on my face—which suited me—but I was curious. My curiosity did not have to wait long to be sated…Aris' tongue flicked over the head of my cock. Searing pleasure shot through me. Moaning against Zoryana's core, my hips jerked as Aris got bolder with his tongue. I did not last long and was not able to warn him. I presumed he moved as my climax exploded, though his hand stayed on me, pumping every last drop. My attentions to Zoryana increased until she flooded my face with her own climax. She collapsed forward, caught by both me and Aris as we guided her to the bed safely.

Looking down at myself, I had exploded all over my tunic and Aris' hand. He looked confused as to what he was supposed to do. Zoryana reached up to take his hand then proceeded to lick my seed off his skin. That woman was enthusiastic, and I loved her for it. Aris' cock was so hard in his pants that there was no way it could be comfortable. I moved off the bed to remove my clothes. I looked at Aris and slowly reached out to start unlacing his pants while Zoryana removed his tunic. I did not want him to be uncomfortable—even though he had been the one to instigate everything, none of us knew what our limits were in this situation. He looked relieved when his cock was freed, standing at attention. He had given both Zoryana and me incredible climaxes. It was his turn. Keeping eye contact to make sure he was fine; I ran my hand over his length. Before all of this, I had thought seeing another man's cock would disgust me…or make me feel insignificant… especially a man as generally huge as Aris. While he was bigger than me—well-proportioned to the rest of his body—I did not feel lesser because of it. He moaned and licked his lips as I gripped him, tugging slightly. Zoryana's smaller hand slid by mine, rolling his balls.

"Do you like that?" she asked him, running her other hand over his chest, racing scars that covered his skin.

"Mmmmhm…yeah…" he replied, voice thick with pleasure. His eyes were closed, and he was starting to thrust his hips a little. Zoryana motioned down to the ground and went down to her knees. Following her, I was curious what she had in mind. She leaned in and added her mouth to my movements on Aris' dick. Then she waggled her fingers at me.

"Kiss me," she whispered, pointing to her lips and Aris' cock. Finally understanding, I too leaned in and we locked lips, Aris' cock resting against our faces for a moment. We parted enough and moved our heads so that his cock could slip between us, two sets of lips and two tongues on him together.

"Gods…" Aris groaned above us. His hands appeared on our heads as we licked and sucked him, determined to get him off together. It did not take long—the culmination of the pleasure he had given, and the different feeling of what we were doing. "I'm coming…" he groaned seconds before his load shot over us. Zoryana took the initiative and slid her mouth over him, catching his climax. Sitting back on my heels, watching Zoryana sucking his orgasm from him was an image I never wanted to forget.

Lying in bed, Zoryana's soft breath on my chest as she slept—peaceful and looking like all her worries were gone—I smiled as Aris' arm slid over her in his own sleep, hand not stopping until it was resting on my stomach as well. War had a way of changing priorities, making things feel more urgent. I did not care if it was only the war and fear that brought us all together the way we had. I was not ashamed to say I loved them both. The Prince of the Sun was in love with the High Queen of the Dusklands and her Shadow. The world was changing, and I just hoped we all lived to see how it emerged at the end.

CHAPTER TWENTY-FOUR
THE DAWN RECLAIMING

ZORYANA

THE HORIZON LOOKED AS THOUGH it was again on fire. Only a tide after receiving the decree from King Aurastes, our scouts returned, a grave update. The Dawn Crusade was marching towards us in full array—banners of white-gold and crimson, the sigils of the Seven Suns blazing even through the mist. The priests and channelers led at the front, torches bound to their staffs, their voices carrying hymns that made my skin crawl. Standing at the edge of the Thornwood, as far as anyone would allow me without putting myself in unnecessary danger, I could not help but feel like I was looking at my demise, and that of my people and culture.

"Aurastes came himself. He always does when he wants to make a story of a slaughter." Aurelian's voice from behind me made me jump a little. He moved up behind me and wrapped his arms around my middle. "See the lines around the camps? They are wards… But they do not just keep things out, they are designed to keep the men inside as well so they cannot run."

Everything was so symmetrical and ordered. It made me uneasy. They seemed to have forgotten the world was never meant to be even. The world was messy and that was what made it so beautiful, the uniqueness. Their stark, geometric camps were not what nature intended. It made me sad that Solnyr had forgotten that so completely.

"Zorya, Aurelian… Everyone is in the central tent," Aris advised. Both of us turned and parted, walking towards him. Smiling sadly, I reached up to kiss my Shadowsworn as I passed him on the way back into the camp.

The air in the tent felt like the moment before lightning. Everyone holding their breath, the tension electric. Maps were laid out on the table, and my advisers and commanders were standing around it. Aris laid out our positions: the Oathbound in the forest lines, the archers on the cliffs, the Weavers ready to collapse the passes if the enemy managed to push through. Aurelian added what intelligence he could—Solnyr's supply routes, their reliance on sun-crystal for ward-fire. Cut that, and their sanctity dies. He did not know if there had been anything new in the months he had been in the Dusklands, of course, but he could help in a way no one else could—he knew what it was like to think like a Solnyrian.

When we finished, I dismissed everyone to finish their preparations and spend time with loved ones. I had allowed families while we were preparing; I had the people I loved with me, it did not seem fair to not allow my people that right too. However, I wanted to make sure those who would not be fighting were safe so their time together was limited. Aurelian and Aris stayed back with me. I braced my hands on the tabletop, looking down at one of the maps, studying the ley lines marked on it.

"At moonfall," I said, "they will try to blind us."

"Then we fight with our eyes closed," Aurelian replied. I could not help the smile that slid over my lips, though it was sad more than amused.

"You sound like one of us now." The words made him smile too. He leaned in and pressed a kiss to my temple.

The three of us stood there together for a long time. We had no other people to spend time with, no family except each other. We slowly packed away the maps and made sure that everything we would need was in easy reach. Leaving the tent, I took in a deep breath. The air smelled clean but crackled with energy. I was not sure anyone else could feel it. The Weave hummed through the air—the faint pulse of a thousand lives linked by oath and pain. When I breathed in, I could feel their heartbeats alongside mine.

The Dusklands will not fall quietly. We will face the dawn and will not bow.

ARIS

The battle began at moonfall as we predicted. The armies of the sun came at us in perfect order—the Seven Suns blazing from their standards, their hymns like a single, blinding note that made me uncomfortable. I knew I was not the only one. I tried to make Zoryana move back but getting that blasted female to do anything that kept her safe above other lives was impossible. I loved her with every fibre of my being, but she frustrated me to no end.

The light struck first, not steel. Every Solnyrian channeler shouted their spells, calling down fire until the sky itself turned white. The air burned; the earth screamed. Our own forces were forced to step back; our bodies were not made for that kind of intense light. I felt blind; my eyes struggled to adjust to the brightness around me.

The Dusklands answered the attack with silent shadow—moving forward as best as we could around our impediment. The ones who had the ability tried to dim the light with magic not designed for combat. They made the wind whip up as if they were trying to blow the light away.

The first hour of the battle was nothing but glare. Shapes, movement, screams—all flattened beneath the radiance. It was almost impossible to tell friend from foe—apart from the general size difference between us and them. It was like fighting inside a sun. We were used to being the ones that could see when others could not but, in this battle, we were at a disadvantage. The plan had never been to bring the Solnyrians into our lands, but it was becoming more and more tempting in an attempt to quell the light.

I could not see Zoryana. I reached out and she was no longer beside me. Our people's attempts at pushing the sun away were beginning to work and vision was starting to come back. I blinked rapidly to bring my eyesight back as quickly as possible. The black blades of my swords were dripping red from the Solnyrians I had managed to cut down in the glare. Looked around, thankful that none of my own warriors were not laying at my feet. I had avoided as many larger shadows as I could manage but the crush had been close. My own blood was seeping from nicks and slashes on the exposed parts of my arms between my armour. I still could not see Zoryana.

Finally, I found her off to the side with Aurelian. I met the other male's eyes and we nodded at each other. We would keep her safe, no matter what, even if is cost one, or both of us. Making my way through the melee, moving with the silent efficiency I had had instilled in me since I had been brought into the Oath-bound fold. Finding Zoryana again, shadows were starting to emerge from her hands, lengthening and solidifying into the veshkar she had manifested at her coronation. It was the first time she had done that in public since then, too afraid she would not be able to control them. The Solnyrian soldiers, Aurelian, and even some Dusklanders around her looked terrified. With the training she too had achieved, she joined the fighting. Aurelian leapt after her, a second bodyguard—I had to admit I did like that there was someone else so devoted to her. It was every Dusklander's obligation, and desire, to keep her safe, but Aurelian and I had more than just the fact she was the Queen as our motives. She was the female we loved and that meant more than the world.

I watched in horror as Zoryana swung her shadow veshkar at an oncoming soldier. The male lifted his shield. Her weapon hit the metal…and shattered. How shadow shattered like that, I would never know. She was thrown backwards, head hitting the ground heavily. She did not move. In a moment of grief, I let out what could only be described as a roar, the exact opposite to my Oath-bound training of fighting in silence. Racing towards her, cutting down everyone in my path, I saw that Aurelian made it to her first. He would look after her while I found the male whose shield had caused so much damage. I did not know what I looked like, but I was easily head and shoulders taller than him, and twice as wide. I could probably tear him apart with my hands. While that was tempting, in my anger, I swung my obsidian blade—gifted to me by the female this doomed soldier had injured. He did not have a chance to raise his shield this time. My sword swiped across his neck, making red pour down his front. Choking, he dropped.

"Grab the shield," I ordered a nearby Oath-bound and ran to Zoryana. She was alive. Aurelian had pulled her behind a tree, her head in his lap. His hands were stained black from her blood—it looked like a lot, and it was coming from her head.

"She is okay. The bleeding is slowing. I promise," Aurelian assured me. He reached up to clasp my face, leaving handprints of black blood on my cheeks. "She will be okay."

I nodded sharply. Leaning in, I kissed Zoryana, then reached up to do the same to Aurelian. "Keep her safe." Then I rejoined the fray. It felt as though the waves of Solnyrian soldiers we never ending. We kept them mostly out of the Thornwood, but we were starting to be pushed back. The channelers were starting to chant again, their rune stones glowing. I did not think we could last another attack of light.

When Zoryana rose, moving towards the front, I felt her magic before I saw her—the ground beneath my feet shuddered, roots coiling, stones groaning. Aurelian was calling after her to stop but she would not. She looked possessed—I wondered whether she was at that moment. The way she had spoken about the magic before, I had no doubt it could take her over if it wanted and that terrified me. When the channelers let loose their light, it raced towards her. She did not even brace or flinch, just stood firm. When it hit her, it fractured—broke apart into a thousand shards that turned the battlefield into twilight, despite the sun high in the sky. She did not shout commands. She simply lifted her hands, and the shadows moved as one to defend her, defend the land, and her people.

I gestured to my surrounding warriors, and we ran from the tree line, coming around the side of the closest Solnyrian force. They had all paused, horror filling their faces at the display of power from Zoryana—looking every inch the Witch Queen they had feared she was. Behind us, Aurelian and his small band followed us into the fray. I was proud of the prince and how far he had come since he arrived in the Dusklands for the first time only a few months ago. He now moved more like an Oath-bound than a Solnyrian, and he was commanding respect from some of the most sceptical warriors.

Like a silent blade, we cut through the golden troops, not stopping to watch them fall, knowing that if we did not kill one, someone following would finish them off. We did not leave wounded—my unit had been trained to leave none alive. Hosts this large did not collect their dying from the field to nurse them; these men would die out there anyway, the least we could do is make that death short.

By midday, the Vale was full of smoke from Solnyrian fires, and the stench of death. The Solnyrian songs faltered. I was grateful to see there were many more golden breastplates on the ground than black ones. Everyone turned as Aurelian's name was called out from the Solnyrian side. His brother, Aurastes, stood in the heart of his army, gilded armour blazing, the sigil of Solnyr carved across his breastplate. He looked untouchable. Divine. Exactly how he wanted to be perceived, from what I had been told. He was clean from the mess of battle, showing that he had pushed his people out for slaughter to save his own hide. In infinite contrast, Zoryana moved through the Oath-bound that surrounded her, covered in blood—both the enemies' and her own—and the grime of battle.

For a heartbeat, I thought the sight of his brother would undo Aurelian. The way his name had sounded coming from the King was not one of calling out to his brother—he was condemning. Aurelian was a heretic, and he wanted everyone around to know. To not trust the Traitor Prince. Aurelian walked forward, meeting his brother in the middle. I followed to protect him in case it was needed…and because Zoryana was also making her way towards him.

"You were meant to bring her to heel, not kneel before her." The look on the King's face could only be described as sneer. Underlying hatred and possibly jealousy of his brother, now made clear and visible.

Aurelian flinched. I could not tell if it was residual guilt at betraying his brother or thought of bringing a force such as Zoryana to heel. "Brother, you taught me to follow the truth. I just learned it was not you."

That answer was not what the Sun King had wanted to hear. Some Solnyrian soldiers shifted their weight. I wondered how many of them had interacted with Aurelian before he defected, had some sort of relationship with him, or at least had had a conversation. How many we could turn to the side of truth with some of his pretty and convincing words.

Aurastes struck so suddenly no one saw it coming. His sword looked like a flame as it came down towards Aurelian's neck. It was actually alight. I did not have time to ponder how he managed that as the Prince rose his own sword—an obsidian blade Zoryana had given him—just in time to block the attack. Light and darkness clashed. The impact drove Aurelian to his knees. Starting to raise my own blade to ensure that was not the end of the Prince, I stopped as the fire along the King's blade twisted and bent as Zoryana's magic caught it. The light that should have cut through Aurelian instead curled upward, turning to glass and ash.

Aurastes faltered—just for a moment—his eyes wild in fear. That was all it was—he, and the kings that had come before him, all the way back to Caelen, had been afraid of the Dusk Queens and their power. That moment was enough—all I needed. My veshkar found its mark. Aurastes fell without a sound. Just a male, not a god. Just a male with a blade in his chest—a blade that even his armour could not stop.

When it was over, Zoryana stood over the body, silent. No triumph, no joy—only a weary grief too old and deep for tears. "So ends the dawn," she murmured, her voice quiet, though it was heard all around. Everyone was silent. "Let them take their king…let them give him the funeral rites befitting his station. We are not monsters." Her order echoed over the field as she turned her back on the Solnyrian army, showing them, she no longer feared an attack. She no longer considered them a threat.

The field stank of blood, sweat, and grime. The sun broke through the clouds just once before setting, and the light that touched us felt…warm and clean. Not holy. Just light.

Aurelian was still kneeling, looking at his brother's body as his people began to gather him up. Making sure Zoryana was safe as she walked back to the Thornwood—the first time she had stepped beyond the border in her life and it was to kill a king—I moved up beside Aurelian, running a hand over his head lightly. He leaned against my leg, taking comfort. We stayed like that until he was ready to stand. I did not want to rush him—the Dusklands 'faith' was based around grief and memory, Aurelian was grieving his brother. No matter how mad and dangerous the King had been, they had had been kin.

"He looked so…so normal. I thought… He just…died…like everyone else…" he murmured sadly at one point. I continued to stroke his hair to comfort him. I did not know what to say—I had been the one that threw the blade that had ended his brother's life.

By the time we headed back to camp, the sky beyond the border was dark, no sun left in the sky. Following the fires, we found Zoryana in our tent, sitting on the edge of the bed. She was staring down at her hands as shadows looped and swirled through her fingers. There was a sense of control that had not been there before. I was glad to see it, and perhaps a little apprehensive about what it all meant for the future. Finally looking up, a relief took over her body. Jumping up, she flung herself at us, arms locking us together. Out of the corner of my eye, I noticed Aurelian tuck his head into her neck. His body shook a little and I knew he was crying. He'd held it off longer than I would have been able to. Zoryana and I tightened our arms, bringing our group in closer to give Aurelian all the comfort he needed to deal with the grief.

CHAPTER TWENTY-FIVE
THE DAY THE SUN FELL

ZORYANA

WHILE I DID NOT THINK everything was over, the magic inside me was starting to settle. It still called for me to help rebuild and heal the land and my people, but it was not overwhelming. I felt calmer, not quite at peace, but the previously uncontrollable fire in my body was not raging. I was able to think clearer, love slower and deeper. My relationship with Aris and Aurelian was growing and I was convinced I would not be able to part with either of them for any reason.

As we rebuilt the villages, constructing new homes, and planting new crops, I could breathe freely. Being around my people, alive and well—though we had lost so many—reminded me of the point of everything. The communities, families—the multi-faceted connections that we had all made with each other. *Love.* Love was the most important point. The love I had towards my people was repaid to me—though I never asked for it. I was grateful, every day they put their trust in me so completely.

The day after the King fell, the Dusklands welcomed our first band of Solnyrian refugees. Families escaping the unknown…into another unknown. I met them at the border myself and I was so happy that my people welcomed them as enthusiastically as I did. We were not monsters; we never had been. We were a land that valued love and connection, and we would welcome anyone genuine into the fold. More refugees arrived over the days since and homes were found for them. They integrated well and immediately picked up on life with their new community. Their resilience, and that of my own people, was inspiring.

Between the rebuilding efforts, I spent time with my advisers and the Memory Circle, attempting to formulate a plan to visit the other kingdoms. I wanted to make sure my people were settled before I thought about leaving them, but everyone agreed that it was best to go out into the world while it was still dealing with the shock of the loss of Aurastes. We also needed to make sure someone worse did not fill the void left by the Sun King. Serian had pointed out that it was possible that, depending on the laws around succession, Aurelian may be the current King of Solnyr. I was sure he would hate to think of that.

Just as much as I hated the way people looked at me when I passed them. Like I was some sort of deity that walked among them. I was no goddess. I did not want to raise to those dangerous heights—they were corrupting and I wanted nothing to do with it. I could not stop them, however, as they bowed lower than they had before, whispered my name in a reverent way, or sang songs about me. I was uncomfortable with it all, but I tried not to let it show—I did not want to offend.

With a plan finally made, and most of the rebuilding efforts completed, I could no longer continue to delay my *royal tour*, the way my advisers said it made me cringe. It sounded so formal and stuffy. I was travelling to the other kingdoms to hopefully broker peace and change the beliefs Solnyr had no doubt sown over the centuries. I was leaving the Dusklands for the first time in my life. I was terrified about what I would find outside the relative safety of the Thornwood, in the sterile light of day.

ARIS

Even having seen the King dead, having been the one to do it, I continued to have a nagging feeling that this was not over. It irritated me to no end—with everything we had to do to provide the people with homes and a revived sense of safety, despite the fact the protective border we come to rely on was literally crumbling, I needed my cynicism to calm down.

Busying myself coordinating the rebuilding efforts, I was happy to have something to do so I did not have time to dwell on everything. I knew Aurelian did not blame me for killing his brother, knowing it was something that had had to be done; I still felt guilty. It was his brother, no matter how much of a tyrant he had been. Aurelian had not let it change how he interacted with me, even with no one else around. He was still affectionate, and tender. Nothing was different. I hoped he was not holding in his grief; it could become a poison.

Zoryana, along with the Dusklands advisers and Memory Circle, had developed a plan to visit the other kingdoms. Some had had strong ties to Nightfell before the Breaking. There was a hope that those ties were still there, buried deep, perhaps, but able to be fostered, nonetheless. I hated the idea of her being beyond the Thornwood. While Aurelian and I would also be accompanying her—I had made it clear that wherever she goes we do too—I could not shake my overwhelming feeling that we were walking into something worse.

AURELIAN

The war was over. That was what they keep saying. But the air still tasted like ash, and the soil was still smoking. Solnyr's discarded banners littered the fields upon which they fell, wind blowing them in rivers. We received word that the sun priests were driven east, their light-wells shattered upon the death of the King. On the other side of the Thornwood, the sun itself felt dimmer, as if it could not bear to witness what had been done in its name.

Zoryana had not spoken of Aurastes' death, beyond comforting me in my grief. No one dared to talk about him, like invoking his name would bring him back to life. We would need to develop a plan for a way forward, but I appreciated the silence for now. The people whispered of the battle as *The Day the Sun Fell*. They had begun carving the story into stone already—a thousand versions of it, each more myth than truth. They would make gods of us, if we let them. Zoryana hated it. I could see it in the way her shoulders tightened when someone bowed too deeply or whispered her name as she passed. She was not a goddess. She was merely a woman who held her land together by sheer will and refused to die when the world asked her to. I thought that was why they would remember her forever.

We spent the day after the battle walking the ruins of the Vale. Where light scorched deepest, the land became barren, and we were unsure if it would ever heal. But where Zoryana's magic had met it head-on, new growth was already pushing through. Black, lush soil, silver roots, and blue shoots glowing faintly under moonlight. The earth remembered her mercy and repaid her with beauty and life.

Aris took command of the reconstruction lines. The plan had been to start rebuilding the villages that had been destroyed by the Solnyrians and help them reseed their lands. There was nothing anyone, not even Zoryana, could do about the broken Thornwood as the trees continued to crumble, opening even more clearings along the border; all we could do was care for the land and the people. Aris moved through the camps like a storm that forgot to be angry. Every soldier followed him without question. That was something—one of the many things—that was so different about the Dusklands, that a man so young could have such a complete hold of his command, with men much older and more experienced following him without so much as a huff or scowl.

He did not speak of his part in killing my brother, and I did not ask. We did not need to speak about it. He knew I did not blame him for what he had to do. Aurastes was my brother, and there was a time that I had loved him, but that time long ago was overshadowed by the monster he had become. No, I did not blame Aris for killing my brother. It was a necessary act to stop the tirade and danger that faced us.

In the days that followed, the people of the Dusklands worked together to begin rebuilding. Younglings ran through freshly tilled earth scattering seeds, making everyone around slightly exasperated at the lack of order, but amused and thankful that they had the chance for that frustration at all, that the future had not been taken from them altogether. Laughter started to return to the people, filling the air with the songs that followed. Houses were rebuilt, magic, and the strength of the Oath-bound making it less laborious than it would have been on the other side of the border. Zoryana, on hands and knees, helped with planting, feeding small amounts of magic back into the land to speed up the growth. The people loved having her among them, helping, hands-on with soil, bricks, and keeping younglings occupied. Her presence gave them hope and affirmed she would be there for them, not behind stone walls.

The day after the battle, the first Solnyrians appeared at the border. Soldiers, stripped of their golden armour and weapons, families with them, asking for asylum. Zoryana met them at the border and welcomed them with open arms, like the Queen of the People that she truly was—the first Queen of the Dusklands to welcome citizens of other kingdoms into her realm since the Breaking. That was a highly significant milestone, though we did not have time to truly honour it. Homes were found for them, sometimes with willing Dusklands families who had extra rooms. Maybe, just maybe, we could make this new world work. A plan had not been devised for what the next stages were—Zoryana wanted her people settled and thriving before she thought about the possibility of travelling to other lands to broker peace, to tell of the lies Solnyr had blinded them all with.

Two days after, I heard the first song being sung about the battle. I would be lying if I said I did not feel a little uncomfortable—hearing my name in a song felt off. I was a second son; songs were not sung of second sons. A second son...who had been the heir to the King of the Sun...who was dead. Damn...did that make me the King of Solnyr? I had defected...but my brother had died without another heir. I did not want the crown, but I did not want to leave them to the mercy of tyrants either. I pushed that to the back of my mind, unable to think of anything that drastic.

I took to standing on the ramparts at night, looking over the land that was now my home. I knew I would not go back to Solnyr—the Dusklands were truly my home. Zoryana and Aris were my home. There was an eerie beauty to the Dusklands that I had noticed when I visited for the first time. When I had made that first journey through the Thornwood months ago, I never would have imagined what would transpire. I had presumed that eventually my brother would declare war, but I could not have predicted that we would have been on opposite sides, that I would have defected, fallen in love with the Queen...fallen in love with another man on top of that. Sound behind me drew my attention. Zoryana walked up to stand with me. No crown. No armour. Not a queen, just Zoryana. We stood together in silence for a long time, watching the world around us start to dim for the night.

"They will think this was an ending," she murmured quietly, her eyes tracking people walking around below. My vision was not as good as hers in the dark, but I was beginning to adjust.

"Every ending is a beginning that costs just a little more each time." I shrugged softly, sad that our new beginning cost so many lives.

She looked at me, tired but alive and endless. "Then let's make sure the cost means something."

Standing together for a little longer, she was the first to turn to leave. She paused at the stairs and said over her shoulder, "I saw you are still writing." When she had discovered my ledger, she had thought it was funny but respected my need to use it as a way to process all the crazy things that were happening to and around me. I had noticed the little notes she had written in the margins on some pages, adding her own little flair.

"Yes. I have to. Someone needs to remember the world as it actually was—not as it will be told." I had taken to writing everything down as it happened, so there was a record of the truth when we eventually became history.

She nodded once. "Then write the truth, even if no one wants to hear it." She smiled and left me alone on the rampart.

The rebuilding was progressing well. People were happy and beginning to thrive again. I liked visiting the towns to see where I could help, making friends and new family. On the eve of the first diplomatic mission Zoryana had reluctantly agreed to embark on, I was walking through one of the towns that we had finished rebuilding in the last day, when writing on a wall caught my eye. Moving closer, surprised that the clean walls were already marked but the words made me pause. It looked as though it should be in a book in the archives, not scrawled on a wall.

When a prince rejects his crown,

when a queen refuses to bow,

when a commander breaks before he bends—

the world will remember the day it was broken,

and choose whether to stay shattered.

And written underneath in another hand was one line that sent a shiver down my spine.

The prophecy is upon us…

My heart hammered in my chest. Zoryana and Aris were both back at the castle preparing for the journey. I had come down to see how everything was progressing, not expecting to see a prophecy on a wall that clearly referenced us. *A commander breaks before he bends* was undoubtedly Aris, *a queen refuses to bow* was Zoryana, The Queen Who Would Not Bow, and *a prince rejects his crown*—that had to be me. Confused and more than a little concerned, I rushed towards my horse, swinging up onto his back, riding home faster than I had ridden on the way to the town. I needed to tell someone what I had seen before I forgot it.

AURELIAN'S LEDGER
RECLAIMING THE NIGHT

The Road to Varakhrei

Day Four of Kavreth (Cavrios in Solnyr), Year 1003 After the Breaking

"When a prince rejects his crown,

when a queen refuses to bow,

when a commander breaks before he bends—

the world will remember the day it was broken,

and choose whether to stay shattered."

Zoryana had told me to not worry about the words on the wall. They sounded too much like a prophecy for my liking. I could not just let them leave my thoughts. Nor the added words below them, like someone had come along after and affirmed them - *"The prophecy is upon us…"*

We ride to Varakhrei, the closest kingdom to the Dusklands, and one that had the strongest bond with the High Queens before the Breaking. They were also one of the more spiritual of the Five Kingdoms—Six Kingdoms now the Dusklands were a part of the world again. Perhaps I could find some answers about the apparent prophecy there. I had never been one to take muck stock in prophecies or anything of the sort, but with everything that had happened, my dreams of Zoryana before I'd even known she existed, the way we had bonded, and the way Zoryana, Aris and I had come together in our relationship. I could not see past it.

For now, I will be content to travel the kingdoms, basking in the sun that irritates my companions, learning from Serian—who I was sure was Zoryana's father—and enjoying the time with my lovers, exploring more of each other's bodies and desires, and how we fit together in and out of bed. Until we arrive in Varakhrei and we are forced to confront the Solnyrian lie or perhaps be welcomed with open arms.

The war might have been over.

But, it seemed, the story certainly was not.

- Aurelian

ARCHIVIST'S ADDENDUM

Date of authorship disputed

The following fragment was recovered from a sealed Solnyrian cache during the later years of the Dawnbound Court. Its authenticity was contested, dismissed in several official histories as apocrypha or deliberate subversion. Subsequent corroboration rendered those dismissals untenable.

Fragment, hand attributed to Aurastes Solnyr IV

The world believes I died beneath the sun, righteous and aflame.

I did not.

Let the lie remain. It has always served its purpose.

The crown she wears remembers what was taken.

I remember the blood that will answer for it.

This is not the end of the war.

It is the moment it resumes.

Archivist Lyra Daeven
Keeper of the House of Memory

Annotation added post-Reckoning:
Survival was not the story he required.
Control was.

GLOSSARY

- **Vesmor:** The name of the ancient, unified land before The Breaking. Vesmor encompassed the Dusklands, Solnyr, and a collection of other smaller kingdoms. It was ruled by a High Queen from the Dusklands, and a High King Consort—a king or prince chosen from one of the other kingdoms, primarily Solnyr.

- **The Weave:** A magical well in the Dusklands that holds all living memory. The Dusk Queens can draw directly from the power of the Weave.

- **The Breaking:** The event in which High Queen Seravine's magic exploded, causing the Dusklands to be cut off from the rest of the world by a dark impenetrable forest.

- **Shadowsworn warrior:** An elite Oath-bound chosen by the crowned Queen to be her personal guard. They swear a new oath and a bond is created with the Queen, giving them heightened awareness and some say they could even tap into the Queen's magic if needed in battle.

- **Oath-bound:** Dusklands soldiers. All soldiers in the Dusklands take an official oath to the crown to serve.

Their oath is for life, though most queens will release soldiers who ask. They are elite fighters and move like shadow. Every move they make in battle is deadly, and the fight without a sound.

- **Younglings:** (Dusklands) Children aged Birth-10 years.
- **Starlings:** (Dusklands) Children/teenagers. This age group starts around the age of 10, however has a different end for each individual, depending on when they choose to undergo the Rite of the Shadowborne. Most undertake this Rite between the ages of 16-18, however some as young as 15 years old have succeeded.
- **Shadowborne:** (Dusklands) The adult stage of life that begins after they succeed their Rite. This gives people the ability to buy property, work, start a family, etc, making them a fully-fledged member of society.
- **Firstfire:** (Solnyr) Children aged Birth-10 years.
- **Sparks:** (Solnyr) An affectionate shorthand for Firstfires. Sometimes used in a derogatory way.
- **Dawnbreak:** (Solnyr) Teenagers aged 10 to 16 years
- **Brightborne:** (Solnyr) The adult stage of life in Solnyr beginning at the age of 17. This gives people the ability to buy property, work, start a family, etc, making them a fully-fledged member of society.
- **The Rite of the Shadowborne:** A sacred coming-of-age rite moving people from their starling years to Shadowborne. During the Rite, initiates are relieved of the names they had as children and are given a new name to carry through their lives—half is given by their families, the other half they choose themselves. They then walk a path of ember barefoot to prove their strength and dedication. To conclude, initiates are branded with a crescent shaped burn on their wrists.
- **High Fae:** Beings with magical abilities, increased speed, strength, and healing abilities. They exclusively

live in the Dusklands as their magic and that of the land is sacred and it is where they are safe. All citizens of the Dusklands are considered High Fae, regardless of their status in society.

- **Lesser Fae:** Basically humans. The lesser fae category is large and covers all other humanoid beings that do not reside in the Dusklands, including the Solnyrian royalty. A note on Solnyrian royalty: They are considered to be of higher strength and abilities and had smaller amounts of magic. Due to this, they were preferable as consorts for the High Queens of Vesmor, leading to their bloodline having some High Fae blood, even centuries later.

- **Shadowmare/Dusk Stallion:** Similar to ordinary horses, except they are only found in the Dusklands. Their coats are black as night and their eyes are like the moon. Fiercely loyal and highly intelligent. History says there are only ever 1 pair in existence at any point and they bond to their riders for life.

- **Memory Circle:** Important group of spiritual leaders who keep the records and memories from every branch of the Dusklands society. Lead by The Archivist, the full Circle consists of The Armourer (military history), The Astronomer (the stars), The Artist (the arts—songs, paintings), and The Architect (building of society).

- **Tides:** 10-day cycles similar to a week. There are 3 in each month

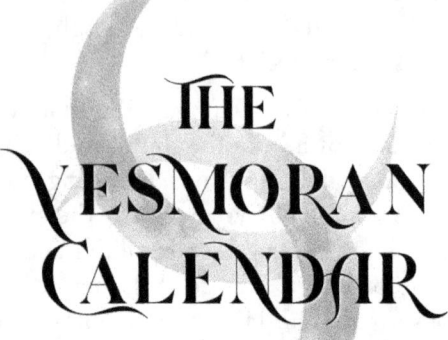

THE VESMORAN CALENDAR

ADAPTED BY THE DUSKLANDS AND Solnyr after the Breaking—the Vesmoran calendar consisted of twelve equal months, all consisting of thirty days each. Each month is broken into 3 equal 10-day cycles called 'tides'.

The year ends with five days of stillness that do not belong to any month. These days are sacred, so much so that neither land changed the names after the Breaking.

The entire year-cycle consists of a total of 365 days.

The months and seasonal cycles are outlined below. Each month has the ancient Vesmoran name, still used by the Dusklands, in addition to the adapted name used by Solnyr.

#	Vesmoran/Dusklands Name	Solnyrian Name
SUMMER		
1	Solmiren	Solmera
2	Threnval	Threvos
3	Kavrethis	Cavrios
AUTUMN		

#	Vesmoran/Dusklands Name	Solnyrian Name
4	Varoneth	Varenius
5	Draesum	Draelis
6	Noxareth	Noxeris
WINTER		
7	Velkaren	Veloris
8	Havorel	Aurivor
9	Serathel	Serium
SPRING		
10	Tirisen	Verales
11	Moralune	Lunaris
12	Aravess	Avaris

Days of Stillness

- Day 361 - Day of Echoes: remembering the dead
- Day 362 - Day of Weave: repairing wards, renewing bonds
- Day 363 - Day of Flames: offerings to Sun or Hearth
- Day 364 - Day of Shadows: vigils and rituals. The Rite of the Shadowborne is held on this day
- Day 365 - Day of Beginnings: vows, oaths, reconciliations. Solnyrian coronotations are held on this day

Each month has 3 Tides:

- Waxing Tide (days 1–10) — beginnings, planting, strength
- Hearth Tide (days 11–20) — trade, diplomacy, labour
- Fading Tide (days 21–30) — endings, magic, visions

Days of the Tide

Day #	Vesmoran/Dusklands Name	Solnyrian Name
1	Shadeborn	Dawncrest
2	Ferrin	Highsun
3	Tarsul	Goldmarch
4	Veyrith	Blazefall
5	Ostrel	Sunward
6	Sarn	Brightforged
7	Korlath	Crownflame
8	Mirun	Sundusk
9	Veshrin	Embercall
10	Shadowsrest	Restfire

ACKNOWLEDGEMENTS

WHERE DO I START? HONESTLY this part is more stressful than the entire book—making sure I don't forget anyone.

Firstly, I have to thank my Mum, of course. She has always been my Number 1 fan, always been in my corner, supporting whatever crazy scheme I came up with (even if that was just sitting on the couch with a movie for a few months). Without you and your support, your cheerleading, this would not have happened. I can't even begin to thank you enough for everything you do.

To Benny, my little brother, for distracting me with silly reels at the right (and sometimes wrong) times (Never say I don't value you… look I put you in my book).

To my Girl Squad (I don't think we've ever been called that but that's what we are now): Catriona, Teagan, and Bree—for putting up with all my 'how would you feel if's, 'how does this sound?"s, and other random questions.

To my guys—Jay and Joel, my loudest fanboys—for keeping me on track and my head above water when I was 100% sure this was trash and I wasn't good enough to publish.

My alpha and beta readers: Hughes, Jordjah, Joel, Hannah

(and the English Proper team), and amazing ARC readers—without your valuable feedback and insights I may not have had the confidence to actually go through with this. Thank you so very much!

And of course—thank YOU! Without you reading this book, it really means nothing in the long run. So thank you from the bottom of my heart for taking a chance on Zoryana and her boys.

Jade x

About the Author

Jade is an author based in Western Australia, drawn to stories shaped by power, grief, loyalty, and the lies people learn to survive. She has a deep love of world building, particularly histories that fracture, distort, and echo through generations. Her work explores the emotional cost of truth and duty in imagined worlds. The Vesmor Chronicles is her debut series.

You can connect with me on:

Web: jadelouiseauthor.com

Socials: @jadelouiseauthor on FB, IG, TT

Newsletter: beacons.ai/jadelouiseauthor

www.ingramcontent.com/pod-product-compliance
Lightning Source LLC
LaVergne TN
LVHW011815060526
838200LV00053B/3791